PENNE DREADFUL

AN ITALIAN CHEF MYSTERY

CATHERINE BRUNS

Poisoned Pen
PRESS

Published by Poisoned Pen Press, an imprint of Sourcebooks
P.O. Box 4410, Naperville, Illinois 60567-4410
(630) 961-3900
sourcebooks.com

Printed and bound in Canada.
MBP 10 9 8 7 6 5 4 3 2 1

For Frank

Thank you for believing in me

ONE

THE RICH AROMA FROM THE MIXTURE of tomatoes and onions cooking wafted through the air, hitting my nose with a distinct perfume. It was a soothing smell that blanketed me in its warm hold. If alone, I would have been content to stand in front of my stove all day.

I stirred the sauce and listened as my cousin Gino Mancusi flipped through the sports section of the newspaper at my breakfast counter and grumbled about his beloved Giants losing again.

"The season is pretty much over. I actually thought they might get another ring this time." He sighed and pushed the paper aside. "You shouldn't have gone to any trouble, Tessa. A sandwich would have been fine."

"It's never any trouble." I enjoyed watching others sample my creations and had vowed years ago that no one would ever leave my home hungry. Part of this obsession came from my love of cooking, but I attributed the rest to my Italian heritage. Italians are passionate about almost everything in the world, and food is at the top of the list.

"It's rare for you to go out for lunch," I said. Gino was a police detective in our hometown of Harvest Park. "Did Lucy tell you to come over and check up on me? Is it your day? Oh wait, let me grab the calendar."

"Stop being a smart aleck." He left the counter and came into the kitchen to grab ice cubes out of the freezer for his soda. On his way back, he stopped and planted an affectionate kiss on the top of my head. "That's what family is for, Tess. We're all worried about you."

I squeezed his arm and turned off the burner. "Grab the parmesan cheese out of the fridge, will you? I grated it this morning."

Gino nodded without another word. I appreciated all that he and the rest of the family were doing, but I was determined not to start crying again today.

It was still difficult to talk about my husband's death, even with loved ones. I'd spent the last five weeks in a trance—or perhaps shock was a better term. Thanks to my mother, cousins, and my friend Justin, I had finally started to come around. Whenever I thought I'd fully recovered though, a kind word or a nice gesture from anyone would make me dissolve into a puddle of tears again.

Last night, my elderly neighbor Stacia from across the street had brought me a fresh baked apple pie. "I know how much you love them, dear." She'd beamed at me from underneath a mass of pink foam hair curlers. Apple pie—anything apple, actually—had been Dylan's favorite, but I didn't have the heart to tell her so. Instead, I'd cried after she left and then devoured a huge slice.

Gino placed the cheese on the breakfast counter. He had classic Italian good looks complemented by dark hair, an olive complexion, and brown eyes that could either be sympathetic or suspicious. I suspected that the latter one was a cop thing.

"Right here at the bar is fine, Tess," he said. "Don't bother setting the table. I have to get back to work in a little while anyway."

"Okay, it's all ready." I ladled the ruby-red sauce onto his plate of penne, inhaling the rich savory smell. It was a little bit like summer, with the sweet fragrance of vine-ripe tomatoes complemented by the minty smell of fresh basil from my garden.

"It smells great," Gino said as he sat down. "Then again, I've never eaten anything of yours that wasn't top-notch. You need to give Lucy some pointers."

"Lucy's a good cook. She's too busy taking care of those devilish twins of yours to do much else. I've got a little bit of extra sauce if you want to take some home to her."

Gino's eyes widened as he swallowed a bite of pasta. "A *little*? Come on, Tess. I saw your extra sauce." He wiped his mouth on a starched white linen napkin. "When I opened the freezer, there were at least twenty ziplock bags in there. Maybe you're a bit obsessed with making sauce, huh?"

Like the rest of my family, Gino's focus was strictly on how the food tasted. For me, there was more to it. I loved the aromas, the spices, the way preparing food made me feel—relaxed, confident, and in control. I'd been cooking for twenty years, since the tender age of ten. My grandmother, a fabulous cook herself, and I had shared a special bond. Whenever we went to her house, I'd head straight to the kitchen to watch her make dinner, and we'd chat the afternoon away. My love of cooking came from her. On my thirteenth birthday, she gave me a special present—her secret tomato sauce recipe. She passed away when I was sixteen, and I took the recipe and made it my own over the years, with the help of a few special ingredients. Although I could make just about anything, tomato sauce was my passion and specialty, always bringing to mind wonderful memories of our time together.

"No, I'm not obsessed." There was silence in the room, except for the clink of Gino's fork hitting the china plate. He didn't understand. No one did. My love of cooking also helped soothe the grief of losing my husband, at least temporarily. Dylan had passed away a little over a month ago in a tragic car accident that would probably give me nightmares for the rest of my life.

This wasn't supposed to happen to us. We'd been young, in love, and trying to have a baby. Dylan and I were married for almost six wonderful years. Although by no means rich, we'd lived comfortably enough. Dylan had been employed as an accountant for a large healthcare firm, We Care, in Albany. As a certified CPA, he'd prepared taxes privately for several clients outside the firm as well. To add to our modest income, a couple of months before Dylan's death, I'd begun working as a cook for the Sunnyside Up Café. Back then, my main goal in life—besides starting a family—had been to run my own restaurant someday.

Dylan had been extremely supportive of my passion.

He'd always teased that he couldn't wait to quit his job and call me "boss," serving as my maître d'. Kidding aside, I knew he'd been as excited about the venture as I was. Still, we didn't have anywhere near the funds necessary to make it happen. Since we'd bought the house only two years ago, we'd been trying to put money away every month, but there were times when real life intervened. A new roof and hot water tank had helped derail the savings process for a few months. We remained hopeful that it would happen within the next couple of years.

Five weeks ago, my dream had been replaced by a nightmare. My new goal in life was to simply make it through a day without crying, and my restaurant ownership dreams had been put aside indefinitely.

After the accident, I'd asked my mother to call Sunnyside and tell them I wouldn't be returning. I'd only been there for a few months, and it wasn't fair to leave them hanging, although they'd been very supportive of my situation.

Even selling the house had crossed my mind a few times in the last couple of weeks. The first time the real estate agent showed us the light-blue Cape Cod, Dylan and I both instantly fell in love with its charm. Although only about fourteen hundred square feet, it was perfect for us, with its large bay window, hardwood floors, and steepled roof.

Now, however, it was difficult to stay here alone. There were memories of Dylan everywhere I looked, such as the empty window boxes built into the white shutters where we'd planted annuals together every spring. I missed so many things about him—his deep-throated chuckle, the way he held me in his strong arms on lazy Sunday mornings in bed, and the long walks we'd take, hand in hand, after dinner on picturesque autumn days, much like this one. Early November in Harvest Park, although chilly, was the perfect time of year to watch multicolored leaves fall from the trees.

The house was an ideal home for a young married couple and even had the classic white picket fence in the backyard. The only things missing were the standard two-point-five kids and dog, which I'd mistakenly thought we had plenty of time for.

Luigi squawked from the floor and stared up at me expectantly. A spoiled tuxedo kitty, he was looking for his share of lunch too. I cut up a small piece of sausage and set it on a paper plate in front of him.

"That cat eats better than most people do," Gino commented. He took another bite of the pasta and groaned with pleasure. "Amazing as always."

This was the therapy I needed. "Thanks."

He watched me closely as I stood on the other side of the counter. "Aren't you going to eat?"

I shrugged and fiddled with the newspaper. "I'm not hungry."

"Tess." His voice was gentle. "Maybe it's time you went back to work. I'm sure you could get another job as a cook easily enough."

I stared down at my hands. "I don't know. I guess I'm afraid that I might break down in front of someone." My voice trembled. No, I wasn't going to do this now. I could—and would—make it through one day without bursting into tears. Dylan wouldn't have wanted me to carry on like this.

Gino rose from his chair and walked around the counter. He took my hand and led me into the combination living and dining room. "Come on. I need to talk to you about something."

I dropped onto the navy love seat, and Luigi jumped in my lap, curling into a ball on my knees. Gino sat across from me in the matching armchair, a line creasing his broad forehead. "You're probably going to hate me for telling you this."

"What? The sauce was too spicy?" I joked.

He didn't laugh. "I should have told you sooner, but you've been so upset, I was afraid it might send you over the edge."

Now he had my full attention. My stomach twisted at his words. "What's wrong? Is someone in the family sick? Lucy or one of the twins?" I didn't think I could handle any more bad news.

Gino shook his head. "It's nothing like that." He exhaled a deep breath. "It's about Dylan."

"What about him?" I asked sharply. "Just say it."

He reached forward to cover my hand with his. "We have reason to believe that Dylan's death wasn't an accident."

My body went rigid. There was no sound in the room except for my heavy breathing and Luigi's purring as he snuggled against me. "Are you saying that someone intentionally killed my husband?"

Gino's mouth formed a thin, hard line. "It looks that way. We believe that somebody tampered with his vehicle."

Anger quickly replaced shock. "You said before that it was a car malfunction. How long have you known about this?"

"A few weeks."

"Meaning since his death." I hated Gino in that moment. For God's sake, he was family. If you couldn't depend on your own family to tell you the truth, who could you trust? "So why am I only hearing about this now?"

"Look, Tess," he said quietly. "It's an ongoing investigation. We don't have all the details, and nothing has been released to the public yet."

Startled, I rose to my feet, forcing Luigi to jump down and scamper out of the room. "Who cares about the public? I'm his wife and you're my cousin! How could you keep this from me?"

Gino's face flushed, and he put a hand on my arm. "You were so out of it those first couple of weeks. I was afraid if I told you, then maybe you'd do something crazy, like—"

"Like what? Take my own life? Join my husband in the hereafter?" I shook his hand off and moved to stand in front of the bay window, looking out at my lawn covered with its gold and orange leaves. "Please leave."

But Gino didn't leave. Instead, he came up behind me and put his hands on my shoulders. As a result, I crumpled. My shoulders started to sag, and the tears I was holding back finally broke free. So much for my new determination.

He held me in his arms while I cried. "I'm so sorry. I wasn't at liberty to tell you anything at first, and then as time wore on, I was afraid. That's the real reason I came over. Gabby said you seemed almost like your old self yesterday. She mentioned that you stopped by her store last night for the first time since Dylan died."

I straightened up and wiped my eyes. "I brought cookies for her club." Gabby was Gino's younger sister and owned a small bookstore, Once Upon a Book, that was three streets over from where I lived in the center of town. She was my dearest friend, the sister I'd never had.

"Like I said, nothing has been released to the public, but details may have already started to leak." He looked faintly embarrassed. "I've been questioning some people around town, and so has another officer. Unfortunately, he let it slip to someone that the car was tampered with, so it probably won't be long before the news starts to spread."

"I see. In other words, you wanted to make sure you told me before someone else did." Furious, I almost wanted to slap him.

Gino wrapped an arm around my waist and led me back to the couch. "That's not it. I swear that I was going to tell you, but you're right, I shouldn't have waited so long." To his credit, his face was full of misery. "Should I go on?"

I inhaled a large gulp of air. "Yes. Tell me everything."

He hesitated for a second. "I don't *know* everything. As we told you from the beginning, a fuel leak was the cause. But it looks like someone tampered with his engine by loosening a fitting, which caused the car to catch fire. Passersby reported seeing flames shoot out from under the vehicle right before Dylan crashed."

"Okay, stop." I had lied. I didn't want to hear that part again—not about how my husband had been trapped in a burning car before crashing into a tree. He'd already been dead when the EMTs had pulled him from the wreckage, but I would always wonder what suffering he might have endured in those final moments.

Gino held tightly to my hand. "I did some checking around. Dylan always brought his vehicle to the Car Doctor, right? Matt Smitty wasn't around the day before when Dylan brought the car in, but his mechanic Earl said they only did a tire rotation. He swore he didn't touch the engine." Gino paused, weighing his words before continuing. "You know that Smitty's not one of my favorite people."

I didn't want to get into this now. Matt had been

my high school boyfriend. I'd broken up with him after he became too possessive, and Gino had never liked him. "But…" The words refused to fall from my mouth. I paused for a second and tried to get my bearings. "That can't be right. Why would someone want Dylan dead?" The thought was incomprehensible.

Gino replied to my question with one of his own. "Did Dylan have any enemies?"

I gave him what I hoped was an incredulous look. "How can you ask me such a thing? Everybody loved him."

"Are you sure about that?" Gino's tone was suspicious. He was using his cop voice, as Gabby called it. "Maybe he screwed up someone's taxes? Reported someone to the IRS for doing something illegal? Did a coworker have it in for him?"

"No. No one I can think of." But Gino had planted a seed of doubt in my head. Maybe there was a disgruntled client Dylan hadn't told me about. "Did someone tamper with his car while he was at We Care? Have you checked out his office?"

"I thought he parked in the garage adjacent to their building. Isn't that for employees only? Plus, there are cameras on every floor."

I nodded, racking my brain. "He had eaten lunch right before it happened. You were the one who told me his car was parked in the alley behind Slice before he…died." It still hurt to say the word. There was such finality attached, and I suddenly felt as if I was reliving that day once again.

Gino had been the one to come to my house to deliver the news. I was grateful it hadn't come from a stranger but had immediately gone into shock. Slowly, the memories returned, and then I recalled Gino mentioning Slice Pizzeria, the restaurant that Dylan constantly frequented.

A light bulb switched on in my head. "Do you think that someone at Slice would know anything?"

Slice was a small restaurant situated at the end of the main street in Harvest Park and owned by New York City native Anthony Falducci. I'd met him a couple of times when Dylan had brought me there for pizza. The building was a bit of an eyesore from the outside. It needed a new roof, and the brown paint was peeling in various spots. The surface of the blacktop in the adjacent parking lot was cracked in several places. Regardless, it was still a staple in the community and served mouthwatering pizza with a variety of delicious toppings.

"It's possible." Gino was silent for a second. "Actually,

that's another reason why I wanted to come talk to you. I had a chat with Anthony, but he didn't have much to offer. I've been trying to get a line on his restaurant but can't find anything. I'm suspicious though. Slice may be the only place where someone could have had access to Dylan's vehicle that day. You guys have a two-car garage, and it would be difficult for someone to tamper with the vehicle at his office building."

I nodded but kept my thoughts to myself. If I could track all of Dylan's activities in his last few days, maybe it would lead me to whoever had killed him.

Gino went on. "Anthony seems golden. He got a speeding ticket a couple of years back, but other than that, he's clean. The guy's been a pillar of the community for almost two decades. His brother Vince recently started working at Slice, and his daughter helps out when needed."

It was well known in Harvest Park that Anthony donated to several organizations every year. On Christmas Day, the restaurant was open to anyone in need of a free meal, no questions asked. When word spread of Dylan's accident, Anthony had taken the news hard. I vividly remembered the tears in his eyes during Dylan's wake.

"Dylan spent a lot of time there."

"He did. Especially lately." Gino raised his eyebrows pointedly.

I bristled. "What does that mean? Why is it a big deal that he liked to go there for lunch? Dylan did Anthony's monthly taxes, so obviously, they were close."

"It's just another angle to check out," Gino replied. "All I'm saying is maybe there's a connection."

I swallowed hard and locked eyes with my cousin. "Tell me one thing. Are you positive Dylan's death was no accident?"

I could always tell when Gino was lying. I remembered one especially frigid winter day when he and Tommy Harper were twelve and they pelted Gabby and me with snowballs while we waited for the school bus and then tried to pin it on someone else. His mother had seen through his lie as well. Policemen were trained to have unreadable faces, but this was my cousin. I could always see through the mask he wore.

His voice was sober. "No, it wasn't an accident, Tess. I'm so sorry."

I bit into my lower lip as tears flooded my eyes. "Then I want to know who did this." Someone had ended Dylan's life and destroyed mine in the process. They needed to pay.

Gino stroked his clean-shaven chin in a pensive manner. "I knew you would feel this way." He hesitated for a moment. "If you really want to find who did it, you may be able to help us."

"Anything. What'd you have in mind?"

"There's a *Help Wanted* sign on the front window of Slice." He took a deep breath before continuing. "They need a cook."

If Gino had wanted to light a fire under my butt, he'd succeeded. I squared my shoulders, prepared to do battle. "Well, it looks like I'm going on a job interview today."

TWO

"HOLD ON A SECOND," GINO SAID. "For the record, I knew you'd want to do this. Hell, I want to know the truth too. But there's no rush. Think on it for a few days before you make a decision, okay?"

I ignored him and walked into the kitchen to remove my stainless-steel pot from the stove, placing it in the sink to soak. "Forget it. The job could be filled by then. Do you think Anthony will hire me?"

"Why wouldn't he?" Gino asked. "You're a fantastic cook. Everyone in town knows that. You could get back to what you're meant to do and help the police department at the same time. A win-win situation."

"All right, you've already convinced me. If I can take down the guys who killed—"

He cocked an eyebrow. "Whoa. Easy there, cowboy. You're not taking down anybody. I just want you to keep your ears open and find me a legal reason to get a warrant to search the place. *If* there is a reason. Got it?"

I nodded, but he wasn't finished. Gino frowned at me and started using his cop voice again.

"Don't do anything but listen when people are talking. That means don't ask questions, don't search through drawers and other places you have no right to. And please, don't give them a reason to believe you suspect Dylan's death was anything but a car accident. I want you cooking—it's what you were meant to do. Also listening, but mostly cooking."

"Oh-*kay*. I'll be a fly on the wall, minding my own business and making pizzas. If they hire me."

He crossed the room and stared out the front window. "When I came in I noticed one of your tires might be a little low on air. Want me to check it for you when I leave?"

"Sure." I was grateful for the attention. With Dylan gone, auto maintenance was an item on my to-do list that never seemed to get done. "So, when did you see the sign last? They may have already hired someone."

"I doubt it. It was there this morning," Gino replied. "I drive by there a couple of times every day. Did Dylan ever mention that there was anyone at the restaurant who didn't like him?"

"No. He talked about Anthony, and we went there for pizza a couple of times. I kind of had a feeling that Dylan didn't like to bring me there."

"Why not?"

I shrugged. "It was his hangout, not mine. Maybe he thought I'd go in and criticize the place."

"You, criticize a kitchen? It could *never* happen."

"Very funny." Maybe Slice wasn't my ideal restaurant, but a little bit of money and creativity could work wonders for the place. I let myself ponder the possibilities for a moment, recreating the dream restaurant I had built in my head so many times before Dylan had died. If I owned Slice, the first thing I'd do would be to take out all those awful orange booths and replace them with square oak tables and matching chairs. It would be a family-type restaurant, but with an air of elegance. A place where you would feel comfortable enough to bring your three-year-old child or your eighty-year-old grandmother. Family was important to Harvest Park's close-knit community, and I certainly wouldn't have made it through the last month without mine.

\ \ /

An hour later I had pulled into a parking spot outside of Slice, taking note of the crooked *Help Wanted* sign in the window with an exhale of relief. I climbed the two steps of the small cement porch and was about to push open the front door when a teenage boy exited the building in a flurry, the corner of the pizza box he held poking me as he brushed by.

"I'm sorry, ma'am." He flushed slightly and, with an apologetic look, hurried down the steps, not waiting for my response.

As I stepped through the doorway, I took in the familiar surroundings. The room for restaurant seating was directly in front of me, with the service counter and kitchen in the back. A tall man came out from behind the orange Formica-topped checkout counter and stared over my head and out the door, clearly annoyed. "Sorry about that, miss. Sam knows he's supposed to use the kitchen door for deliveries. *Kids*. You can't teach them anything these days." He was over six feet tall and extremely good-looking with a mess of curly, black hair that poked out from underneath a Yankees ball cap he wore backward on his head.

I followed him back to the service counter. Still irritated, he punched some numbers into the register, opened the drawer, and glanced up at me. "Are you here to pick up?"

I shook my head. "My name is Tessa. I'd like to see Anthony, if he has a minute."

He smiled at me, his eyes dark and warm, like freshly roasted coffee beans in the morning. "Sure thing." The man turned away from the counter and walked through the open prep area, then stopped in the doorway of an adjoining room in the back of the kitchen and stuck his head in. "There's a woman named Tessa here who wants to see you."

As I waited for Anthony, I took a moment to study my surroundings. I hadn't been inside Slice for several months, and the place looked shabbier than I remembered. A black phone, a cash register, and a plastic container holding laminated menus occupied the counter of the checkout station. Behind this area was the open-concept kitchen featuring a granite work surface to the right sprinkled with flour, probably used for prepping dough. Next to it was a large metal prep table that held a variety of pizza toppings inside. The wall oven ran behind it, and farther down on the same side of the kitchen was the doorway the tall man had disappeared into, Anthony's office, where Dylan had brought me to meet him before.

On the left side of the room was a refrigerator, two bay sinks, a dishwasher, a six-burner gas stove, and a black utility storage cabinet. The doors were shut, but I assumed they held ingredients such as flour, sugar, canned tomato paste, and oregano. Empty pizza boxes were stacked on top of the cabinet and on a small metal table next to it. There was a steel door on the other side of the table that most likely led to a cooler or freezer—maybe both. The once-white walls had yellowed, no doubt from grease, and the entire room was in serious need of organization. It wasn't my ideal kitchen, but then again, I wasn't here for the ambience.

The good-looking guy came back and leaned his muscular arms over the counter. I studied the intimidating tattoo of a scorpion on his left bicep. "I'm Vince, Anthony's brother. His much *younger* brother." His eyes scanned me up and down, and he gave me a sly wink.

Surprised, I took a step back.

He ran a hand over the scruff of a beard forming

around his sensual looking lips, and his perfect white teeth gleamed against his bronzed complexion. "Why don't you and I meet up and have a drink together later?"

"Vincenzo." Anthony was standing a few feet behind his brother, glaring at him. "What the hell do you think you're doing?"

Anthony Falducci was in his late fifties or early sixties, dressed in a short-sleeved black T-shirt like his brother with a white bib apron tied over it. He came around the counter to where I stood, wiping his hands on his apron. His once-dark-brown hair was now dominated by gray and cut short. He ran a hand through the sparse hair on top of his head as he regarded me.

Anthony's brown eyes were set in a round, pink face that broke into a wide grin. "Tessa, how nice to see you." He nodded at the other man. "Don't get any ideas. This lady is off-limits."

Vince stared at him, his expression puzzled. "What's that supposed to mean?"

"Her husband was Dylan Esposito. Remember? The guy who—"

"Oh man." Vince gave me an apologetic look. "I'm really sorry, miss. I had no idea."

"It's okay," I reassured him, desperately wishing I was somewhere else.

The phone rang, and Vince snatched it up in a hurry, as if grateful for the distraction. "Slice. Pick up or delivery?"

Anthony turned back to me. "What can I do for you?"

I pointed in the direction of the front door, where the *Help Wanted* sign hung. "I'm looking for a job."

Anthony's eyes widened. "That's right. You're a cook, and a good one too. Dylan said so." There was an awkward pause, and then he crooked a finger at me. "Follow me, hon." We walked away from the carryout station into the large dining area where only two booths were in use. A young couple deep in conversation was seated at one, while a woman with three small children occupied another. Anthony motioned toward a booth with red checkered paper place mats on top of the surface. "Can I get you something to drink?"

"No thanks." Dylan had raved about Anthony's homemade pizza, although he was always careful to mention it wasn't as good as mine, reminding me of the old adage—a way to a man's heart is through his stomach. I'd always kidded my husband that I shouldn't have prepared dinner for him on our first date. It became a standing joke between us that my chicken parmigiana was what had convinced him to propose.

The restaurant was fairly clean but had started to show its age. Pieces of the dull tile flooring were broken or loose in several spots. The orange vinyl-covered seat underneath me sported several cracks and a large hole near one of its seams. The overhead light fixtures appeared spotty, and a few of the bulbs had blown out, giving the dining room a depressing and foreboding-like atmosphere. I knew that Slice was primarily a takeout restaurant, so perhaps Anthony didn't see the point of spending additional funds in the dining area. Still, I could think of a dozen ways to make the place brighter, cheerier, and more appealing to the public. I visualized looped cable lights hanging from the ceiling to echo draped pasta noodles. Red-and-white-checkered linen napkins adorning the spotless wooden table surfaces. Perfection.

Anthony cleared his throat uncomfortably. "So, the truth, honey. How've you really been doing?"

"Not great." The words were no lie, and the object *was* to make Anthony feel sympathetic enough to hire me. Still, I detested pity of any sort. On the day of Dylan's wake, if I'd had to experience one more person muttering "Sorry for your loss," I might have screamed out loud. Yes, it was a difficult situation for everyone involved, and what else was there for people to say? But it had been agony to endure all the same.

Anthony nodded in understanding. "Dylan was a great guy. One of my best customers and a whiz with my taxes. I really miss him."

"Me too," I managed to choke out.

He reached across the table to pat my hand awkwardly. "This has got to be hell for you. My wife, Luisa, she drives me crazy, but if I didn't have her around—" His face grew red as he said the words. "Well, you know what I mean. So, what kind of experience do you have cooking?"

I folded my hands on the table. Fortunately, I didn't have to lie about this part. "I've been cooking since I was ten. I went to college as a business major, then quit after two years to go to culinary school." My parents had not been happy with that decision, but as far as I was concerned, it was the best one I'd ever made. When I started at the culinary academy, I knew I'd found my niche. "After that I worked as a waitress, then a short order cook." I didn't explain that I'd wanted to learn how to do every particular job in a restaurant because my dream had always been to run my own someday. "I started a new job at Sunnyside Up Café three months ago. When Dylan's accident—" Suddenly, I couldn't go on.

Anthony waited patiently. "Take your time. It's all right."

I let out a deep breath. "Sunnyside was a nice place, but I didn't know when I'd be able to return, and it wasn't fair to keep them waiting. Besides, my specialty is Italian food. It's also my favorite to make. Before Sunnyside, I worked as a chef at Magnifico's Restaurant."

He looked impressed. "Wow. That's a nice place...er, was. Didn't they go bankrupt last year?"

"Unfortunately, yes." Magnifico's had been a fancy Italian restaurant, about a half hour's drive from Harvest Park. I'd worked there for two years and enjoyed the experience, except that the constant competition with other employees, specifically the other two chefs, had been a major turnoff. Everyone was always looking out for number one, while my only desire had been to make the customers happy. It was a family-owned place with people who had no idea how to run a business and all the drama you would expect from that scenario.

Anthony seemed to regard me with new respect. "Tessa, you probably have more culinary talent than the rest of us here combined. Didn't your tomato sauce win first prize in some big competition recently?"

The mention made me flush with pride. "Yes, at the New York State Fair last year." I'd also won a thousand dollars in prize money but didn't mention that part. The certificate, framed and on the wall of my kitchen, meant more to me than the cash.

Anthony pursed his lips. "That's what I thought. Wow. I need a cook but honestly don't think I can afford you."

"It's not about the money." Also not a lie. "The location is convenient for me, and pizza is one of my favorite dishes to make."

"A clever girl like you should be figuring out how to license that fantastic sauce of yours instead. You might be sitting on top of a gold mine, honey." His eyes lit up. "Have you ever thought about selling your recipe? Didn't that Neiman Marcus cookie sell for a small fortune?"

I laughed. "I could care less about the money. The recipe originally belonged to my grandmother before I made a few tweaks. I'd never consider selling it."

"Ancient family secret, eh?" Anthony smiled and leaned forward. "I'll level with you, honey. I've been looking for a cook for a couple of weeks now and haven't had any bites yet. Vince, who you met, is a great cook. He's actually a sous chef. Trained in New York City. But he doesn't want to be tied down in the kitchen all day. Vince is a real impatient sort, and he's used to doing as he pleases. I need someone I can rely on, five days a week."

"Well, you wouldn't have to worry with me," I assured him. "There's no place I'd rather be than in the kitchen." I gave him my most eager smile but sensed that something was holding him back. Could it have anything to do with Dylan?

Anthony pursed his lips, as if conflicted. "Why don't you let me think about it for a few days and I'll get back to you? Leave me your phone number."

"No." I put a hand to my mouth, but it was too late. The word had already slipped out between my lips. Impatience crept into my bones, and my emotions might start to show if this went on any longer. I needed to stay calm and not give myself away. "I'm sorry, Anthony. This is a one-time offer. There's another restaurant that wants to hire me as well." Okay, another white lie, but he didn't need to know. "I prefer a closer commute, and that's a major reason why your place is appealing. I promised to give them my answer today."

Anthony looked torn. He leaned back in the seat and studied me for a few seconds, the lines deepening on his forehead. I could almost see his mind at work as the sharp, dark eyes weighed both the pros and cons. His expression brightened, and when he gave me a reassuring smile, I knew the decision was in my favor. "You've got a lot of spunk, Tessa. Okay, it's a deal. Welcome to Slice."

Relief swept over me. "Thank you so much."

He leaned closer. "What I said about Vince, that's between you and me, okay? Plus, I don't know how long he plans on staying in Harvest Park."

I remembered what Gino had said about Vince being new to the restaurant. "So, he's only here temporarily?"

Anthony shrugged. "We're closed on Sundays, so how about you start the day after tomorrow?"

"Sounds good." I nodded. "What time?"

Anthony thought for a moment. "Come on in at noon. We're running short on dough, so you can start laying up a fresh supply. We need to freeze more. How's that sound?"

At that moment, a vision of Dylan entered my mind. The pain in my heart was so sharp, it managed to dull my senses. There was no reason to suspect Anthony had anything to do with Dylan's murder, but he'd spent a lot of time here and it was the last place his car was seen before the accident. This could prove to be a dead end, but I was determined to find out what had happened and who was involved. I owed that much to my husband.

"Tessa? Did you hear me?"

I jerked my head up and forced a smile to my lips. "Sounds perfect."

We walked back around the counter and into the kitchen area where Vince was placing anchovies on a pie. The prep table was open, displaying a range of toppings such as pepperoni, sausage, olives, peppers, and various types of cheeses. Vince didn't strike me as the most organized of cooks. Dough, spatters of sauce, and toppings speckled the work surface. I was a stickler for a tidy kitchen.

"Let me grab the new hire forms from my office, and then I'll see you out," Anthony said in a cheery tone as he left me standing there with Vince.

Vince looked up as Anthony walked away. He noticed me watching and raised an eyebrow in return. "I guess congratulations are in order," he said sourly, his former friendly face now twisted in a scowl.

Before I could respond, he strode across the room and disappeared into the cooler, slamming the door behind him.

Anthony emerged from his office and handed me I-9 and W-4 forms. "If you could fill these out and bring them back with you on Monday, that would be great." The phone rang, and he gave me a quick pat on the shoulder. "Enjoy the rest of the weekend. You can go out the kitchen door if you want." He reached past me and picked up the phone. "Slice. Pick up or delivery?"

I was headed in the direction of the back door when it burst open, engulfing me in a rush of chilly air. A skinny boy who looked about fifteen, different from the one I'd seen earlier, almost knocked me over. They seemed to be coming at me from all different directions. His lips twitched into a grin when he saw me. "Sorry, honey."

I hated it when anyone younger than myself called me honey. The kid's eyes boldly scanned me up and down. "So, who are you? Vince's new babe? Or maybe Anthony's getting a little action on the side?"

Besides the obvious smart mouth, the kid had dyed platinum-blond hair and a narrow face as white as flour with sunken cheeks. His eyes were bloodshot, as if he hadn't slept in days. He held a black warmer bag in his hand and wore jeans with holes in the knees.

"Shut up, you two-bit punk." Anthony had ended his phone call and moved back across the room toward us in time to hear the wisecrack. "Eric, this is Tessa. She'll be working here from now on. You treat the lady with respect or *else*. Understand?"

Eric snorted. "Yeah. Whatever."

Anthony stuck a finger in Eric's face. "We've been getting complaints all afternoon that you've been running late. I even had to give one guy a free pizza because he was so pissed off."

"I couldn't help it. My car stalled," he complained.

"Sure, it did." Anthony folded his arms over his chest. "Keep it up. You can easily be replaced."

Eric opened his mouth to say something, then shut it without comment. He pushed past me and grabbed the pizza boxes Vince had set on the work table.

"See you Monday, honey," Anthony called over his shoulder as he went into the office and shut the door behind him.

Eric rushed past me to hold the door open, like a gallant gentleman. "So, sweet thing," he said. "You married?"

Being near this kid was causing my skin to crawl. "My husband died in an accident a few weeks ago." My voice shook slightly as I said the word *accident*, but I wanted to gauge his reaction.

"Bummer." Much to my dismay, he continued to walk

alongside me as I fumbled for car keys in my purse. "What kind of an accident?"

This part was so difficult for me to say. Would it ever get easier? "His car caught fire, and then he crashed into a tree."

He stopped dead in his tracks and turned to me, veins bulging in his neck. "Wait a second. Are you Dylan Esposito's old lady?"

Now it was my turn to ask a question. "You knew my husband?"

The smile faded from his lips. "Yeah, I knew him. Anthony treated him like his son."

"Sounds like it bothered you." I forgot the revulsion I felt for the kid for a minute, curious to know what exactly he'd thought of Dylan. Maybe he'd been jealous of his relationship with Anthony.

He laughed bitterly. "Nah, not *me*. But—" He stopped, paused, and looked around. "Let's just say that not everyone at Slice liked your husband."

I inhaled sharply. "Who didn't like him? Vince?"

He ignored my question as he pulled open the door of his rusted, dark-red sedan with the *Slice* sign on top, depicting a single piece of pizza hovering in the air above the remainder of the pie. "I heard your old man tell Anthony once that you were an awesome cook." Eyes that had been dull and listless now regarded me with interest. "How come you want to work in a hole in the wall like this, and why would Anthony hire you?"

This kid was more intelligent than I'd given him credit for. "Why wouldn't he? I love Italian food, and my husband loved Slice. I think it would help me to work here—make me feel closer to him." Sure, that part was bogus. I felt the closest to Dylan in our own home, but hopefully Eric wouldn't see through my ruse.

Eric laughed. "Yeah, right." He got into the car, and the window whirred down as he continued to watch me thoughtfully. "Tell you what. Maybe you could fix me a private dinner sometime, and we'll have a nice, long chat about your husband." His eyes roamed over me one last time. "See you soon, beautiful."

THREE

AFTER LEAVING SLICE, I DECIDED TO stop over and visit Gabby at her bookstore. Once Upon a Book was only about a quarter of a mile from Slice and located on the same side of Harvest Park Avenue. The brilliant sunshine temped me to walk, but I didn't want Anthony to become suspicious if he found my car in his lot after he thought I'd left.

I needed to talk to someone besides Gino. Gabby always gave sound advice, and she never pulled any punches. Although I adored both my cousins, Gino was still a cop, through and through, and overprotective to the core. He didn't realize that I intended to take snooping at Slice to a whole new level when I began working, nor would he be happy about it.

While I had no siblings, Gino and Gabby had always felt like a brother and sister to me. My father had passed away from a sudden heart attack five years ago, and my mother now lived alone in the house where I'd grown up in Harvest Park. My mother had one sister we seldom saw, and she preferred to spend time with my father's sister instead. Aunt Mona, Gino and Gabby's mother, was divorced from their father and spent her spare hours reading Danielle Steel novels and pretending that she lived in one.

I parked my car in front of Java Time, a coffee shop that was two doors down from Gabby's shop, and glanced around at the town with an air of contentment. Although a bit chilly, the sun was shining in a glorious blue sky, giving hope that winter was still a ways off. Leaves crunched under my boots as I got out of the car and locked it with my remote. Harvest Park was a small town located outside the city of Albany. There was an historic feel to the place, with lots of brownstones, cobbled streets, and a peaceful air about it. Close to a dozen shops peppered the streets on either side of the town's main attraction—a beautiful park rich in greenery during the summer but still quite beautiful in mid-November, despite the almost bare trees.

During the summer, the park was always populated with mothers taking their children to play on the swing set and jungle gym while dogs pranced happily about on leashes. Tulips in various colors bloomed every spring, and the grounds crew set out pumpkins in the fall and a festive tree lighting display for the holidays.

The park was also the primary location for the Harvest Park Apple Festival that had occurred every October for years. For an entire weekend, local restaurants set up booths, with vendors selling everything from Buffalo chicken wings to Manhattan clam chowder. A live band provided entertainment, and there were plenty of activities like coloring contests and face painting for children. In the past few years, Dylan and I had enjoyed stuffing ourselves silly with fried dough and salted pretzels. We'd stroll hand in hand along the grassy path and watch the sun set while kids played in bouncy castles and waved to their parents from a lit-up merry-go-round.

I'd been especially excited to secure a booth this year and had decided to sell my homemade stromboli, which I took immense pride in layering with pepperoni, freshly grated mozzarella, and tender pieces of baked ham, wrapped in my homemade pizza dough brushed with butter. Dylan had planned to take orders while I prepared the food. His death had occurred a week before the festival, and this was the first time I'd let myself think about the event. I hadn't even asked for my deposit back or remembered seeing the crowds around the town, which were always so prevalent that particular weekend. It was amazing how one's priorities could change in the blink of an eye.

As I walked toward Java Time, I glanced over at Gabby's store, checking for the *Open* sign on her door. Her store was in a prime location as far as I concerned. All the main necessities in life were located on the same side of Harvest Park Avenue—the Meat and Greet where I'd occasionally stop for spare ribs to add to my sauce and sirloin roast to make my braciole, Java Time Coffee, Sweet Treats Bakery, and Gabby's store. On the other side of the park was Spice and Nice, which carried every kind of seasoning imaginable, the Flower Girl, a florist that specialized in exotic flowers, Grab and Go Grocery, and Suit Yourself, a men's clothing store that had counted Dylan as one of their most frequent customers. Once I could see the *Open* sign and soft light coming from Gabby's front window, I pulled open the door to Java Time and basked in the nutty smell of fresh coffee.

Archie Fenton owned and operated Java Time. He was like your friendly bartender dispensing advice, but instead of alcohol, he served up specialty drinks along with my favorite type of coffee, his rich, dark roast. He also had French vanilla cappuccinos and mocha lattes to die for. I was especially fond of his peppermint hot chocolate with homemade whipped cream, which he only served around the holidays. The shop was closed on Sundays, but other than that, he never took a day off. His wife had died several years back, and their kids were grown and had moved away, except for one son. The shop and its customers had become Archie's extended family.

He watched me now from behind the front counter, a Giants hat on top of his bald head, his large jowls drooping as his mouth formed an enormous grin. He handed change to a customer and immediately came out from behind the register to greet me.

I put my arms around him and squeezed. "Hey, Arch. What's the special of the day?"

"Tessa." His voice was gruff as he gave me a quick peck on the cheek. "It's so good to see you out and about again."

My eyes started to fill. "Thanks. I've missed you."

"Chin up, honey. Right now, it's hell to get through a single day, but things will get easier with time. I promise you that."

He took my left hand in his, and I noticed the wedding

ring that he still wore, ten years after Ella's death. I glanced down at my own gold band and diamond solitaire, remembering how I'd cried happy tears when Dylan had placed them on my finger. It seemed like such a long time ago.

"I'm here if you ever need to talk."

"I know." The lump in my throat expanded and I had to remind myself to breathe. "Hey, how about two of your fabulous dark roasts to go?"

"Right away." He went behind the counter and started to fill the paper cups from a machine. "I'm guessing one of these is for your book-loving cousin. I haven't seen her all day. Must be busy."

"She usually does well on Saturdays," I agreed, glancing around the shop. Archie's place was pleasant and warm, smelling of cinnamon and coffee beans. There were a few tables and a solitary booth in the back of the shop that were all currently vacant. The entire shop was inviting with its dark, wood-veneer walls and pine-beam ceiling overhead.

Archie placed the cups in a cardboard tray on the counter and took the money I handed him. "I'll miss seeing your other half in here. Dylan always lent an air of elegance to this place. Whether he was in a suit and tie or sweats and T-shirt like the last time I saw him, your man always reeked of class."

I smiled. It was true, Dylan had always looked like a million bucks. He was a firm believer in dressing for success. "You must have seen him on a Saturday." I almost didn't realize I'd spoken the words out loud. Dylan had often worked out on Saturday mornings with his friend Justin but over the summer had started cutting back on the exercise and went to the office instead. He claimed his workload was getting unmanageable and We Care, his employer, wouldn't allow him an assistant.

"Nope. It was the day before he—" Archie lowered his eyes to the floor. "You know. I remember it well. I wish I'd gotten a chance to talk to Dylan more, but he was with some other guy, and I was swamped at the counter anyway."

"Oh. A Thursday then." Dylan had died on a Friday—a beautiful fall day filled with sunshine and unusually warm for the time of year. My forehead wrinkled at the memory. Dylan hadn't taken the day off from work that Thursday. I always left before him, but on that particular day I hadn't felt well and decided to call in sick. He'd come into the bedroom to kiss me goodbye, and I remembered that he was wearing a three-piece, dark-blue suit. It was my favorite because it went so well with his eyes. Archie must have gotten the dates wrong. "Are you sure that was the right day?"

He tapped the side of his hat proudly. "Positive. There's no cobwebs in this brain. My memory is as safe as money in the bank."

I tilted my head to the side and studied him. "Who was he with? Justin?"

Archie shook his head. "Definitely not Justin. This guy had gray hair. Real greasy looking too. Dylan came up to get their coffee, and the guy had his back to me, so I didn't get a good look at him. By the time I got a chance to go over and say hi, Dylan was sitting by himself. He seemed a bit out of it too. I asked him if he was all right, but he just nodded and left."

Maybe it had been a client. "Did they argue?" I asked.

"Don't think so. They had their heads bent together pretty well." Archie's face sobered. "I didn't think much about it then, but if I'd known that would be the last time I'd see or talk to him—"

I interrupted, not wanting him to finish the sentence. "You don't know if this guy lives in town?"

"Well, I didn't see his face, so no, I can't swear to it. But

I might recognize him from the back of his head." He tried to make a joke out of it but must have noted my pensiveness. "Something wrong?"

"No. It must have been someone he did taxes for." Dylan often met personal clients at our house or in various parts of town if we didn't know them well, so that part seemed normal enough. What struck me as odd was the fact that he'd been in sweats and a T-shirt in the middle of a workday. Dylan was the consummate professional and never wore sweats unless he was at the gym or we were relaxing at home on a weekend. Even when he came home from work at night, he'd often stay in his slacks and dress shirt until bedtime. If Harvest Park had ever nominated a man for *GQ*, Dylan would have won hands down.

The door of the shop opened and a crowd of five gathered behind me, waiting for service. I moved out of the way and waved to Archie. "I'd better get over to Gabby's. See you soon."

He winked. "Don't be a stranger, honey."

I pushed the door open, nearly hitting a man on his way into the shop. The cardboard tray started to slide from my hands, and Matt Smitty, my former boyfriend, reached forward and grabbed my drinks before they fell to the floor.

"I'm so sorry." Running into Matt was always awkward, although Dylan and I had used him as our mechanic for years. My purse had slipped from my shoulder, and I knelt down to retrieve it from the floor. "I should have been more careful. Thanks for your help."

"Anything for a pretty lady," Matt said, smiling down at me. I straightened up and stepped outside onto the sidewalk while Matt held the door open for me. To my surprise, he followed. I always wanted to believe that Matt had changed for the better since our breakup, but I still felt a bit uncomfortable around him at times and tried to avoid him when possible. But this was my opportunity to ask a few questions about Dylan's last day, and I wasn't about to pass it up.

"Thanks. How are you?" The last time I'd seen him was at Dylan's service, and his wife, Lila, had been with him. She was a delicate-looking blond who had moved here from the South a few years back, but I didn't know her well.

"Seems like I should be asking you that instead." He ran a hand through his dirty-blond hair, pushing the bangs out of his eyes. Even at thirty, he still had the same pronounced baby-like features I remembered from high school, complete with a rounded chin and cheeks, wide-set hazel eyes, and a dimple on the right side of his mouth. "I was wondering how you were holding up."

"Weren't you going inside?" I motioned toward the door.

He stuffed his hands into his jeans pockets and straightened up to his full, lanky six-foot height. "It can wait. I'd rather hear how you're doing first."

I withdrew one hand from the tray and wiggled it back and forth. "Coping, thanks. One day at a time. Actually, I'm glad I ran into you."

"Are you now?" He gave me a slight, almost teasing smile that reminded me of better days, when we'd been good friends before getting involved with one another. Matt and I had known each other since elementary school. Late in our junior year, he'd asked me out and we'd dated for a few months. He'd professed over and over to love me, and although I'd been fond of him, I had never felt the same way. When he started to become too possessive, I'd broken things off, and Matt hadn't taken it well.

I clutched the cardboard tray tightly. "Yes. I was wondering if you had talked to Dylan the day he brought his car in. You know, the day before he…his accident."

Matt's two-bay garage repair shop was about ten minutes away from my home. It had been convenient for

Dylan on his way to work, plus Matt was an excellent mechanic, the best one around for miles.

The smile on Matt's face disappeared, and something dark stirred in his intense hazel eyes, bringing back other memories for me—more painful ones this time. After our breakup, Matt had taken to following me around constantly—at school, at work, and to my house—with stalker-like tendencies that had frightened me. Finally, my father had threatened Matt with a restraining order if he didn't leave me alone. Matt had then apologized and didn't come near me again.

Then came the rumors that he'd started using drugs after high school. I'd fervently hoped they weren't true but couldn't be positive. I'd been away at college, then culinary school, and hadn't seen him again until after Dylan and I had become engaged, and by then it seemed that Matt had turned a corner. We'd both moved on with our lives—me with Dylan and him with Lila—and whenever I saw him around town with his kids, he'd struck me as an attentive and devoted father. Still, there was always a small flicker of possession in his eyes whenever he looked my way that warned me to keep my distance.

"I wasn't at the shop that day," he said. "Earl worked on his car. I already told your cousin that."

"Oh. Of course." What else could I say without tipping him off to the fact that Dylan's accident had in fact *not* been an accident? Or did he already know this, thanks to Gino's coworker with the set of loose lips?

I didn't want to sound accusatory with my questions since Dylan and Matt hadn't exactly liked each other. Dylan respected him as a mechanic, and they made small talk whenever he went into the shop, but an argument between them weeks before our wedding had assured they'd never be good friends. One night at a local bar, Matt had come on to me after I told him Dylan and I were engaged. While I had tried to brush off his advances, Dylan had been furious, and a shouting match had escalated from there. Matt had been drunk at the time, and Dylan wasn't exactly sober either, but it was a text from Matt the evening before my wedding the next month that had bothered me the most. He'd said I'd be sorry if I ever married Dylan.

Today, six years later, his former threat was back to haunt me. I'd hidden the text from Dylan at the time, not wanting to restart the feud, but I always wondered if it had been the right thing to do.

As I thought back on Matt's warning, his amber-colored eyes surveyed me intently, as if he could guess what

I was thinking. He folded his arms over his chest. "Why don't you tell me what you really want to know, Tess?"

His voice carried an edge that made me back up against the side of the building. "What are you talking about?"

He put a hand up against the brick facade of the building, inches from my shoulder. "Gino thinks that Dylan's death wasn't an accident."

"Did he tell you that?"

Matt shook his head. "He didn't have to. Another cop came into the shop last week and talked to Earl. He said Dylan's death was, quote, suspicious."

Cripes. I hoped that this guy got reprimanded or something by the police department. I hesitated, not knowing what else to say. "It's…possible. Could I talk to Earl? I was wondering if he might remember how Dylan was dressed that day."

Matt looked at me strangely. "What does that have to do with anything?"

"I don't know," I said honestly. "Is there a chance you could ask Earl and let me know what he says?"

"Sure." He stood motionless, staring down at me, but the suspicion had seeped out of his face. "If you need anything…anything at all, call me. Day or night." He glanced around, but we were alone on the street. I almost expected to see Gabby's shop door open and her to appear with a pair of binoculars or maybe even a baseball bat. Like Gino, she hated Matt.

For some reason, his offer of help unnerved me. Although Matt hadn't done anything wrong, I was getting strange vibes, and it reminded of all the reasons why I'd left him back in high school. I swallowed a knot of fear in my throat, smiled, and forced out a hoarse, "Thanks."

Matt reached forward and put a hand on my shoulder while I stiffened slightly. "Remember, Tess. I'm never far away."

FOUR

"HE IS SUCH A WEIRDO," GABBY declared as she sat cross-legged on the floor of her shop, arranging books on a bottom shelf. "Why you ever went out with that guy is beyond me. Hand me that James Patterson novel, will you?"

Gabby's bookstore was warm and inviting, like its owner. There were plenty of shelves for readers to browse, and she'd set up old-fashioned armchairs upholstered in red velvet throughout the store for those ready to crack open a spine. Near the back were several padded chairs and an oval, dark-wood table that Gabby used for her weekly book club meetings. About forty people belonged to the club, but not all the same members came every week. They would discuss a certain book for an hour, while Gabby provided coffee and homemade cookies—the latter usually from me. The only requirement for membership was that they buy the book from Gabby's store.

I handed the book to my cousin and watched as she tried to decide where to place it on the shelf as she mumbled under her breath. I'd already filled Gabby in on Gino's visit, and as expected, she was furious that he'd kept the truth from me about Dylan's accident. Her annoyance had been further fueled when I told her about my run-in with Matt.

"Like I said, that guy is bad news," she said. "But I think it's great you're going back to work. If there's something shady going on at Slice, you'll definitely figure it out."

I closed my eyes for a minute and let myself drink in the delightful scent of Gabby's store. It smelled of crisp, new books mixed with the lingering scent of fresh apple cider, which Gabby put out for her customers every morning during the fall season. It was a gorgeous 1920s building with a high ceiling, a rustic, Mediterranean-style hardwood floor, and bookshelves made of knotty pine. Gabby had stumbled upon the property at the perfect time. The former owners had run a candy store out of it for several years and were well into their seventies when they'd decided to retire and sell the building to her at a very reasonable price. My cousin had taken out a small business loan, installed new shelves, and stocked the store with everything from Agatha Christie to Dr. Seuss.

A silver-framed picture of Gabby and Stephen King adorned the wall behind the front counter. Gabby had met him at a signing last year and had been bold enough to put her arm around him in the photo. From the look on his face, it didn't appear that he'd minded. No one was immune to Gabby's charm.

Even though Gabby had been in business for less than a year, she'd already done an outstanding job with the place, despite everyone's warnings that the store didn't have a chance of making it in our small town. Some weeks were better than others; however, Gabby was planning more events in addition to her regularly scheduled author signings to increase foot traffic, and weekly speakers and kid's activities were already becoming a big draw. She loved to read, and I admired her for following her passion, something I once did before the accident derailed my restaurant dream.

My thoughts returned to Matt. "Maybe it wasn't the best decision I ever made to date him," I admitted, "but that was a long time ago. He has a wife and three kids now. You should see Matt's face when he talks about his boys." Every time I saw him, he proudly pulled out their latest photos. It was always a safe topic for us to talk about. "People can change, Gabs," I said with forced conviction.

Gabby quirked her eyebrow, registering the false note, and rose to her feet. "Yeah, he has three kids, but the rumor mill says that he and his wife aren't so happy anymore. And I've seen the way he still looks at you. When he came to Dylan's wake, he couldn't take his eyes—" Gabby's face turned the color of a ripe tomato. "Oh, Tess. I'm sorry. That sounded really crass."

"It's all right." I swallowed another mouthful of the dark roast, savoring the taste as it rolled over my tongue. How I had missed Archie's coffee. Time to change the subject. "Did your book club enjoy the cookies last night?"

She beamed. "Every one of them vanished before we were done. Seriously, you should open your own bakery, girl."

"It's always fun to make them." Gabby had been thrilled when I'd come in with my jelly cookies, which consisted of buttery shortbread with raspberry preserves in the center, and my double chocolate chips that were so soft and chewy, they practically melted in your mouth. The baking had put me in a better frame of mind, and even though she'd offered to come and get them, I'd decided it was time for me to venture out of the house. Gabby had encouraged me to stay for the meeting, but I'd refused. This was a work in progress for me. Baby steps, one at a time.

Gabby reached for her cup and stood next to me at the front counter, her dark, exotic eyes looking slightly upward as they rested on my face. "Matt always has that smug look on his face. I don't want to be anywhere near him."

I watched my cousin as she sipped her coffee. Gabby was a true beauty, inside and out, with her curvy figure and short, ebony hair styled in a blunt cut. Even though we'd grown up in different households, we were as close as sisters and had always been each other's main confidante. Gabby had never made any bones about not liking Matt, and the feeling had been mutual.

"He's the best mechanic around—maybe in the entire state. You still can't let that incident in sixth grade go, huh?" I teased, remembering the time she'd given him a fat lip when he'd put gum in her hair.

"It's more than that and you know it," she huffed. "There's something about that guy that has always rubbed me the wrong way. He's the proverbial thorn in my rosebush, so to speak. And he's apparently never gotten over you."

"What are you really trying to say? That you think Matt killed Dylan? What would have been his motive?"

Gabby looked at me like I had two heads. "Well, if he and his wife are getting divorced, and you suddenly became available, there's your motive."

I finished my coffee and threw the cup in the trash. "Matt's not a killer."

She studied me carefully. "If you're serious about finding out who did this to Dylan, then you have to look at everyone as a potential suspect. No one is exempt." She grabbed the empty cardboard box off the floor and flattened it between her two graceful hands. "Plus, you'll need an assistant, so I'm applying for the job."

I barked out a laugh. "An assistant?"

"Sure. All the great detectives in books have assistants. Sherlock had Watson, while Nancy Drew had her two best friends, Bess and George."

"Gino will be furious if you get involved."

Gabby waved a hand in the air, as if swatting at a fly. "Ah, don't worry. I can handle him."

Well, this was a new one. Gabby acted as if a confrontation with Gino was a mere walk in Harvest Park. The truth was, Gino had always been super protective of his little sister—and me as well. It didn't bother me as much since I had no siblings of my own to deal with, but he'd always driven Gabby nuts. At least he still didn't follow her and her boyfriends around on dates like he'd done in high school. I hoped not, anyway.

She must have noticed the look of skepticism I wore because she merely shrugged. "Never mind my brother. So what's your game plan?"

I blew out a breath. "Maybe the best thing would be to trace all of Dylan's movements during his last couple of days. You know, find out where he went, who he saw. I figured I should start with his office at We Care."

Her eyes widened. "That makes sense, I guess. He spent the most time there."

"Correct. They're closed on the weekend, so I'll check them out on Monday morning."

"You can't go in there asking questions," Gabby said. "Why not wait until you've worked at Slice for a few days?"

"Give me a little credit, would you?" I asked. "Dylan's personal effects are still at his office so I'll call his receptionist and let her know I'm picking them up. Who knows? I might find something useful."

Gabby nodded. "But what about the family dinner tomorrow night? Are you going to tell anyone else about this?"

I shook my head. "Of course, if I find out anything significant, I'll share it with Gino. But this is *my* husband we're talking about. I'm not about to sit around and wait for the police to find this person. No offense to Gino, but they're doing a lousy job so far."

She reached out to squeeze my hand. "I don't blame you. And I think your getting back to cooking full time will help to put everything into perspective. Whatever happens, you know that I've got your back."

"I've never doubted it for a second."

FIVE

"SO." MOM BEGAN TO SET THE table. "When do you start your job as head chef at Anthony's? Oh, and don't forget about the biscotti and *genetti* for the Altar Rosary Society next Saturday night. Will you still have time to make them?"

The smell of my Bolognese sauce beckoned me, and I dipped the wooden spoon in for a taste. Ah, yes. The meat and onions blended perfectly with the herbs. A little extra pinch of oregano and it would be perfect. Some fresh, chopped parsley would make a nice garnish as well. I stirred a smaller pot on the stove with pastina for Gino's twin boys, who were fussy about what they ate. They preferred the tiny pieces of pasta with egg, butter, and cheese mixed in. It had been a favorite of mine as a child and still served as a great comfort food on a cold winter's night.

It was almost six o'clock on Sunday evening, and I was

hosting dinner for my family. This was a practice I enjoyed doing weekly, but it was the first time since Dylan's death that I'd felt up to the task. Gino, his family, and Gabby would be joining us any minute.

I washed the spoon off under the faucet before submerging it in the sauce again. "I'm *not* head chef, Mom. They don't even have such a thing. I'll be working in the kitchen, making pizzas and some dinners. That's all."

Mom came into the kitchen with a glass of red wine in her hand. She offered it to me, and I shook my head. "I don't understand. Why would you even take such a position?" she asked. "He can't be paying much."

I wanted to tell my mother about Dylan's not-so-accidental death, but it was not a good time, and the fewer people who knew, the better. My mother loved gossip but not when it concerned her family. Chances were that she might not believe me anyway, but I didn't want to take the risk. In some ways, she still treated me like I was five years old, not thirty. She missed my father terribly, and I think she'd secretly hoped I'd move back in with her after Dylan's death.

"Do you know much about Anthony or his family?" I asked in an attempt to change the subject. Harvest Park had a fair share of Italian families, mine and the Mancusis being among them, but then again, so did several Upstate New York towns. Dylan's mother had actually been born in Sweden, and he'd inherited his classic blond hair and blue eyes from her, but his father, like mine, had been 100 percent Sicilian.

I'd only met my in-laws twice—at our wedding and his funeral. They lived in Florida, and Dylan didn't have much contact with them during our marriage. He had confided to me once that he'd never measured up to their expectations. They'd wanted him to become a doctor, not an accountant, and were furious when he quit medical school after one semester. Their relationship had never been the same after that. His parents had been broken up over his death, and it saddened me that they'd never been able to repair their relationship.

"Anthony is one of the largest donors we have at Heavenly Angels Church. He arranges a toy drop-off at his restaurant every Christmas." Mom tapped a finger against her dark hair, piled high on top of her head in a dramatic updo. "When I was in there last week, he asked how you were doing. He was so upset about Dylan. I know it's a difficult situation, honey. A senseless and tragic accident."

I kept quiet while she prattled on, arranging linen

napkins on the white lace tablecloth. "I heard that Belladonna's is looking for an experienced chef. You could have that job in a heartbeat. Dylan was a wonderful man, but let's face it, sweetheart: a hundred-thousand-dollar life insurance policy won't go far these days. He should have provided for you more."

"He was only thirty years old. We didn't think death was in our immediate future." I hated to admit it, but she was right. We should have planned better.

She sighed. "Well, at least you don't have to worry about taking care of any children by yourself."

Her words sent a pang through my chest. My biggest regret was not trying for a baby sooner. We would have been married six years on Valentine's Day, but I was the one who had wanted to wait to have kids. Dylan had been anxious to become a father, and at times I still pictured him with our make-believe family—playing ball with a dark-haired son or carrying a daughter around on his shoulders, her blond hair the spitting image of her daddy's. Sadly, it would never be more than a dream now.

Mom's face reddened, as if she had guessed my thoughts. "That was insensitive of me, darling. Now getting back to this…job." She frowned, as if the word made her ill.

"The DeNovo boy works for Anthony, doesn't he? His first name is Butchy. Have you met him yet?"

The sauce bubbled while I stirred, and I longed for my mother to stop talking so I could venture into my safe, happy place. "No. I saw a delivery kid named Sam and met another one named Eric."

"Butchy's such a lovely young man," she gushed. "He was at the Grab and Go last week and carried my groceries to my car for me. Anthony always hires the politest kids. I heard one of the boys couldn't find a job so Anthony hired him, even though he didn't need three delivery boys. Isn't that wonderful? Butchy's mom, Angela, is on the Altar Rosary Society with me. She's running for president this year. It's terrible to say, but I hope she doesn't win."

"Why? I thought she was one of your friends." I didn't know the DeNovo family, except for Angela whom I'd met a couple of times when she'd been with my mother. They'd moved to Harvest Park a few years back, after Mr. DeNovo had passed away. Like my mother, they were devout churchgoers. I'd started to drift away from the parish after I married Dylan, who had not been very religious.

She paused to refill her wineglass and then placed the bottle back on the table. "Because she's starting to lose it.

Angela's in the beginning stages of dementia and comes out with the strangest things. The other day she told me Butchy's the manager at Slice."

"Oh boy."

"Exactly." My mother shook her head. "It's so sad, especially since she's only a few years older than me. Anyhow, are you sure the cookies won't be too much trouble? We could buy them, but yours are so much better. I'll reimburse you for the ingredients."

"It's no trouble, and I'm not worried about the money."

"You need to have some fun, darling. How about taking a cruise with me? I'm thinking about going to the Caribbean after Christmas."

I did a mental eye roll and didn't answer right away. My mother was a cruise enthusiast and thought a vacation could cure any ailment.

"I'm sure Justin would watch Luigi." Mom continued, her glass perched elegantly against her full red lips. "He'd do anything for you. That man has always had his eye on you."

My mother's ramblings usually gave me a mild headache, but this comment flat out annoyed me. Justin Kelly and Dylan had been best friends since their college roommate days at the University at Albany. Dylan and I met two years later when I returned home one summer to be in a wedding where he and Justin also happened to be groomsmen. The first time I'd laid eyes on Dylan, I'd fallen hard, and Justin's friendship had always been part of the deal.

As Dylan was starting out at We Care, Justin had graduated from the fire academy and immediately secured a job at the Harvest Park Station. He and his wife, Natalie, had married about a year after Dylan and me, and we'd often gone out together as a foursome. We'd bought our house shortly after they had—in fact, their ranch home, where Justin now lived alone, was on the next block. Natalie and I had been on pleasant enough terms, but our friendship was nothing like Dylan and Justin's, or even mine and Justin's, for that matter.

We were shocked when Justin revealed they were divorcing because of an affair Natalie had been having with one of her coworkers. Since she'd moved out a year ago, Dylan and I had tried to lend Justin support in any way possible. I constantly invited him over for dinner, but he seemed to prefer Dylan bringing a plate over to his house instead, although he'd always call or text me a thank-you afterward. He'd been a rock for me since Dylan died, despite the fact he was grieving too. Justin never made any inappropriate advances, and my mother needed to know that.

"That's ridiculous. Justin has been a godsend since Dylan's death."

"He's a good man," my mother agreed, "and he didn't deserve the way Natalie treated him. I simply said for you to watch out. He's always been interested in you. A mother knows these things."

She didn't understand. "He helps out with repairs around the house. You know, fixing the sink and stuff like that. We both miss Dylan terribly, and it's nice to talk to someone who loved him as much as I did."

Mom wagged a blood-red acrylic fingernail in my face. "Theresa, listen to your mother. A man isn't that helpful unless he wants something in return."

She reached down to pet her two Jack Russell terriers, Parmigiano and Reggiano, or "Parm" and "Reggie" as we all called them, after the King of Cheeses. She hardly ever went anywhere without the dogs. They were more spoiled than most children. Excited by the attention, the dogs began to run around the room in circles.

"Mom! They're scaring Luigi." I pointed at the cat,

who was trotting up the stairs in a panicked effort to get away from them.

We were interrupted at that moment by a knock on the door. Gino, his wife, Lucy, the twins, and Aunt Mona were ready to descend upon us.

Aunt Mona was my father's younger sister. She and my mother had always gotten along famously, even though they were like day and night. Mom was delicate and petite, while Mona was big boned everywhere and immensely proud of it. She wore her grayish-brown hair in an outdated beehive hairstyle, and every winter, she donned the same faux-fur coat, along with black sturdy boots that looked as if she'd stolen them off a Viking.

My mother and Aunt Mona were even closer now that their spouses were no longer in the picture. She and my Uncle Hal had divorced when Gabby and Gino were still in elementary school. He'd since remarried, and last we heard, he was living in California.

Lucy put her arms around my shoulders and hugged me tightly. She smelled good, a mixture of violet perfume and the crisp clean air outside. Lucy was blond and petite, with green eyes that shone like expensive jewels. She and Gino made a striking couple. The Mancusi family genes had dominated, and their twins, Rocco and Marco, were exact replicas of their father. Darling little imps who some days I was convinced came airmailed straight from hell.

"Aunt Tessa!" Rocco started to jump up and down. "Where's Luigi? How come he won't come see me?"

"Because you pulled his tail last time," his mother admonished him in a soft voice. "That's why you two can't have a pet."

"I get to pet Luigi first!" Marco yelled as he ran up the stairs with his brother following closely behind him.

"Can't have a pet?" Gino called over his shoulder to his wife as he raced up the stairs after them. "They've got two lizards, a snake, and goldfish. What do you classify those as?"

Lucy ignored him and turned to hang up the kids' coats. "Do you need some help in the kitchen, Tess?"

"Thanks, but everything's ready to go." I brought the sauce and salad to the table while my mother followed with the rest.

Gino arrived at the bottom of the staircase a few seconds later, carrying one twin and dragging the other behind him. He sat them down at the Little Tikes table I kept on hand especially for these occasions. "I'd better not see either one of you throwing garlic bread this time," he warned.

"Aunt Tessa, Luigi's in your bathtub." Rocco giggled. "He's drinking water out of the faucet."

I smiled. "He does that a lot."

Marco turned as if to go back upstairs. "Uh-oh. I shut the door so he can't get out."

"That's all right," I assured him. "Luigi can open the door if he wants to." The cat was long and lean, and the doorknob of the bathroom was positioned slightly lower than the other ones throughout my house. To tell the truth, he was probably happier in there for now. Luigi hated the dogs and wasn't fond of the twins either.

As we all sat down, there was a tap on the front door. I turned to see Gabby standing in the small vestibule. I crossed the room and took the bottle of merlot from her hand as she hung up her coat. "I have wine. You didn't need to bring any."

Gabby grinned. "There's never enough wine. Follow me out to the kitchen so we can talk for a minute." She raised a hand in greeting to everyone as she walked past the table.

"Aunt Gabby, will you sit with us?" Rocco pleaded.

"Sure thing, little man. As soon as I get done helping Aunt Tessa."

Gino watched us, his fork raised in the air. "All the food is already out. What are you two up to?"

Lucy patted his hand. "Eat, dear. You're way too suspicious of everyone these days."

"It's that easygoing nature of his," Gabby called out grandly as we went into the kitchen. She grabbed a crystal goblet out of my overhead white cabinets with the glass panes in front. "What have you been doing since we talked yesterday?"

I folded my arms over my chest. "Not much. Besides cooking all day, I've been trying to plot my strategy for tomorrow. I'm making a mental list of people I want to speak to, but I'll be limited because of work. I need to talk to Justin, but he's out of town until tomorrow and then he's working. I already texted him and asked if he'd stop over Tuesday night when he gets done. I don't want anyone else to tell him what happened, but I couldn't exactly say it in a text either."

Gabby opened the bottle of merlot she'd brought and then poured herself a glass. "Who's on your list?"

"I thought I'd start with Carlita." Carlita Garcia owned Sweet Treats, the bakery next to Gabby's store, and she was notorious for knowing all the Harvest Park gossip. Dylan had been laying off desserts for a while and claimed he was gaining weight, although I certainly hadn't noticed it. Still, if he'd been out and about town the day he died, she would have seen him. Carlita had eyes in the back of her head.

"I guess it wouldn't do any harm," Gabby admitted. "The chances that she saw something aren't very good though."

"Can you take a quick break and meet me over there tomorrow, say about ten? I have to be at Slice at noon. My shifts are going to be twelve to nine o'clock, so I won't be able to do much digging after work, but I should have enough time to stop by Dylan's office in the morning as well."

She gave me a small impish smile, which made me think she had something up her sleeve. "Liza doesn't get in until ten, but I'll try. Text me in the morning, and I'll help conduct your first official interview." Liza Fowler was Gabby's lone employee. She was a few years older than Gabby and myself and a fellow book worshipper like her boss.

My cell buzzed from the kitchen counter. Before I could grab it, Gabby glanced down at the screen and did a double take. She held the phone out to me like it was diseased. "Why the hell is Matt Smitty calling you?"

A prickle of uneasiness shot through me, but I tried to

act casual with her eyes glued on me. Ignoring the question, I put the phone to my ear. "Hello?"

"Hey, Tess. It's Matt. Hope I didn't catch you at a bad time."

"No, this is fine." Gabby stuck her finger down her throat, and I rolled my eyes. "What's up?"

Matt spoke in a low tone. "I was on the phone with Earl and asked him about how Dylan was dressed the day he came in. Funny thing is that Earl did remember. He said he made a comment to Dylan because he was wearing sweats, and Earl said it was the first time he hadn't seen him in a suit and tie. He asked Dylan if he was slumming it for the day."

I clutched the phone tighter. "Does he remember what time he saw Dylan? Did he drop the car off or wait for it?"

"Earl said he waited for it. I checked, and his appointment was for three o'clock. Earl said he did notice a suit hanging in the back of the car. Maybe Dylan got off work early?"

I grabbed a Post-it Note off the counter and wrote down the time. I had forgotten to ask Archie what time Dylan had stopped in for coffee that day but could always check back with him. Why had my husband wanted me to think he was going to work when he evidently hadn't? "Thanks, Matt. I appreciate it."

"Tess." Matt's voice turned husky on the other end. "I feel really bad about what happened to Dylan. Please let me know if you ever need anything. You can call me anytime, even if it's in the middle of the night."

I raised an eyebrow at Gabby, who had inched closer to me and was trying to listen in. Matt might have meant to offer me comfort, but this struck me as odd. We were not friends anymore. Why would he think that I'd call a married man in the middle of the night? "Thanks, Matt." I hung up, at a loss for further words.

Gabby's eyes searched mine. "What did he want?"

"He said that Dylan was wearing sweats the day he brought his car in and Earl spotted a suit in the back seat. It must have been the same one he was wearing that morning when he left the house."

She gave me a sharp look. "What else? Come on. It's written all over your face."

"It's…no big deal," I said uneasily. "He said for me to call him if I needed anything."

Gabby pointed a finger at me. "You see? I told you. He's still carrying a torch—"

She never finished the sentence, because at that moment, Gino peered his head in the doorway, and we both jumped.

A muscle ticked in his jaw as he stood there, watching us in silence for a few seconds. Had he been listening in on our conversation?

"The pasta's getting cold, ladies," he said between clenched teeth. "You should come back to the table. If you're done with your gossip session, that is."

Oh yeah, he'd probably heard more than we wanted him to.

SIX

MONDAY MORNING DAWNED GRAY AND OVERCAST, but at least snow hadn't been predicted. Even though the calendar only said November, it wasn't unusual to see a Nor'easter this time of year.

I stood in front of my bay window with a mug of coffee in hand and watched the two little girls across the street board the school bus. It would be easy to stay home, in the confines of my warm, comfortable kitchen with its light-blue Formica countertops and stainless-steel gas stove. I could lose myself in an abundance of flour and sugar and get my baking underway for the upcoming holiday season. But I knew I couldn't hide from the world any longer. A new determination had filled me in the last couple of days. I could not—and would not—rest until I found the person responsible for my husband's death.

In the past, I had always been a huge fan of the holidays and spent most of December wrapping presents and baking an abundance of Christmas cookies. I usually made between fifteen and twenty different varieties. Instead of sending cards, I delivered homemade treats. My most popular variety among adults were the *genetti*—a soft-textured, glazed Italian cookie with nonpareils on top. Children loved my famous gingerbread men made with rich molasses and my butter cookies dipped in melted fudge and adorned with plenty of colorful sprinkles.

I gave cookies to everyone I knew—family, neighbors, coworkers, friends, and even the mailman. Since I loved making them and never wanted to disappoint anyone, I would bake again this year, but the magic was gone from the season for me. At this point, I wasn't sure if it would ever come back.

With dread, I tried to prepare for my first holiday season as a widow. I already knew from my mother and her experience how difficult all the "firsts" could be. Plus, I still had Dylan's birthday to get through in a few days. Maybe I'd look into helping out at one of the local shelters this year. Keeping busy was the key to combat the loneliness. I couldn't let myself sink back into the well of despair I'd fought so hard to climb out of.

A hazy mist had settled over the horizon as the sunlight behind the clouds struggled to break through. The glow expanded in the sky, its sudden light giving me hope. A new day had dawned, and its message was abundantly clear to me. *Time to start over.*

I was somewhat nervous about going back to work in a kitchen other than my own again. I simply had to resign myself to the fact that my dream restaurant—the one Dylan and I had talked incessantly about for years—would never happen.

A noise from the kitchen startled me out of my thoughts, and I turned to see Luigi sitting on the breakfast counter as if he owned the place. His enormous green eyes gazed at me, watching my every move with intense curiosity.

"Hey, you know better than that." I tried to sound stern, but his expression was so comical that I couldn't help but laugh. I gathered him up in my arms, and he purred contentedly against my chest. Luigi's V-8 engine noises continued while I filled his food dish with star-shaped kitty crunches, and then he couldn't scramble out of my arms fast enough.

It was five minutes after nine, so I picked up my cell and dialed the main number for We Care. Olivia Moore, the receptionist on Dylan's floor, should be in by now. She answered on the second ring. "Good morning, We Care. How may I assist you?"

So perky for a Monday morning. "Hi, Olivia? This is Tessa—Tessa Esposito. How are you?"

There was silence for a few seconds. "Oh, Tessa! My God…it's…uh…so nice to hear from you."

Her voice had gone from upbeat and cheery to cautious and confused. "Thank you. I'd like to ask a favor."

Another brief pause. "Of course. What can I do for you?" she asked.

"I was wondering if I could stop down and pick up Dylan's personal items this morning before I go to work. I'm sorry I haven't been in sooner but—" What was there left to say? *Sorry, I wanted to wait until I wouldn't cry in front of you?*

"Oh." Her voice sounded puzzled. "Didn't you pick those up already?"

Why would she think that? "No. I completely forgot about it until now."

"That's totally understandable," Olivia assured me. "Um…I need to ask Mr. Reinhart first. Would you mind holding for a minute?"

I glanced at my watch. "Sure. Um, I could be there in a half hour if that would—"

But it was too late. Olivia was already gone, and I was left alone with Sirius's seventies station. I kept the phone pressed to my ear as I emptied the dishwasher and listened to Barry Manilow's "Copacabana." The song had reached the part about Lola drinking herself half blind when Olivia came back on the phone.

"Tessa, I apologize," she said. "Apparently Mr. Reinhart thought you'd picked up the stuff already. Our intern, Sandy, is the one who boxed up Dylan's items. She went out on medical leave right afterward. We thought she'd called you, but the boxes are still sitting in his office closet. I'm terribly sorry for the inconvenience. Mr. Reinhart said you could come by tomorrow."

I'd really hoped to go today but didn't press the issue. "Of course. That's fine."

Olivia sounded hesitant. "I wanted to say...well, I'm sorry about everything that happened to Dylan."

"Thank you," I said quietly. "It was quite a shock."

"His death must have been too," Olivia agreed. Another line was ringing in the background. "I have to go. See you tomorrow." She clicked off before I could say another word.

Her words left my brain in a muddled state. What on earth had she meant by that? *His death must have been too?*

I'd met Olivia at the office Christmas party a couple of years ago. She had gotten married last year, and Dylan mentioned once that she was expecting a baby. He'd also commented that Olivia was a bit on the ditzy side, complaining how she always forgot to give him his messages or would interrupt when he'd specifically asked not to be disturbed.

I shot off a quick text to Gabby. Can't go to Dylan's office today. Meet me at ten thirty at Sweet Treats? I didn't wait for a response and quickly jumped into the shower. After I had finished washing my hair and toweled off, I went to the closet in search of clothes to wear and pulled on jeans and a tunic sweater.

My eyes fell upon the unmade king-size bed, and a wave of despair swept over me. Perhaps the worst part of Dylan being gone was sleeping alone. For a moment, I was sorely tempted to fall back into bed and spend the day weeping, but pity parties solved nothing. My sole mission now was to find out what had happened to my husband.

After I had pulled my hair back into a tight ponytail and applied mascara to my lashes, I gazed critically in the mirror at my reflection. I felt much older than my thirty years today. My brown eyes stared back at me with faint circles of weariness under them. I applied some concealer as my thoughts returned to the conversation with Olivia. Along with being nervous about poking around We Care, I wasn't looking forward to going through Dylan's stuff, no matter how necessary it was. It was a chore I'd been putting off since the accident, but I knew I'd have to sort through Dylan's clothes and other belongings in our bedroom and study sooner or later.

I went downstairs to give Luigi a hug and picked up my phone from where I'd left it on the bay window seat. Gabby had texted, Works for me. See you then. With purse in hand, I went into the garage, settled myself in the front seat, and backed the car out. Then I headed for the center of town.

I found a parking space in front of Meat and Greet and locked my car. Through the glass window of Sweet Treats, I spotted Carlita behind the bakery display case, chatting with an elderly couple. She gave no indication that she'd seen me, but it was a given. Carlita missed nothing.

"Hey, girl." Gabby was walking briskly toward me down the sidewalk, her hands buried deep in the pockets of a black-and-red-plaid jacket. Her dark hair whipped around her face, and her cheeks were pink with excitement. She linked her arm through mine. "My favorite detective, Nancy Drew, is ready to crack this case wide open. It's so good to see you getting back to your old self again. Now, let's get this party started."

"Hola, lovelies," a heavily accented female voice greeted us as the row of silver bells jingled over the door. The paper cut-out turkeys that decorated the glass in honor of Thanksgiving—most likely made by Carlita's grandkids— flapped their orange-and-brown crayon-colored wings clumsily in the chilly wind.

Carlita was counting change back to the elderly couple. She said *adios* to them, and they smiled as they made their way around us to depart. Carlita stepped out from behind the case and immediately threw her plump arms around me, her strength crushing me. "So good to see you, my beauty."

In her midfifties, Carlita was of Spanish descent while her husband, Giuseppe, was one hundred percent Italian. The best of both worlds, Carlita said, and she alternated between speaking in Spanish, Italian, and English. She was about my height and heavyset, although she carried the extra weight gracefully.

Carlita's sharp, dark eyes were somber as they examined my face. "I am so happy to see you, Theresa." Like my mother, she always called me by my given name. She clucked her tongue. "Sorrow—it makes you skinny. That is why I am here. What can I get you?"

Like Archie, Carlita missed little that happened in Harvest Park, and if she wanted to know something about your life, she was never shy about asking.

If I told her I wasn't hungry, she would be insulted. "I'll take one of your apple fritters." Dylan and I had always been huge fans of the pastries. I'd made them a few times myself, but mine didn't come close to Carlita's. Prepared with flour, fresh apples, and cinnamon, they were then fried and coated with a rich, sugary icing. They were always mouthwatering and even better when served fresh and hot out of the oven. Dylan would often bring one home for me along with Archie's coffee if he'd gone to the gym on a Saturday, but he'd stopped going altogether last summer and started working at the office instead.

"Ah." Carlita nodded in approval. "Your sweetie's favorite. I give you two—one my present. You need to fatten up." She glanced at Gabby, who was examining the contents of the case. "What you want, love?"

"Hmm." Gabby's face was pensive. "A couple of your butter cookies, please."

Carlita pointed a finger, almost in accusation, at Gabby. "I hear you have new boyfriend *again*." Carlita herself was married with six children and numerous grand-kids, whose framed photos decorated the stark white walls of the bakery.

"Jeez, Carlita, we've only been out a couple of times. I wouldn't exactly call him my boyfriend," Gabby said. "How do you know this, anyhow?"

"Giuseppe saw you with him the other night. He see you going into the movies." Carlita ducked behind the counter to gather our goodies.

Giuseppe was happy to leave the socialization part of the business to his wife and spent the majority of his day baking in the back room. Carlita's two eldest daughters also worked at her shop.

"Nothing is a secret in this town," Gabby whispered to me.

"Carlita," I said. "Do you remember the last time you saw Dylan in here?"

Her heart-shaped face grew sympathetic. "He used to come in every Saturday morning." She patted her stomach.

"He say he go to gym, work out, and then stop here to fatten up again." Carlita sighed. "I miss that boy."

Tears clogged my throat, and I said nothing.

She continued. "Then he stop coming. Except day he died, he come in for a loaf of Italian bread. Say you no have time to make and wanted him to pick up. But he did not talk much. I ask him if he want fritter to go and he say, 'No, thank you.' Say he not eat them anymore."

I had forgotten about the bread. If I didn't have time to make some fresh, I would often ask Dylan to pick up a loaf on the way home, and I'd add my garlic topping to it. Dylan loved my garlic bread, and I usually made it two or three times a week, but now that Carlita had mentioned it, he'd stopped indulging and limited himself to only one piece with dinner over the past several months.

My mind was jumbled with details. I tried to focus on the scant ones I knew about Dylan's last day. He'd stopped at Carlita's for my bread and then gone over to Slice for a late lunch. According to the information Gino had given me right after Dylan's death, the accident must have occurred around midafternoon. Had he gone to work for the morning and left early? The day before he'd been dressed in a suit when he kissed me goodbye but was seen by Earl and Archie wearing sweats in the middle of the day. He'd also had coffee with a man he was not fond of. I wrinkled my brow. This was like a puzzle with a thousand pieces and none of them fit. I hoped the visit to his office tomorrow would help answer some of my questions.

Carlita started to put the goodies in two white paper bags, then stopped. "You beauties eat here?"

Gabby shook her head. "I'll eat mine back at the store."

"I'll take mine to go, please, so I won't be late for work." I handed her a ten-dollar bill. "Ring up both orders together. My treat."

"*Sì*?" Carlita's eyebrows wiggled slightly as she took my money. "You work at Slice now, I hear."

Damn, she was good. "That's right. I'm cooking in the kitchen."

"Ah, you work with the handsome Vincenzo. He stop here all the time. He love my almond cookies. Say this bakery better than all the ones in New York City." She touched two fingers to her lips. "That one—he is *bellissimo*."

"Do you know him well?" I asked.

She wiggled her hand back and forth. "Sometimes he talk to me, sometimes not. He a bit moody."

Yeah, no kidding.

"I've heard he's cute." Gabby grinned. "Does he have a girlfriend?"

Carlita stabbed a finger into her own well-endowed chest. "*I* be his girlfriend. He come in here so often that he either love my cookies or I am the main attraction."

I laughed. "Always so modest, Carlita."

"Of course. When you've got it, flaunt it, right? But that one." She sighed. "He have those big, dark eyes that I could lose myself in. He own restaurant in New York City before. Food critics give it five stars," she said as proudly as if it had been her own.

"He told you this?" I asked.

"*Sí*. He tell me he tired of big city life. He come back home to help his brother." Carlita crooked her finger at us, indicating for us to lean closer across the counter, even though there was no one else in the shop. "But I hear other things. That his business in big trouble."

"Again, how do you know this?" Gabby demanded.

Carlita gave us a teasing smile. "I know *everything*. No, just kidding. We have same food distributor. He like to talk."

So things had gone sour for Vince with the restaurant. "What sort of trouble?"

She shrugged. "Ernie—my food guy—he say that maybe their tax man turn them in. They take money from their own restaurant." She furrowed her brow. "Stealing money from your own business?"

"It happens more often than you think," I said.

"Very strange." Carlita handed me my change, then her dark eyes gleamed with sudden recognition. "Aha! I remember now. He walk out that day when your young man come in for the bread. They act like they know each other."

I struggled to keep the excitement out of my voice. "Did they talk?"

"Your sweetie hold the door open for him and Vincenzo—he grunt in return. Very rude. I ask Dylan if he know him and he say, 'Yeah, unfortunately.' And that was all." Carlita raised her pencil-thin eyebrows at me. "Why you want to know?"

"Oh, no reason." I tried to sound casual, but it was definitely time to have a little chat with Vince Falducci.

SEVEN

I ARRIVED AT SLICE TEN MINUTES early and entered through the back kitchen door. As I hung my coat on one of the hooks and tied on an apron, two male voices carried from the walk-in cooler adjoining the kitchen. I recognized the first as Vince's.

"I think we should sell." His rich, deep tone resonated through the room. "You're barely making it as it is. It's nice to be charitable, but you're running a business here, for God's sake. And there was no need to hire that woman."

"Her sauce is great," Anthony insisted. "It won top honors at the fair and I have no doubt it will be *very* profitable to us."

What was that supposed to mean? Was he going to advertise my sauce on the menu somewhere? *Penne topped with Tessa's tantalizing award-winning tomato sauce.* Had that been the reason Anthony hired me? No matter. All I wanted was an opportunity to snoop around and see if someone at Slice had disliked Dylan enough to want to get rid of him.

Vince snorted. "Oh, okay. I see what you're doing. Still, it wouldn't hurt your daughter to help out once in a while and save you some on payroll."

"Izzy doesn't like working here," Anthony said.

"Really?" Vince held back a laugh. "You could have fooled me. She never had a problem hanging around when Esposito was in here."

My entire body froze. Anthony's voice became a low, angry growl. "Shut up. That's bull and you know it. Besides, she may have started off liking him but things changed…and you know what happened then."

A knot formed in the pit of my stomach as I listened to their exchange. Anthony's daughter had disliked my husband. Why? Was there a chance she could have killed him?

"Izzy's getting married in a few months," Anthony went on. "She'd never look at another man."

"She's only marrying Rico because he's rich," Vince said sharply. He walked out of the cooler with Anthony following. Both men fell silent when they noticed me standing there.

Instead of acting embarrassed, Vince scowled and moved past me into the office, slamming the door behind him. Anthony shut the cooler door, and for a moment, we both stood there in uncomfortable silence. Finally, he cleared his throat. "Vince…he…uh…gets these strange ideas in his head sometimes. Dylan was a good boy. Like a son to me."

I bobbed my head up and down. "Sure." The news that Anthony's daughter may have had something against Dylan was totally unexpected. Would Vince be willing to tell me anything further? What was the deal with him anyway? The other day he'd been pleasant and polite when he thought I was a customer, but now, he acted like he couldn't stand me. Or was that his way of covering up the embarrassment when he'd tried to ask me out?

Anthony handed me a name tag, which I pinned to my apron. "I brought some dough out of the cooler for you to start prepping pizzas. We just got an order in for one." He placed the slip next to me and pointed at the peel on the table, an aluminum shovel used to place the pizza inside the oven. "I've filled the prep table with all the toppings, and if you need spices, oregano, or basil, they're in the utility cabinet next to the stove. That's where you'll find canned tomatoes and paste for sauce too. Are you going to be all right on your own in here for a while? We got a reservation for thirty people for dinner. It's an anniversary party."

"Sure, I'll be fine." I went to the three-bay sink to wash my hands. Even though I wasn't sure about the timing on the wall oven yet, it was great to be back in my element again. I was already making mental notes of items Anthony should add to his menu. "Thirty people is a lot for you, right?" I sprinkled flour on the work surface from the shaker he'd put there.

"We don't usually get parties that size," Anthony admitted, "so it's a big deal. They're friends of the family. I hope Izzy shows up."

"So, you don't know if she's coming in?" I asked.

"If the mood strikes her, Izzy will be here," Anthony said. "She's busy planning her wedding. That takes a lot of time, you know."

"Of course." Before I could say anything further, the phone rang and Anthony went to answer it. I covered my hands with flour and started to knead the dough, excited to lose myself in the task for a while.

Vince came out of the office and tied an apron on. He shot a surly glance back in my direction as he went to the register but made no attempt to speak to me, so I took the bull by the horns. "Hi, Vince."

"How's it going, Mrs. Esposito? So happy that you came back today." His tone was thick with sarcasm.

"Have I done something to offend you?" I asked.

Vince refused to turn and meet my gaze. "No, ma'am. I'm not offended by you."

Yeah, okay. I gripped the ball of dough tightly between my hands. "Slice must seem small after running your own restaurant in New York City."

His head jerked up, and dark, dangerous eyes met mine. "How did you know about that?"

"Someone mentioned to me that your place closed recently. What was the name of it again?" Already, I could tell that my questions were not welcome.

"Oh, really?" Storm clouds brewed behind his eyes. "Did they also mention why my restaurant closed? Are you afraid to work with someone who doesn't do everything by the book…like your husband so obviously did?"

His tone was sharp, and I bristled at the comment. "No, of course not." I turned away from him and slid the metal pizza peel underneath the dough. Did this guy have a major chip on his shoulder or what? And why was he bringing Dylan into it?

Vince rang up a customer who had come in for takeout. Anthony emerged from the office and placed an order slip in front of his brother, then handed me a menu. "Are you familiar with our dinners, Tessa? We have more than pizza here. Customers can get chicken or eggplant parmigiana, lasagna, or spaghetti and meatballs. Vince prepares a certain number of dinners every day, and if they don't all get used, we freeze the rest."

I scanned the laminated menu. "What about garlic bread?"

"It comes with all the dinners," Anthony said. "We don't sell it separately."

I added sauce, pepperoni, and cheese and placed the pie into the oven. It slid easily off the peel, which I then brought back to the table to start another pizza. As far as I was concerned, there was nothing quite like massaging one's fingers through the lumpy dough and feeling the texture change from the softness of a warm marshmallow to a tacky and slick final product. Perfect for pizza crust. "Have you ever thought about featuring stromboli on the menu?" I asked.

Anthony merely shrugged his shoulders. "Can't say I ever did." He looked at Vince, who had turned back into the kitchen. "Do you know how to make stromboli?"

"Of course I can make it." Vince's tone was snippy and accusatory. "No one's ever asked for it though."

I wiggled my fingers. "I make a pretty mean one if I do say so myself. How about adding a couple of penne dishes to the menu? Penne is so much more attractive looking than linguini or spaghetti. I have a great shrimp alfredo recipe you could use. Or maybe penne with a lemon garlic sauce for a healthier option?"

Anthony leaned forward, his eyes as round as pepperoni slices. "Those are great ideas, Tessa. Say, after you finish that pizza, could you make up a pot of your tomato sauce? I think I'd like to feature it with all the dinners from now on."

I smiled graciously. "Of course. I'd be happy to."

Anthony pointed at the utility cabinet on the other side of the kitchen. "There are stainless-steel pots inside and a couple more in the oven. You should find all the ingredients you need for the sauce in the cabinet as well— unless you've got a secret one that I need to run out and pick up?"

I smiled but said nothing. He wanted to know what was in my sauce—that much was certain. Too bad for him I wasn't sharing.

Anthony went on. "Leave the sauce in the pot, and I'll take care of freezing it." He turned to his brother. "What do you think about adding stromboli to the menu?"

"Sure." Vince sounded bored as he watched me brush the dough with olive oil and ladle the rich tomato sauce over it. I reached into the prep table and grabbed fresh mozzarella cheese, sprinkling it liberally on top. For a finishing touch, I added several pieces of sausage and a pinch of oregano, the spicy smell permeating my nose. "Little Miss Penne seems to have all the answers to making your business a success, Anthony."

My eyebrows rose in confusion. "I was only saying—"

He cut me off. "Hey, maybe when it's slow later, you can make up a batch of your healthy lemon penne with a side of stromboli for us to sample." He elbowed Anthony in the side and laughed. "But for now, do as the boss says and get the sauce cooking, sweetheart."

Heat rose through my face. I didn't appreciate Vince's attempt to mock me. I'd obviously made him angry when I brought up his former place. My intention was to find out more about the restaurant, why it had closed, and if Dylan had something to do with it. From his rude comment and the information Carlita had given me, it was obvious he hadn't liked Dylan, but why? Vince also seemed to think he could run circles around me in the kitchen. Well, he was wrong, and I would prove it.

"You should let me make up a few loaves. I get complimented on my stromboli all the time." I addressed Anthony but watched Vince out of the corner of my eye to see how he'd react to my next statement. "It was Dylan's favorite."

At the mention of Dylan's name, Vince removed the peel from my hands and thrust the pizza into the brick oven with remarkable force. I winced inwardly as I watched him.

A party of six had made their way into the dining room, talking and laughing loudly. Anthony grabbed some menus from their place at the checkout counter and addressed Vince. "Better grab more pepperoni out of the cooler."

"Sure thing. I'll get some more dough for the Penne Princess too," Vince said sourly as he went into the cooler.

His rudeness irked me, and I was about to say something snarky in return when the phone rang. Since no one else was around, I made a grab for it. "Slice Pizza."

There was a pause. "*Bellissimo.*" A man with a heavy Italian accent spoke into the phone. "Anthony, you never sounded so good before!"

"Can I help you? Carryout or delivery?"

"Sweetheart, it's Dom. Come on, Isabella, you should know this voice. And how come I didn't get an invitation to that big shindig wedding of yours? Papa Anthony's laying out big bucks for it, no?"

"You don't understand," I protested. "I'm not—"

"*Molto bene!*" he laughed. "Tell your papa I'll take the usual. Go heavy on the black olives. Lots of friends coming over to sample it."

I scribbled away on an order pad. "So, was this a twelve or twenty-four cut? Any sides with that? We have mozzarella sticks or calamari."

A deafening silence met my ears. When Dom spoke again, his tone was more formal and annoyed. "Who the hell is this?"

I glanced up and saw Anthony headed my way. I placed a hand over the receiver. "Dom's on the phone. He wants his usual with extra black olives."

Anthony nodded and handed me an order slip. "I'll take care of it, honey. Nothing for you to worry about.

Dom's a regular and kind of fussy about his pizza. Would you mind filling this drink order for me?" He took the phone and cradled it against his ear. "Dom!"

There were loose cans of soda located in the walk-in cooler. I crossed the room and opened the door. Slice's kitchen was too cluttered for my taste. I preferred a more orderly place to work, but then again, this wasn't my restaurant. If this had been my place, the first thing I'd do would be to build some extra shelving along the walls for the empty pizza boxes. I'd also put in a drink dispenser and lose the canned soda. That would save some money for sure. I grabbed two diet colas, one regular, and three orange sodas. As I returned to the kitchen, I laid the cans on the counter and reached for a tray.

"We don't have black olives today, buddy." Anthony made a note on his pad. "Okay, yeah. Green peppers to substitute. I'll get Butchy to deliver. He'll be back any minute, and then I'll send him right over. Yeah. I'm expecting more olives tomorrow."

Vince was at the register, ringing up a customer with a takeout order when the back door swung open. Eric entered the kitchen and, without a word to anyone, went directly into the cooler. He came out a minute later, empty-handed, and grabbed the pizza boxes waiting on the table next to me, stuffing them into a warmer bag. His bloodshot eyes connected with mine for a brief second, sending a chill through my body. Still silent, he made his way over to the back door, wrenched it open, and slammed it behind him.

Eric's behavior unnerved me. Why would a delivery driver need to go into the cooler? He hadn't taken anything, so what was really going on? No one was paying attention to me as I wandered into the cooler and stole a look around, eager to inspect my surroundings.

A thermometer on the door registered forty degrees. The room itself was about ten by twelve feet with a connecting door at its opposite end that I suspected led to the freezer. Boxes lined the shelves, labeled with ingredients and expiration dates. Scanning the room, my eyes landed on a box near the ceiling with *black olives* written on it in block lettering. Huh. Hadn't Anthony said they were out of black olives?

The wall outside the freezer's door held another thermometer, and this one read zero degrees. I pushed the door open and looked around. More cardboard boxes occupied the metal shelving along the walls. Some were labeled *dough* and a few *pepperoni*, but nothing seemed out of place.

As I walked back into the cooler, rubbing my arms quickly to get rid of the goose bumps, my name tag fell off my apron, landing underneath the bottom shelf. I probably hadn't pushed the pin all the way through. I dropped to my knees to grab it and noticed an open cardboard box filled with several empty mason jars. Next to the box, a small plastic baggie sat on the cement floor with a white powdery substance inside. My heart raced at the sight of it. Was that…cocaine? My mind went back to Eric exiting the cooler. Of his bloodshot eyes and the first time we met, and the realization hit me fast—Eric's doing drugs in Slice. Fingers shaking, I reached down to grab the bag when I heard a high-pitched, squeaky voice from behind me.

"Who are you?"

Startled, I straightened and whirled around, afraid the guilt might show on my face A woman in her early twenties stood there, her left hand propped on the door and the other one on her hip. She was wearing a pink lace top and jeans so tight that I wondered how she managed to draw a deep breath without pain. She was about my height, with skin so pale it seemed transparent. This must be the famous Isabella.

I extended my hand. "Hi, I'm Tessa. I just started work here." I purposefully left out my last name, Vince and Anthony's earlier conversation still fresh in my ears.

Her dark, wide-set eyes studied me for a moment before she reluctantly extended her hand. A glittering diamond the size of a walnut shone on her ring finger, and I remembered Vince's comment about her fiancé's wealth.

"I'm Izzy," she said. "Anthony's daughter. Nice to meet ya." Her accent was a bit on the Bronx side, and I recalled Dylan telling me that Anthony had been born in New York City but had relocated to the Upstate area several years ago. Her eyes flickered down to the floor for a moment but she said nothing. Izzy held the door open for me, and I had no choice but to follow her back into the kitchen, my heart pounding loudly in my chest.

I crossed back to the granite-topped prep table and started dough for another pizza order that had come in while I was in the cooler. As I formed the pie, I watched with interest as Izzy hung her expensive leather jacket on one of the hooks and grabbed an apron. She placed a pink ball cap over her short, russet-colored hair. Anthony was still on the phone but gave her a warm smile.

Vince looked up from his pile of receipts and shot Izzy a malicious grin. "Ah, look at this. The queen has arrived."

Izzy wrinkled her nose at him, the tiny diamond piercing on one side winking in the bright light from above. "Go to hell," she snapped.

"Nice way to talk to your uncle." Vince's attractive face creased into a generous frown as he regarded his niece, then he pushed his curls back from his forehead. I noticed a large, angry scar above his left eyebrow.

The animosity between the two was evident and didn't sit well with me. I finished the pie, adding green pepper, onion, and sausage, then started to gather the ingredients to make my sauce. I longed to get back into the cooler, but Izzy was now leaning against the door, therefore blocking my path. She folded her arms across her chest, presumably bored with all of us, and examined her French manicure while waiting for her father to get off the phone at the front counter.

Vince pointed at me. "Have you met our newest employee? This is Tessa."

She shrugged. "Yeah, I met her. So?"

"Let me rephrase. That's Tessa Esposito." Vince's eyes lit up as he said the words and waited for her reaction.

Great. Thanks a lot.

Izzy roused herself from her slouched position against the wall and stared back at me. Her eyes were cold as she scanned me up and down. "You're Dylan's wife?"

I nodded, not knowing what else to say.

She continued to watch me. "It's a terrible shame what happened to your husband. Sorry for your loss."

Her mouth quivered into a slight smile before she looked away. Call me crazy, but I suspected Izzy was anything but sorry.

\ \ | /

My body was beyond exhausted as I unlocked the front door to my home and made a note to leave a light on next time I worked. I hated coming home to a dark and empty house. It was almost ten o'clock, and all I could think about was curling up in my warm, comfortable bed to snuggle with Luigi and watch a rerun of *Seinfeld*.

Izzy had avoided me and thankfully was kept busy waiting on the large party for most of the evening. When I'd finally had a chance to return to the cooler about an hour later, the baggie with the powder was gone. Damn. Had Izzy been the one to remove it? Anthony had gone into the cooler for more dough and then Vince to grab a box of pepperoni. Izzy had even walked back there while on her cell phone, most likely for some privacy. Although she hadn't spoken to me again, I'd felt those dark eyes glued on me all night. Her behavior made me wonder if it had something to do with Dylan or if she knew I'd seen the baggie.

Although it was only my first day, I'd already discovered several people whose behavior made them key suspects in my husband's death. Vince obviously didn't like Dylan, so they must have had some type of previous relationship. Izzy was angry at him, although I wasn't sure why. Eric was either doing drugs or selling them at Slice, perhaps both. If Dylan had discovered this, he might have threatened to report the kid, placing him high on Eric's unfavorable list.

Despite the friction between the other employees, it had felt wonderful to be back in the kitchen, prepping meals, stirring my sauce, doing what I'd always been meant to do. I thought I'd done fairly well and only burned one pizza, a mistake that I chalked up to the time difference between the brick oven and my gas one at home. It bothered me that there was so much untapped potential in Slice. With some tender love and dough—dough in one's wallet, that is—Slice could make a wonderful family restaurant.

All evening, I'd visualized smiling moms, happy dads, and chattering children eating at the restaurant. A gas fireplace warming everyone on cool evenings, and a piano player entertaining the crowded restaurant on Saturday nights.

Back to reality. I glanced idly at the pile of envelopes I'd collected from my mailbox. Most likely they were bills and advertisements for credit cards that I had no interest in looking at right now. Sighing, I tossed the envelopes on top of the pile already accumulating on my coffee table.

Luigi appeared at the bottom of the stairs, blinking at me with sleepy, half-opened slits of eyes. He yawned and stretched, then trotted into the kitchen, jumped onto one of the stools at the breakfast counter, and stared at me expectantly.

I stroked his head. "Did you have a good day?"

He meowed and lifted a paw in the air. Dylan and I used to joke that this was his attempt to high-five us. I'd been enamored with this cat ever since I'd first laid eyes on him four years ago when Dylan had brought him home as a Christmas present for me. Dylan had often talked about getting Luigi a lady kitty to socialize with, but that was one more thing we had never gotten around to.

I stared into the fridge. There was some penne left over

from dinner last night, but it didn't hold much appeal. I looked in the freezer, behind my accumulating bags of sauce, in hopes of finding a frozen cheesecake, but I'd eaten them all. Instead, I went with a cup of raspberry herbal tea. Paired with television, it sounded like a great way to unwind.

After I changed into my nightgown, I washed my face and got into bed. Luigi wasted no time snuggling up on Dylan's pillow. I clicked through the channels, but nothing interested me. I put the remote aside and grabbed my steno pad off the nightstand. I always kept one there in case I came across a recipe on the cooking channel I wanted to try. I divided the sheet into two columns, one titled *People of Interest* and the other, *Motive*. It seemed a bit amateurish, but hey, I had to start somewhere. I thought of Gabby's words. "No one is exempt."

As much as I hated to, I wrote Anthony's name down at the top of the page. Motive? I wasn't sure. Maybe Dylan found an item in his taxes to incriminate him. Could Anthony be hiding something? There must be a connection there.

Izzy was next. According to Vince and Anthony's conversation, she'd liked Dylan at first, and then something had happened. Had he done something to anger her? I needed to find out more about the queen of Slice.

Vince. Did he only know my husband from Slice, or was Dylan the one to turn him in for embezzlement at his previous restaurant? Carlita had mentioned that Vince didn't seem to care for him, and Eric's words from the other day came back to me. *Not everyone at Slice liked your husband.*

Sam, Butchy. I hadn't formally met Butchy yet, but he came with a glowing report from my mother. It was difficult to get a read on Sam from the brief encounter I'd had with him the other day.

Eric. He was definitely the vilest of the three delivery drivers and had hinted that he had information. Plus, I was now convinced he was doing drugs. Was he bluffing about having information?

I hesitated for a long time before writing down the next name. *Matt.* I didn't want to believe Matt had anything to do with Dylan's death. However, Dylan's vehicle had been at the Car Doctor for service right before the accident. If the opportunity had presented itself for Matt to knock Dylan off so easily, would he have done it?

Mystery man at Archie's. I didn't know who Dylan had met for coffee the day before his death but intended to find out.

I glanced around for my phone, then remembered that

I'd left it in the living room. I set the paper and pen down on my nightstand and padded out of the bedroom and down the stairs in bare feet to the darkened front room. After I'd located my cell, I spotted the bright LED lights of a vehicle approaching through my front window. The car pulled up to the curb directly in front of my house, and then the headlights went out.

Suddenly uneasy, I snuck behind the silk curtain panels of my bay window and peered out into the street. The lamppost on my lawn cast a shadow over the vehicle, and I could tell that it was a dark sedan. My heart knocked against the wall of my chest as I waited. Five minutes must have gone by, and the car still remained, with no signs of movement.

Fear rose in my throat. I had just decided to call Gino when the car turned around in the street and drove away. I went to the front door and opened it, watching the car turn off my street, and then the headlights came back on. There was no way I could make out the license plate from this distance. I locked the door and leaned against it, waiting for my breathing to return to normal.

If someone was trying to scare me, they were doing a heck of a good job.

EIGHT

TRAFFIC IN ALBANY WAS LIGHT AS I crossed Pearl to Green Avenue and proceeded down a one-way street to the fifteen-story office building where Dylan had worked. I found an empty spot at a meter across the road, nearly blinded by the morning sunlight reflecting off the full-length glass windows. I locked my car and walked briskly toward the entrance.

Dylan had never talked much about his job during the three years he'd been employed at We Care. He said it was boring, mundane, and assured me that better things were coming our way, namely our restaurant. We'd attended the annual Christmas party, and occasionally he'd go to happy hour with his coworkers but that had been the extent of his socialization.

Gino had left me a voicemail while I'd been in the

shower, but there hadn't been time to call him back yet. He wanted to know how my first night at Slice had gone. I definitely needed to fill him in on Izzy's reaction to me, the powder substance I'd seen in the cooler, and the car that was parked in front of my house last night.

My brown, low-heeled leather boots clacked against the black-and-white linoleum floor of the pristine lobby. I pressed the button for the elevator and waited. Most of the floors in this building were dedicated to the health service corporation, but my destination, floor eight, was occupied solely by accountants, payroll clerks, and other administrative workers.

I opened the heavy glass door and spotted Olivia behind the receptionist counter in the middle of the floor. She rose to her feet when she saw me.

"Hi, Tessa!" She came around the counter to give me a hug. Olivia was tiny, only about five feet tall, and I felt like a giant next to her. Her shoulder-length, light-brown hair touched the side of my face during our embrace and smelled of lavender. Her hug was actually only a slight squeeze, since her protruding belly stood in the way. She had to be due in the next month or so. "It's wonderful to see you."

"You too, Olivia. How are you feeling?"

Olivia's blue eyes shone as she patted her stomach. "I had terrible morning sickness for the first six months, but now I'm tired all the time. And running to the bathroom every five minutes." She laughed. "I'm due at Christmas."

"Congratulations. You and your husband must be very excited." It bothered me that Olivia hadn't come to Dylan's wake or funeral. She'd sent a lovely card, but I'd thought it was a bit strange that Ned Reinhart, Dylan's boss, never made an appearance either. As a matter of fact, I didn't recall any of his coworkers showing up.

Olivia gestured for me to follow her down the long, plush-carpeted hallway. For a strange reason, my heart began to pound, and I was afraid I might hyperventilate. How ridiculous. It was only his office and some material things. It was almost like I still expected to find Dylan in there, smiling as he looked up from his calculator, waiting to go to lunch with me.

The nameplate was gone from the door of his office. I peeked inside, not sure at first what to expect, but the room was empty, save for the desk and a metal file cabinet in the corner. There was nothing on the surface of the desk except for a black office phone and large calculator. Even the framed wall photo I'd given him when he'd started was gone. It was a poster featuring a beagle with glasses using a calculator with the caption *I'm auditing you but really have no idea what I'm doing* underneath. Staring at the sterile office was more depressing than viewing his personal effects would have been. It was almost like Dylan had never existed.

Olivia opened the small closet next to the file cabinet and pointed at two banker's boxes inside. "I can get a handcart for you if you like."

"No, it's fine. I'm parked right across the street." I stared down at the boxes and thought again how sad it was that three years of my husband's life had been relegated to this. "Are the boxes heavy?"

She shook her head. "Just files and a few pictures, I think. Of course, Mr. Reinhart had someone go through them first. You know, after everything that happened."

Puzzled, I stared at her. "After what happened?"

Her cheeks became tinged with pink. "When Dylan was fired, of course."

I blinked. No, I must have heard her wrong. This was some sort of mistake. "What are you talking about, Olivia? Dylan wasn't fired."

Olivia's eyes widened slowly, and she started to stammer. "Um, if you'll…ah, excuse me, I need to get back to my desk. I think I hear the phone ringing." She headed for the hallway.

"Wait a minute!" I grabbed Olivia's arm. "Please tell me what you're talking about."

Olivia stared down at the floor. "God, Tessa, I—"

"What makes you think Dylan might have been fired?" It was impossible. He'd deposited money faithfully in the bank every week. He never missed a day of work. She must have gotten it wrong.

She traced a pattern in the carpet with her low-heeled, black mules. "I don't know exactly what happened. It was a few weeks before he died and seemed to come out of left field. Everyone was shocked when they found out. Dylan stormed out of here one day without a word to anyone. The next day I needed his signature on something, and Mr. Reinhart told me that he wouldn't be coming back."

Relief soared through me. "So maybe Dylan wasn't fired. He might have quit instead." Although I had no idea why he'd do something like that without consulting me first.

Olivia shook her head. "Judy, who works in the office

next to Mr. Reinhart, said he was definitely fired." She flinched under my gaze. "Please don't say I told you. I don't want to get into trouble."

For a minute all I could do was stand there, dumbstruck. I placed my hand on the box to steady myself. "Why was he fired, Olivia? Did the company have to downsize? I don't understand what happened."

She gave a small shrug. "I'm not sure either."

"Where is Mr. Reinhart?" I poked my head out Dylan's door and peered into the hallway.

Olivia started inching away from me, down the hall toward her desk. "Um, he asked that he not be disturbed."

"Forget it." I dismissed her with a wave of my hand and started in the opposite direction. "I remember where his office is."

Olivia hurried after me as fast as her bulging belly would allow. "No, you can't!" Her voice was panicked. "He hates being disturbed when he's in the middle of something."

"Well, this can't wait." I strode to the office at the end of the hallway. Ned Reinhart's door was partially open. He was on the phone and sitting behind a marble-topped desk with his leather swivel chair facing the window as he stared out at the busy streets of Albany below.

"Yeah, that's right," he muttered into the receiver. "The woman's threatening to sue because she claims the doctor came on to her. This would be extremely high profile, and we can't have that. Get our legal department involved right away."

He must have caught sight of my reflection in the window because he suddenly whirled around to face me. Recognition set in immediately, and the look on his face changed from one of irritation to shock. "I'll call you right back." He slammed the office phone down into its cradle and stared up at me. "Mrs. Esposito. I thought you weren't coming till this afternoon."

Olivia was standing to my left, a distressed look on her face. "I'm so sorry, Mr. Reinhart. I said that you asked not to be disturbed."

He glowered at Olivia. "You can waddle back to your desk now, Mrs. Moore."

His words horrified me, but Olivia merely bowed her head and backed out of the room in a hurry.

I'd met Ned before, but we'd never exchanged more than a "Nice to see you" or "Happy holidays." He was the image of a professional with his immaculate gray suit, white oxford shirt, and black-and-gray-striped tie. I judged him to be in his midfifties.

Dylan had never liked his boss but in the last few months had stopped complaining about him, which I took as a sign they'd reached a truce. But as Ned stared at me now, he seemed anything but friendly. I paused, suddenly feeling foolish. "I promise not to take up much of your time."

He grimaced. "I have a conference call in ten minutes, so let's make this quick. What do you need?" Grudgingly, he gestured at a light-blue padded chair in front of his desk. "Sit down, if you wish."

I accepted the chair and clutched my purse tightly in a useless effort to keep my hands from shaking.

Ned cleared his throat and looked uncomfortable. "Uh, I'm sorry about Dylan's passing. It was a shock to all of us. Did you need any help with transporting his personal items to your car?"

In my opinion, he didn't act sorry. Was this why no one at Dylan's workplace had barely acknowledged his death—because he'd been terminated? My patience was wearing thin, so I cut right to the chase. "Why was Dylan fired, Ned?"

His eyes went wide with alarm, and he rose from his seat to shut the office door. "I'm afraid I'm not at liberty to give you any information about that."

Then it really was true. I bit my lower lip. "Please. I only recently found out. Dylan never mentioned it to me."

Ned's jaw went slack as he sat back down. "He never told you that he was fired?"

I shook my head.

He studied me for a second, doubt registering on his angular face. "How could you not have known? That was what—almost two months ago?" He ran a hand nervously through his disheveled gray hair. "Pardon me, Mrs. Esposito. Your private life is none of my concern."

"Please." I reached across the desk and touched his hand. "I won't hold you accountable for anything. No one will ever find out that you told me. This is my husband we're talking about, and I need to know what happened." *For my own sanity.* "Was Dylan's work not up to par? Did he call in sick or take long lunches?"

Ned rose from his chair and opened the door for me. "I'm very sorry for your loss, Mrs. Esposito, but it would be best if you left now."

He wouldn't look at me as I passed in front of him, his gaze fixed intently on the plush carpeting. The door closed quietly behind me.

My grief had turned to anger, vicious and bitter in my

gut. Ned was only concerned with We Care's reputation. He didn't care about Dylan and probably never had. My husband was dead. What did it matter if Ned told me the real reason he'd been fired? Ned clearly didn't know who he was dealing with, and I was determined to find answers.

My knees shook as I walked back to Dylan's office and lifted the two boxes from his closet. I was tempted to remove the lids and start sifting through the items right there but forced myself not to. Maybe I should have taken Olivia up on her offer of a hand truck. The boxes were not heavy, but it would be difficult for me to carry both at the same time.

While I stood there debating what to do next, a young man with bleached-blond hair and a gold hoop in his left ear stuck his head in the doorway. "Hey, Mrs. Esposito. Olivia said you were in here. Need a hand?"

Chuck Saxton was a fresh-faced kid barely out of his teens who had recently graduated from a two-year community college. He performed various maintenance and administrative tasks for the firm along with other jobs that the more-seasoned employees threw at him. He'd once even gone out of his way to bring Dylan his cell phone when he'd left it at work. Dylan had said that Chuck was a faithful employee and a good guy to have around.

"Yes, please. If you have a couple of minutes to spare, that would be great. I have to transport these boxes down to my car."

Chuck lifted both boxes effortlessly in his arms. "Sure, no problem. Where are you parked?"

"At a meter across the street." We walked past Olivia's reception counter, empty and silent except for the persistent ringing of her phone. I ran ahead of Chuck and held the door open for him. "Can I carry one of those?"

"Nah, I've got them." He watched me with unabashed curiosity as I pushed the button for the elevator. When our gazes met, he lowered his eyes to the floor. "I was really sorry to hear about Dylan, Mrs. Esposito."

"Thank you." The elevator pinged, and I let Chuck enter first, then pressed *L* for the lobby. Mercifully, we were alone, because I didn't want anyone else to overhear what I was about to ask him. "Actually, I was wondering if you could answer some questions for me about Dylan."

He smiled, but I glimpsed a bit of uneasiness in his bright-blue eyes. "Uh, sure. I wish I could have come to the funeral. It was the same day as my cousin's wedding and I—"

The elevator doors opened, and we walked past a

couple of women chatting in the lobby. "No, that's not what I meant. I was wondering if you knew anything about Dylan getting fired."

He scanned the lobby with a nervous air, as if afraid someone was watching us. "Not much, but yeah, I think all the employees know he didn't quit. Everyone here liked Dylan."

Gingerly, I pushed open the door adjacent to the revolving door and held it for Chuck. He followed me across the street to my car, and I opened the trunk for him. "Are you sure? Was there anyone who didn't like him? Ned, perhaps?"

Chuck's fair complexion turned a deep shade of red as he set the boxes inside my trunk. "Mrs. Esposito, I don't want to get involved."

"Please, Chuck." The urgency in my tone must have been palpable. "No one will tell me anything. Whatever you say will remain between the two of us. You have my word."

He squirmed under my gaze. "I don't know—"

I held up a hand. "Try to see this from my point of view. I only found out today that my husband was fired. He died in a senseless accident, which I recently discovered might not have been an accident at all." Okay, maybe I shouldn't have added that last part, but heck, with the way gossip spread around here, Chuck would probably find out anyway. "It's not my intent to point fingers. I only want to know what happened, for my own peace of mind."

Chuck blinked in surprise. "Oh wow. I didn't realize. That's awful." He ran a hand through his hair. "Okay. He and Reinhart always did seem at odds. I kind of got the impression that Reinhart was happy about Mr. Franklin—his boss—firing Dylan."

I racked my brain to remember the references Dylan had made to Ned when he first started working there—*clueless, a micromanager, and not willing to promote from within.* "Could Ned have had it in for Dylan? Was he jealous of him? Is that why he was fired?"

Maybe Ned had told Mr. Franklin lies about my husband. Dylan had mentioned that We Care's budget was tight, and a few of the lower-level staff had been let go. Perhaps Ned feared his job was next on the chopping block so he'd made up some lame story to get Dylan axed instead.

Chuck swallowed hard, his Adam's apple bobbing up and down. Then he bent his head close to mine and spoke in a voice so low I could barely hear him over the oncoming traffic. "I don't think so."

"Please, Chuck," I begged. "Tell me the truth."

"I don't know much," he confessed. "One day, shortly

after Dylan had left, I overheard Reinhart talking to someone on the phone. I was fixing the ceiling light in his office and had earbuds in, so he probably thought I couldn't hear, but I always keep the music turned real low, in case someone hollers for me, you know?"

"Go on," I urged.

"Reinhart mentioned Dylan's name and said that he had recommended We Care not press charges about the embezzlement, so it didn't leak out to the media. I figured he was talking to his boss, Mr. Franklin. Whoever it was, he assured the person on the other end that no one would ever know."

The blood started to roar in my ears as I quickly added two and two together. "Wait a second. Are you implying that Dylan—" No, I couldn't take it all in. "Are you saying that my husband was stealing money from his company—*your* employer?"

Chuck wouldn't look at me. Instead, he pursed his lips tightly and nodded, his voice barely above a whisper. "Yeah, I'm afraid so."

NINE

THIS HAD TO BE A NIGHTMARE. There was simply no other explanation. My husband wouldn't steal. Dylan had been a good man, and an honest one. The questions started to flood my brain. Dylan was still dressing up for work every day, probably so I wouldn't be suspicious. Where had he gone instead? To Slice? How had he still been depositing money in the bank every week if he'd been fired? It must have been the money he'd embezzled from We Care. Unless he'd been doing something else deceptive as well? A shiver ran through me.

Chuck interrupted my thoughts. "I overheard Reinhart saying on the phone that he wasn't about to lose his six-figure job over some punk who couldn't keep his hands off the company's dough. He told the other person not to worry—that he'd make sure Esposito stayed quiet."

What was that supposed to mean? I struggled to clear my head. "No. This can't be true."

Chuck's expression was pained. "Please don't tell anyone I told you. I don't want to lose my job over this."

"Of course not. I wouldn't do that to you, Chuck, but—" It was difficult to find the right words. "Do you know why Dylan... I mean, *how* did he do this?"

He shrugged. "From what I overheard, he was taking deposits and putting them into a separate account that he'd created. I guess it was discovered during a surprise audit."

His voice sounded far away, as if I was underwater—drowning little by little with each word.

Chuck went on. "We Care is all about their reputation, so they probably didn't think this would look good in the news. You know, one of their own accountants stealing from them. Instead of arresting Dylan, they fired him and refused to give him a reference for another job."

I wanted to clap my hands over my ears and run screaming into the street.

Chuck leaned forward, eyes wide with excitement. "He yelled and swore at Reinhart that day. I didn't know what was going on at the time, but I never saw Dylan act like that before. He always seemed so calm and put together."

He patted the lid of the banker's box. "Guess it happened so quickly that he forgot to take his stuff."

His words, like the wind, whipped around my long hair and sent an aching chill through my bones. I opened my mouth and inhaled huge gulps of the cold, exhaust-polluted air while Chuck watched me with an anxious expression.

"Are you okay, Mrs. Esposito?"

"Fine," I managed to choke out. "Thanks for all your help." I moved around to the driver's side of the car. My legs were shaking so badly that I was afraid I might topple over.

Chuck reached around me to open the door. "Maybe you shouldn't be driving if you're this upset. Can I call you a cab?"

There was no time for a cab. I glanced down at my watch and saw that I was already late for work. *That's where I'm going, right?* For a minute, I couldn't think straight. Nothing seemed to make sense anymore. "No thanks. I'm all right."

I got into my car. I sat there and revved the engine for a minute, my hands gripping the steering wheel tightly for support. Chuck walked back across the street and stood there watching me, hands in pockets, a frown creasing his brow. He was still there when I pulled away from the meter.

After driving for a few minutes, I realized I was headed in the wrong direction. Quickly, I made an abrupt illegal U-turn in the street while several car horns and drivers' middle fingers saluted me. I was afraid I might be sick. There had to be more to the story. My husband did *not* steal. He wouldn't even cheat on his morning sudoku game. One time, a cashier had forgotten to charge him for a dozen eggs, and he went back to the store the next day to pay for them. That's how honest Dylan had been.

The truth had reared its ugly head. Chuck's comment about Ned—"he'd make sure Esposito stayed quiet"— continued to haunt me. I'd been focusing on Slice, but what if it had been someone Dylan worked with at We Care that had wanted to silence him—specifically, Ned?

I should have called Anthony to let him know I'd be late. The lunch hour traffic was in full swing as my car slowed to a crawl. When I reached Harvest Park, I thought briefly about calling in sick, but the distraction at Slice might do me more good than being by myself would. I'd knead some dough for a while and figure out what to do next. Maybe Dylan had a good reason for—*No.* There was no good reason to steal. Anger, hurt, and confusion blew through me like a cold wind. I'd wanted to know the truth behind Dylan's death but never expected this. Why would he do such a thing? Dear, good, upstanding, and honest Dylan. God, what a fool I'd been.

Tears blurred my vision. The pain in my chest was so suffocating that I couldn't draw a deep breath. Too late, I realized that the vehicle in front of me had stopped for a red light. I slammed on the brakes, but my car plowed into the rear end of the small hatchback. The tires screeched and a loud thud followed. My head jerked back against the seat, and everything went black.

\ \ /

Someone was talking as I slowly opened my eyes. "Ma'am?"

Perplexed, I turned my head. A fit policeman with a blond buzz cut had opened my car door and was kneeling next to me. "Stay calm. Everything is all right."

I didn't know what I needed to be calm about. My head hurt, and my brain was a mass of jumbled confusion. For a few seconds I couldn't remember what had happened. Squinting into the bright sunlight, I saw another policeman standing a few paces from my car, directing traffic around it. A middle-aged woman with short, platinum-blond hair was conversing with a third officer. She stood at the curb, next to a vehicle whose back end had been smashed in. My car was positioned awkwardly in the road. "What happened?"

"Looks like you hit the car in front of you and passed out for a minute." His eyes studied my face intently. "Have you been drinking, ma'am?"

"No, sir." I remembered the restaurant and glanced down at my watch. It was 12:30. "I'm late for work!" I straightened up and reached for the key in the ignition, but the officer laid a firm hand on my arm.

"Ma'am, you have to go to the hospital and get checked out. But before you do, I'll need to see your license."

"Oh. Of course." Confused, I glanced around for my purse and found it on the seat next to me. I drew out my wallet and handed him the card.

The officer looked at my license and then at me. "Okay. Now I need you to step out of the car and walk a straight line for me."

A familiar voice drifted toward me. "Not necessary. I'll take over from here, Sawyer."

Gino gestured for Officer Sawyer to move away from the car. "Lou, this is my cousin, Tessa. I'll vouch for her. She wasn't drinking."

Officer Lou Sawyer rose to his feet and handed me

back my license, which I clumsily shoved into my coat pocket. He glanced at Gino. "Are you sure about that?"

Gino nodded and cut his eyes toward me. "It's fine, Lou. She lost her husband in an accident a few weeks ago and has been under a lot of stress." He squatted down next to me, taking the other policeman's place. "Are you okay? What the hell happened?"

I was embarrassed for the other officer to hear my sad life story, so I avoided going into specific details. "I looked away from the road for a second and…uh…didn't see the car in front of me stop. Is the other driver okay?"

"She's fine." Gino cupped my cheek with his palm. "Thank God you are too."

His hand and voice were comforting, and I nearly broke down in tears as everything I had discovered in Dylan's office came rushing back. How could I explain to Gino that the one man I'd loved and trusted for years had managed to betray me?

Gino turned to the blond policeman. "Can you give us a few minutes?"

"Take all the time you need," Lou assured him, his green eyes clouded with concern. "Her car needs to be moved to the curb though. It's starting to cause a backup."

"You want to wait for me on the sidewalk?" Gino asked me.

I shook my head. "I can slide over." I was surprised at the soreness in my body when I moved, even though it was mere inches.

He grimaced as he sat and put the vehicle back into Drive, and the car moved forward. "Your car seems to be okay except for a dent in the front, but it lurched forward when I stepped on the gas."

"That's nothing new," I assured him. "I've been meaning to have that checked."

Gino shut the ignition off and turned to face me, worry etched into his well-defined features. "You're lucky that the airbag didn't deploy. It should have."

My voice trembled. "I'm glad the other woman wasn't hurt."

"Look, Tessa. This is scary. Maybe you shouldn't be alone for a while, until you get things under control. I don't like the idea of you being by yourself every night. Why don't you come stay with Lucy and me? Or maybe think about selling the house. The memories have got to be painful for you."

That was when I officially lost it. "I don't even have

memories to comfort me anymore." Like a faucet, tears streamed out of my eyes, and I started to sob uncontrollably.

Gino put his arms around my shoulders and held me tight against him. "You're not making any sense. What's got you so upset? And why didn't you call me back this morning?"

I hesitated. Gino might be my concerned cousin, but he was still a cop. "Dylan was fired from his job and never told me."

"When did this happen?" he asked.

I shrugged. "Probably a couple of weeks before his death."

"And you never knew?" A deep wrinkle formed between his brows.

Why did everyone feel the need to keep reminding me of this fact? I jutted my chin out in defiance. "He deposited money in the bank every week. There was no reason for me to suspect anything unusual was going on."

Skepticism shone through my cousin's dark eyes. "Where was he getting the money from then? Was it unemployment checks?"

Didn't I wish. "No."

"Tess." Gino spoke gently. "What exactly is going on?"

"Someone told me today that he was fired for

embezzling from his company. I—I can't seem to wrap my head around it."

Gino's eyebrows raised in disbelief. "How much money are we talking about?"

I shrugged. "No idea."

Gino had morphed from devoted cousin into full-blown cop mode. "You have no idea where the money is? Did he hide it in your house somewhere?"

I shrank away from him. "Please don't make this any more difficult for me." My eyes began to tear again, and I grabbed a tissue out of my purse. "And I don't want anyone else in the family to know about this yet. Not my mother, Lucy, or Mona." Gabby was exempt, since I would tell her myself. "You're a cop, and you might feel that you have some duty to—"

He cut me off. "You should know that family always comes first with me. Dylan's dead, Tess. You're not responsible for his actions, and I know that you were not involved in whatever scheme he might have concocted. But if you think you've found something out that's important, I need you to tell me."

Wearily, I leaned back against the seat. "I went to Dylan's office this morning to pick up his personal items.

Someone mentioned they were sorry he'd been fired. Everyone thought I already knew." I stopped to blow my nose. "When I started asking more questions, I discovered that he'd been embezzling funds from his employer. He set up his own bank account and everything. When they found out, he was fired. They agreed not to press charges because they didn't want the media to find out."

Gino's face was stern, and a four-letter swear word popped out of his mouth. "Are you sure about this?"

"Yes. He deceived me. Dylan stole, Gino. Do you know how that makes me feel? Our marriage was based on a bunch of lies." Sure, infidelity would have been worse to deal with, but this almost felt like Dylan had cheated on me, and in a sense, he had. He was no longer the man I'd once thought he was.

"Why didn't they arrest him?"

I twisted the tissue between my hands. "Apparently they didn't want a scandal. One of the employees also told me that Dylan's boss didn't like him and was happy he'd been fired."

This got Gino's attention. "What's the guy's name?"

"Ned Reinhart. He might be worth checking out." I couldn't help but wonder if our entire marriage had been a sham. Were there any other red flags I hadn't thought of until now? If Dylan told one lie, chances were excellent that there were more. I might be opening a fresh can of worms, but I'd rather know the whole truth than be kept in the dark any longer.

Gino nodded. "I'll run a check on this Reinhart fellow. But if Dylan paid the cash back, as I assume they made him do, *and* he was still bringing home a salary, where was that money coming from?"

He was asking me questions that I had no answers to. "Again, I don't know. I can't deal with this right now, Gino. Besides, it's almost one o'clock, and I'm late for work."

"To hell with that place. You need to go to the hospital and get checked out. Plus, we don't know for sure that Slice connects to Dylan's death." He hesitated for a moment, then blew out a long breath. "Look, Tess. I've got a confession to make. When I suggested you work at Slice, it wasn't so you could help the police."

My eyebrows drew together. "I don't understand."

His face reddened slightly. "We were all so worried about you that when I saw the sign at Slice, I thought it might motivate you to go back to work. You know, help you get back to your old self. This way, you'd also feel like you were doing something useful to help with the investigation. If I'd ever dreamed it would lead to this, I never—"

"Thanks so much for your confidence in me," I said bitterly. "So this was all to humor me? Get little Tessa out of the house and back to making pizzas in someone else's kitchen?"

"It was meant in the best possible way," Gino assured me. "I told Gabby that too."

I sucked in some air. "Gabby was in on it too? I'd expect you to do something like that, but certainly not her." He had no idea how this had hurt me.

"Don't be so hard on her," Gino said. "It was my idea. I told her what I had in mind, and she agreed it was worth trying. Gabs said she'd be supportive and would go along with anything you asked of her. We meant well, Tess."

This was too much for me to absorb. "I'll have to think about this later," I said in all honesty. "But I'd appreciate it if you told Gabby she doesn't have to keep the ruse up for my sake anymore. No, on second thought, I'll tell her myself."

Gino had the good grace to look embarrassed. "Now that the jig is up, so to speak, call Anthony and tell him you're not coming back."

"No." I squared my shoulders, preparing for an

argument. "I can't do that, and I *won't*. There's something strange going on at that place. Everyone there had a reason for disliking Dylan, maybe even enough to want him dead. I need to get a little closer to it all. There's a very good chance his killer *is* employed there. Yesterday afternoon I found a baggie with white powder under one of the shelves in the cooler. I'm guessing someone dropped it, and I think there might have been cocaine inside."

Gino's eyes widened with interest. "Where is it? Do you have it? Why didn't you tell me about this sooner?"

I shook my head. "I didn't have a chance. Izzy, Anthony's daughter, caught me before I could pick it up. When I went back later, the baggie was gone. Can you guys raid the place?"

He looked disappointed. "It's not enough. We need probable cause. You can't be positive it was coke. What if it was sugar instead? Now, if you'd brought the substance to me and we tested it, that would be different. Then we'd have enough reason to get a warrant." He pursed his lips. "I'm sorry I came up with this stupid idea in the first place. You don't belong there."

I ignored his comment. "I wonder if Dylan knew someone at Slice was involved with drugs, and maybe he threatened to turn them in. I also found out that Anthony's daughter, Izzy, disliked Dylan, but I don't know why. When she found out who I was, she didn't exactly roll out the red carpet for me."

"Sounds like a great work atmosphere," Gino remarked.

Another thought occurred to me. "Anthony was good friends with Dylan. What if Dylan told him he'd been fired? Could he have become more involved in Slice's business? Slice was not doing well financially. Maybe Dylan was helping Anthony find ways to save money at Slice?"

"Don't say anything to Anthony," Gino advised. "He might get suspicious if you ask about Dylan's work there. Now let me go talk to Lou, and then I'll drive you to the hospital."

Without another word, he got out of the car and spoke to his coworkers. Lou was standing at the curb with another officer and the woman whose car I'd hit. I grimaced as I got out of the car, stiffness already setting into my joints, and went to address her. Like me, she'd been alone in the vehicle. Her car had taken the brunt of the damage, and I winced, thinking about how much my insurance might go up as a result. She watched me approach, a neutral expression on her face.

My cheeks were burning as I put out a hand for her to shake. "I'm so sorry about your car. Are you okay?"

She smiled and extended her hand. "Yeah, I'm fine. Glad you're all right too."

"Thanks. My insurance company will take care of everything." Before I could say anything further, Gino took me by the arm and guided me into his unmarked vehicle.

"You need to be careful what you say, Tess. That woman might try to take advantage of you."

"But it was my fault," I protested. "If she'd been hurt, I wouldn't be able to forgive myself." Besides, I had more important things to worry about than if she tried to extort a few extra hundred dollars from me. I leaned against Gino, who put his arm around my waist to support me, the weight of Dylan's betrayal heavy on my heart. Tonight, after work, I'd look through his personal items and see what else he might have conveniently forgotten to tell me about.

After we were settled in the vehicle, Gino adjusted his seat belt. "You should call Anthony and tell him you're not coming in. He'd understand."

"No. I feel fine, and my headache is starting to go away."

"Tess, you're all shaken up. Your health is more important. We're going to the hospital, and I don't want to hear any more arguments."

I knew he wouldn't change his mind but decided to

see if he might meet me halfway. "If the doctor says I'm all right, I'm going to work afterward."

Gino grunted. "Why is everyone in this family so damn stubborn?" He didn't wait for my answer as he started the car and we moved down the street. "Thankfully, your car is drivable. Lou's not going to write you a ticket, but we can't do anything about the insurance company."

I sighed. "That's the least of my worries."

We both fell silent during the five-minute drive to Harvest Park Hospital, and I called Anthony on the way to explain what had happened. He sounded concerned and told me not to worry about my shift, but I assured him I'd be there eventually.

The emergency room was at full capacity when we arrived, and I groaned. "We'll never get out of here."

"That's a good thing. You won't be able to go to work then." Gino flashed me an evil grin.

The woman at the counter took my medical information, and then we found a couple of empty seats. Despite all the other people, though, I was the next one called. Perhaps Gino's Harvest Park PD jacket had something to do with it.

The doctor did a few tests, held up some fingers, and

asked how many I saw, then typed notes into a laptop. "You might experience some stiffness," he warned. "That's normal after a car accident. But if you have any vision blurriness or severe headaches, come back immediately or go to see your regular doctor."

Gino folded his arms over his chest. "Is she okay to go to work today?"

The doctor frowned. "Yes, but normally I'd advise against it. Given the circumstances, Tessa, I'm sure your boss would understand."

"I have to go." Chuck's revelation had motivated me even more to find out what had happened, and I didn't want to waste another minute.

"Your car is back at your house," Gino said as we exited the hospital's main entrance. "I didn't want you driving, so I had one of my coworkers drop it off."

Puzzled, I stared at him. "How am I supposed to get home tonight?"

Gino opened the passenger door of his car for me and walked around to the driver's seat. "I texted Gabs about your accident. She said to call when you need a ride home. You get out at nine, right? She has some extra stuff to do at the store and will be there until then."

"Wow, that's late for her. Okay, I'll probably take her up on it. Thanks for everything."

Gino watched me soberly. "Are you sure you want to go back to Slice, Tess? I mean, if Anthony and his employees are doing drugs or something else illegal, this could be more dangerous than I originally thought. Sure, it might relate to Dylan's death or maybe something entirely different, but I don't want to take any chances with your safety."

I gripped the side of the seat between my fingers and blew out a sigh. "This is a horrible thing to say, but what if—God forbid—Lucy had been murdered? Then you discovered through your investigation that she'd lied to you and you were forced to question her honesty for the first time ever. Could you forget about it?"

"No," he admitted in a hoarse voice. "But I'm a detective and—"

"I know," I interrupted. "But if you weren't a cop, could you walk away?"

He sighed. "All right, I get what you're saying. God knows I don't approve, but I do happen to understand. Please be careful about what you say to Anthony though."

"Dylan was pretending to go to work every day. What was he doing instead? Who was he doing it with? Maybe it relates to why he was killed." Funny how you think you know a person. I had never suspected a thing. *Well played, Husband. Well played.*

Minutes later, Gino pulled into the parking lot of Slice. "If you have any pain, I want you to promise that you'll call Gabby to come get you sooner. If she's not available, call me."

"I'm fine."

He narrowed his eyes. "No. You're vulnerable and upset, and I'm worried about you."

"Upset yes, but vulnerable no," I admitted. "Not anymore. Angry sums it up much better. I want answers, Gino, and I'm going to find them."

TEN

"IS EVERYTHING OKAY, TESSA?" ANTHONY ASKED. "You look kind of pale. Maybe you should go home. Are you having any pain?"

It was almost two o'clock when I'd finally reached Slice. My head still ached, but I didn't want to go home. I shook my head, wincing from the stiffness in my neck. "It was only a fender bender. How about I freeze some dinners? I'll whip up some of my eggplant parmigiana." My mind was preoccupied with what Chuck had relayed to me earlier, and it was quickly becoming an obsession. *What else had Dylan lied to me about?*

"Whatever you're most comfortable with." He hesitated. "Some more tomato sauce would be great." He handed me an order slip. "And we got a call for two pizzas.

I'll grab some dough out of the cooler for you. Don't worry about making any fresh today."

"The sauce I made yesterday is gone already?" Anthony hadn't heard me, and I was left alone with my thoughts. Was there a way to phrase my questions without making him suspicious? *How often was Dylan here, Anthony? Was he doing other things besides your taxes, like finding creative and dishonest ways to help your floundering business?*

I checked the prep table and saw that the vegetables and cheeses had already been filled. Anthony came out of the cooler with five bags of dough. Before he could walk away again, I stopped him. "Do you have a second?"

"Sure. What's wrong?"

"I was wondering how often Dylan used to come in here. I mean, was it like every day, or maybe two to three times a week?"

He removed his hat and scratched his sparse hair thoughtfully. "I'm not sure. But he did my taxes, you know. It wasn't all pleasure and pizza." He smiled in an effort to keep his tone light, but I detected a curious glimmer in his eyes. "Why do you ask?"

Desperation had settled into my tone. "Was he always alone? About how long would he stay?"

Anthony furrowed his brow. "What's going on, honey? Level with me."

Okay, how to get out of this one. *Gee, Anthony, I was wondering if one of your employees might be responsible for my husband's not-so-accidental death. Or maybe you saw somebody tamper with his car that day. In fact, I kind of think you and him were involved in something illegal! Cooking any books with those pizzas, Anthony?*

Gino's warning floated through my mind. I needed to be very careful about what I said. Sighing, I forged on. "He might have been cheating on me." The lie stuck in my throat, and my voice was hoarse. "I was wondering if you knew anything about it."

Shock registered on Anthony's face. "There's no way. Dylan talked about you all the time. He adored you, Tessa."

"Well, the last couple of months before he died, Dylan started acting really strange. A woman knows when she's being lied to." Then I decided to go a little further. "I think he was meeting someone here."

Anthony carefully stroked the white whiskers on his chin. "No. He was a good boy. I never saw him meet a lady here. He came in a couple of times with a friend of his. It's been a while, so I can't remember the guy's name."

"Tall, athletic guy. Dark hair?" I asked. "A fireman named Justin?"

He snapped his fingers. "Yeah, that's right. Now I remember Dylan saying that he worked for the fire department. Nice-looking boy. But in answer to your question, no. I never saw Dylan here with another lady."

I gripped the edges of the prep table. "That's a relief." I racked my brain for something else to add. "But there was something going on with him. Money might have been an issue, since finances were always pretty tight at home. Did Dylan…" In a sudden panic, I groped for the right words. "Did he ever ask you to borrow money?"

The color rose in Anthony's face. "No. Those pizzas need to be baked, Tessa. Butchy will be back for his next delivery soon. Don't forget the sauce either."

"Sure," I said. "But I made some yesterday. It's gone already?"

Anthony seemed uncomfortable. "I'm freezing some. You can never have too much of a good thing, right? If you want to leave me the recipe, I'll make it myself. I know you're pretty busy in here with the pizzas and dinners."

"No, that's not necessary. I'll do it." I didn't mind Anthony using my sauce for the dishes, but if he thought I was giving him the recipe, he had another thing coming. I tried to work the conversation back to my husband. "Did Dylan—"

"Please, Tessa. The pizzas." Anthony narrowed his eyes and walked into the dining area, where a couple had settled into one of the booths.

Having no choice, I dug my hands into the dough, and an immediate sense of calm washed over me. The pies were finished far too soon, and the urge to keep my hands busy was overpowering. I was tired and stressed, my body stiff and sore from the accident. It probably had been a mistake to come in, but I was off for the next two days and could rest up then. There was no time to waste.

After I had started the sauce and the pizzas were in the oven, I thought that perhaps some creativity would help ease my anxiety and decided to make some stromboli. I scanned the reach-in fridge of the prep table and placed diced ham, pepper, onions, and mushrooms into separate bowls. I greased a frying pan on the stove and added the ingredients one by one, ladling tomato sauce on top to simmer for a few minutes. As the mixture cooked and the delectable smell of onions and frying ham filled the room, I rolled out pizza dough on to a cookie sheet and cut it in half. I covered the pieces of dough with pepperoni slices and added the warm, rich mixture from the pan. Then I folded the dough around it and brushed the top with melted butter. As I placed the loaves in the oven, the back door slammed, and a young man walked toward me.

He appeared to be barely out of his teens and, at about five foot seven, wasn't that much taller than me, and he looked so thin, I thought I could quite easily pick him up. Dressed in a pair of faded blue jeans, white sneakers, and a black hooded jacket, he waited patiently as I removed the pizzas from the oven one by one, slid them off the peels and into the cardboard boxes, and used the rocker knife to cut even slices.

He smiled at me politely. "You're Mrs. Esposito, right? Eric told me you'd started working here. I'm Butchy."

I returned his smile. "It's nice to meet you, Butchy. My mother knows your mother from church."

"Oh?" His ruddy complexion deepened. "My mom gets really ticked off when I miss Mass. She once made me go to confession and tell the priest I hadn't been to church for a whole month. He was okay about it, but she forced me to say a ton of Hail Marys."

I laughed and turned to take the loaves out of the oven.

Butchy sniffed at the air. "I love stromboli and those smell great. Your husband said you were an awesome cook." His face froze. "I'm sorry for your loss, by the way."

Intrigued by his words, I glanced around the kitchen. Vince was in the office with the door shut, and Anthony was now sitting in a booth with some of his regular patrons, laughing loudly. "Thank you. Did you know Dylan well?"

He shrugged. "Well enough, I guess. He always stopped to talk to me and ask how things were going. Real nice guy. He spent a good deal of time in Anthony's office with him when he was here."

How interesting. "Was Dylan here every day?"

He paused to think. "Pretty much. At least it seemed like he was always around, especially in the last month or so before he—" Butchy lowered his eyes. "I figured he was working for Anthony full time as his accountant."

I leaned forward on the table eagerly. "Did you ever see Dylan come in here with anybody? Or was he always alone?"

Butchy's amber-colored eyes became wary. "I'm not sure what you mean. Like, was he ever with another lady?"

"Anyone. Man, woman, it doesn't matter."

He studied me carefully. "Why are you asking so many questions?"

Have a little tact, Tess. He's getting suspicious. If I tried the ruse about the other woman, maybe he'd provide some information and not worry about my motive. "Okay, you've got me. What I really meant was, did you ever see him with another woman?"

Butchy glanced out into the dining room, as if he was checking on Anthony's status as well. "No, but Izzy would go into the office sometimes when he was there." He fidgeted under my gaze. "I think she kind of liked him. And one time—" He hesitated, then grabbed the pizzas and began to stuff them into the black warmer bag. "Never mind."

I reached out and touched his arm. "One time, what? Please tell me."

He stared down at my hand, positioned on his elbow. Flustered, I removed it, but he still refused to look at me. "I walked by the office one night and heard her talking to Dylan. Anthony wasn't here, and Vince was on the phone. She asked Dylan if he wanted to—you know."

Blood pounded into my face. "If he wanted to *what*?"

Butchy practically squirmed with discomfort. "If he

wanted to go back to her place after work. She told him she'd make it a night he'd never forget."

Speechless, I stared at Butchy and prayed this was some type of joke.

He didn't wait for my response. "Dylan told her to get lost, Mrs. Esposito. He didn't take the bait. Then he said something to Izzy about how she should be careful that her fiancé didn't find out about her promisc—I mean her behavior. Jeez, I can never say that word right."

"Do you mean she's promiscuous?" I asked.

Butchy nodded. "Yeah, that's it. One night when Dylan and I were leaving, she was in the parking lot making out with some guy in a BMW. It wasn't Rico either."

"Who's Rico?" I asked, trying to remember where I'd heard the name.

"He's Izzy's fiancé. She got real angry when Dylan mentioned it and told him to mind his own business—or else."

Fear settled in my stomach. "What do you think she meant by that?"

"I'm not sure," Butchy admitted. "But you don't ever want to get on Izzy's bad side. That broad has enough venom in her to make a snake jealous."

Dylan had made quite an enemy of the seductress Isabella. How far would she go to protect her secret from her fiancé?

Butchy seemed oblivious to my internal thoughts and prattled on. "Between you and me, I can't stand her. If I had enough guts I'd have told Anthony about her and that other guy, but I was afraid he'd fire me, so I kept quiet. It's not my business, and I need this job, Mrs. Esposito. I've got seven brothers and sisters at home and have to help out all I can."

"Of course," I said, feeling immensely sorry for him.

He took a step toward me, his features softening in the light from above. "After that night, I don't think Izzy went near your husband again. She kind of acted like he had the plague, you know what I mean? I even heard her tell Anthony one night that he should get rid of him."

The hair rose on the back of my neck. "Get rid of Dylan?"

"You know," Butchy said. "Fire him. Find someone else to do his taxes."

"Oh, right." Relieved, I tried to swallow the lump in my throat.

He glanced at the clock on the wall. "I've got to run. Please don't tell Anthony about any of this, okay?"

"Your secret's safe with me," I assured him.

He gave me a feeble smile. "Have a good night and don't worry. Things will get better soon."

I watched him disappear out the kitchen door and tried to pull myself together. At least something had gone right today. Butchy seemed willing to talk and, unlike the others, wasn't treating me like an alien. He might even turn out to be an ally.

The door to the office opened and Vince came out, sniffing the air. He stopped short by me and pointed at the loaves on the table. "What'd you make those for?"

"I had some extra time and thought that maybe we could put them up for sale."

Vince scowled and ran a hand through his unruly hair. "We won't be able to sell them."

A woman leaned over the checkout counter, staring in at the both of us. "Hi, I called in a pizza. Last name is Hunter."

Vince waved a hand dismissively at me. "I've got this." He took a pizza box off the wall shelf behind me, stepped over to the counter, and laid it down in front of the woman. "Fifteen dollars."

The woman eyed the loaves that I was wrapping in foil with interest. "Oh my. Is that stromboli I smell?"

"Fresh out of the oven." I smiled.

Anthony reappeared from the dining area and nodded politely at the woman. "Hello, Mrs. Hunter, how are you today?"

"Fine, Anthony, thanks. How much is the stromboli?"

Both Vince and Anthony turned to look at me, but I simply shrugged and said nothing. Let them figure it out for themselves. The satisfaction in proving Vince wrong was priceless.

"Uh, twelve dollars a loaf," Anthony said with uncertainty.

"I'll take both of them." Mrs. Hunter glanced down at the little girl who was clinging to her coat and whining. "Can you give her a slice, please? She's driving me crazy."

"No problem." I cut off a thick slice, placed it on a paper plate, and handed it to the woman. "It's still very warm, so be careful."

Mrs. Hunter broke off a piece for the child, then helped herself to one. She took a small bite and closed her eyes as she chewed. "Oh my, this is delicious. Will you be featuring this on the menu from now on? My family loves stromboli."

Vince and Anthony exchanged a glance between them. "Sure," Anthony hedged. "We could do that."

Mrs. Hunter paid for her order, then she and the child left. Anthony turned to me with an apologetic smile. "You did real good, honey. Before you suggested it, I never even thought about putting stromboli on the menu."

While Anthony may have been happy with the results, Vince was not. He flashed me a clear look of contempt. "Congratulations on making employee of the month."

What was this guy's problem?

Anthony disappeared into the office, and I busied myself with ladling the tomato sauce into containers for him to freeze while Vince waited on a new customer.

The back door banged open, and the kid who'd bumped into me the other day appeared. He was tall and slim, with carrot-colored hair and blue eyes that stared at me curiously under long, dark lashes. He placed a black warmer bag on the table and nodded at me. "Hi, I'm Sam. You must be Mrs. Esposito."

"Call me Tessa." I smiled. "Nice to meet you."

He jerked his head toward the office door. "Is Anthony in there? I want to ask him if I can cut out early."

I put on a pair of plastic gloves. "Yes, he—"

Vince strolled over, his eyes narrowing at me as he addressed Sam. "You don't have to tell this lady anything, Sam. She's an employee—same as you. I'll inform Anthony you went home early."

I bit into my lower lip, determined not to say something I'd regret. This was no time to get myself fired from Slice. I had a great deal of work ahead of me.

Sam looked from Vince to me as if he didn't quite understand Vince's behavior himself. "Okay, sure. Thanks." He started to walk away, then glanced over his shoulder at me. "Nice meeting you too."

"Take care," I said. Vince took the containers of sauce I'd packaged and brought them into the cooler without another word. *Jerk.*

Anthony reappeared from the office. "You've had a long day, honey, so go ahead and knock off early. I can take care of things for the rest of the evening, and I'll still pay you for your regular shift. Plus, Vince is here to help."

"Lucky me." Vince shut the door to the cooler. "Anthony, wait up. I need to talk to you in private." They went into the office together and shut the door while I pulled out my phone to call Gabby. Since there were only a couple of hours till closing, I wasn't about to argue with Anthony. I wanted to go home. It had been a long, strange day.

Gabby's phone went to voicemail, and I cursed under my breath. I disconnected and shot off a quick text to her. She wasn't expecting to come get me for a couple more hours and might be in the middle of something at her bookstore.

Eric walked by me with a black warmer bag in hand. "Hey, sweet thing. What's up?"

I hadn't even heard him come in. "Nothing. I'm trying to reach my cousin to give me a ride home, but she's not answering."

A sly smile crossed his face. "I suppose I could give you a ride, after I make this last delivery."

I hesitated for a moment. The repulsion I felt for this kid was trumped by my curiosity ever since he professed to know something about Dylan's death. Plus, I was convinced that the drugs I'd found in the cooler belonged to him. Did I really want to drive with someone who might be under the influence? But it was the only way to ensure our conversation wouldn't be overheard.

"Don't worry. I'll be good." He winked.

"All right, thanks." I accepted before I could think better of it, then grabbed my purse and coat.

Eric opened the passenger door for me to his beat-up Chevy. A creep with manners—how nice. He started the engine, and we zoomed out of the parking lot. "Where do you live?" he asked.

I glanced around the car. There were empty soda cans, bags of chips, and candy wrappers scattered everywhere. The entire vehicle smelled like gasoline, and I caught the faint odor of marijuana mixed in with it. The windshield was so dirty that I wondered how he managed to see where he was going. "I'm at 42 Seasons Way. Three blocks over from the park."

"Yeah, I know the street." Eric accelerated. The legal speed limit around here was 30, but the kid had to be pushing over 50 miles per hour. He studied the order slip in front of him. "Sorry to hold you up, but this guy gets his panties all in a bunch if I'm late with his pizza. From the size of him, it wouldn't hurt him to wait a while."

This kid had no filter. "That's fine. It will give us more of a chance to talk."

"Oh yeah?" He reached out and ran a finger suggestively down my arm. Furious, I smacked it away. "What? I thought you were interested in me. Nights have got to be pretty lonely for you since your stuck-up suit of a husband kicked the bucket."

I fought to control my temper. "Sorry, but I'm not looking for a replacement." *Especially from a punk kid like you.*

"Then what did you want to talk to me about?"

I decided to be honest with him. "I think you know something about my husband's death. You don't believe it was an accident."

He placed a cigarette between his lips and reached for the car's lighter. "But we both know that, don't we? Come on. I've heard that you've been going around asking questions about your old man. What's the deal?"

"You tell me."

Eric blew a plume of smoke in my face, and I did my best not to gag. "Thanks to that windbag of a cop, it's all over the streets. Somebody tampered with your dude's car and baked him to death."

My stomach twisted in a knot at his words. "Did you see who did it?"

He stared straight ahead, a smug smile playing on his lips. "I might have."

Was he pulling my leg? I honestly couldn't tell. "Does this person work at Slice?"

"I didn't say that. Your old man's car was parked in the alley that day. Anyone could have come along and fooled with the engine. Chances were pretty good that no one would see either. But—maybe someone did, you know?" He gave me a sly wink.

Even though I despised him, I sensed that Eric was telling the truth. "Just come right out and say what you want."

"Take it easy, babe. Get me some cash, and I'll tell you everything I know."

God help me. If Gino ever found out I had agreed to a bribe with this creep, he might shoot me with his gun, but I was desperate enough to agree. "How much do you want?"

"Five grand."

I sucked in some air. "I don't have that much lying around." I thought of the life insurance policy that should be arriving any day now. "But I'll have it soon."

"I don't take IOUs, baby." Eric sucked on his cigarette. "I've got to think about my future, you know?" He laughed. "The perks of this job are great, but there's no future in it. What I'd really like is an office job. I'd make a great CEO somewhere. The ladies would all be chasing me then."

"Look, you can understand my position, with Dylan being gone. I can get you a grand today and the rest within a week or so."

He picked up my left hand before I could stop him and studied the one-carat solitaire I wore with my wedding band. "That baby's got to be worth a couple of thousand at least."

I gritted my teeth and snatched my hand away. "Forget it."

Eric held up his right hand, as if making a promise. "Only as collateral until you get the rest of the dough. Scout's honor."

Right. Because Eric was definitely the type of kid who helped old ladies across the street and returned valuable property that was loaned to him. I wasn't handing over my ring, but I let him go ahead and think that it might happen. From my wallet I withdrew five twenties, which I arranged into a fan and held out to him. "Fine. After you deliver the pizza, take me to the ATM. I'll get you the other nine hundred and give you the ring. But first you tell me what you know, or it's no deal."

Eric pulled into a long blacktop driveway in front of a beige Colonial. He placed the car in Park and snatched the bills out of my hand. "Wait here. We'll talk when I get back."

Conniving little creep. I watched him swagger toward the door with the warmer in hand. My phone buzzed, and I drew it out of my purse. It was a text from Gabby. I'm so sorry! I got hung up at the store and missed your call. Are you still at work?

My fingers flew over the phone's keypad. No, I'm with Eric the delivery guy. He's giving me a lift home. I think he knows who fooled with Dylan's car. Call you when I get home.

As I pressed Send, Eric opened the car door, and a loud popping noise filled my ears. A moment later, an engine roared to life and burned past us. For a few seconds I didn't register what had happened. With horror, I watched as Eric slumped to the ground beside the car and a steady stream of blood flowed from his body to the blacktop underneath him. He lay there, motionless.

"Oh my God!" I screamed and covered my eyes.

The sound of running feet on pavement drew closer, and I looked up. Eric's customer was shouting at me and gesturing with his hand. My legs shook with fear as I somehow managed to get out of the car. The man reached my side. He was shirtless and heavyset, carrying an iPhone in one hand. He reached out to me with the other. Despite the cold and his half-naked body, his bald head shone with perspiration. Sweat trickled down the sides of his face, and he breathed heavily. "Hurry, lady! Follow me!"

"What are you doing?" I shrieked as he tried to pull me up the driveway. "We have to get him some help!"

"Don't bother," he panted. "The kid's dead. Now let's get the hell out of here before someone tries to pop us next."

ELEVEN

"ALL RIGHT." GINO GUIDED HIS UNMARKED vehicle through a yellow light that changed to red as we flew underneath it. "Tell me what happened from the beginning. Yes, *again*."

I turned toward the side window so that he couldn't see me roll my eyes. It wouldn't do any good to complain. After the police had arrived, they had transported the customer and me down to the station where we'd been subjected to over an hour of intense questioning. First thing, I'd called Anthony, who'd been horrified when I told him what transpired. When I divulged my relationship with Gino at the station, my cousin had personally come to escort me home. It was after nine and I was too tired to even try to argue with him.

"I was sitting in the car, waiting for Eric to make a delivery. As he got back inside the vehicle there was a loud noise, like a firecracker. When I looked over, he was lying on the ground."

Gino swore under his breath. "I knew that it was a mistake for you to be working there. Plus, I said to call if you needed a ride. Why were you with that hoodlum?"

"Because I think he knew something about Dylan's death. He hinted that he might have seen who tampered with the car."

He eyed me suspiciously. "Eric could have been lying, you know. Why didn't he say something before now?"

I shrugged. "Maybe he was holding out for the right price." Oops. Wrong thing to say.

Gino pulled his car into my driveway and placed it in Park, the engine idling. He turned to me, his brown eyes snapping. "Did you offer that kid money?"

I didn't answer.

"Damn it, Tessa," he said in disbelief. "You did, didn't you? That punk was nothing but a scam artist with a record. He assaulted an officer last year and was arrested for possession of drugs. Did you ever think he was trying to make a quick buck off you?"

"He knew something about Dylan's murder," I insisted. "I think someone wanted to shut Eric up—for good. Maybe before he could talk to me? Whoever did this might be the same person who killed Dylan. We need to find out who's behind it."

"*We?*" A muscle ticked in Gino's jaw. "There's no *we*. This has gone too far. I'm officially firing you from Slice. First thing in the morning, call Anthony and tell him you won't be coming back to work."

I counted to ten in my head before answering, knowing Gino's macho stubborn streak. "Sorry, but I can't do that."

"Can't or won't? Why did I even tell you about the job? I never thought you'd take it this far." Gino's expression darkened. "What if you'd been shot instead of Eric?"

I shivered at his words but remained silent. The same thought had already occurred to me.

"Well?" he asked again.

"I have to find out what happened to my husband. I have a right to know. I *need* to know. There are a couple of employees at Slice who might be willing to talk." Butchy came to mind, and I wanted to have a chat with Sam too.

He sighed. "Tess, I don't want someone coming into Anthony's shop one night and taking a potshot at you. My goal was to get you cooking again—not *killed*."

"These days, that sort of thing can happen anywhere."

His eyes glittered as he leaned in closer. "Yeah, but I don't want it happening to my cousin. Did anyone ever tell you how stubborn you are?"

I shot him a grin. "It must be a family trait."

"No doubt." He pinned me with a long, hard stare. "So what else have you found out?"

"There are people I'm suspicious of at Slice," I confessed. "Carlita from Sweet Treats told me that Vince Falducci and his former partner were stealing from their restaurant in New York City. She said it's a possibility their tax guy turned them in. I don't know if it was Dylan but plan on looking through his personal records tonight to see if I can find anything. Vince got very angry when I asked about the business and wouldn't even tell me the restaurant's name. I was planning to check around on the internet to see what I could find."

"Don't bother. I can run some searches on him easily enough," Gino said. "A check through DMV at the very least. Anything or anyone else that I should know about?"

Heat flooded my cheeks. "Anthony's daughter, Izzy, had a crush on Dylan and offered him a good time. Apparently, Dylan saw her making out with another guy, and she might have been worried he'd tattle to her rich fiancé about it. Even Anthony seems a bit shady to me now, and he doesn't like talking about Dylan. Someone may have been watching my house last night too." I told him about the car that had been parked on the street with the headlights off.

Gino gritted his teeth. "You should have told me about this sooner. Plus, you're forgetting a key suspect."

"Who?"

"Your ex-boyfriend," Gino said darkly. "I'm watching that guy like a hawk."

"Just because Dylan's car was at his shop the day before he died doesn't make Matt a killer," I pointed out.

"It's the same thing as Dylan's car being at Slice right before he died. Okay, I'll be honest," Gino confessed. "I've never liked Matt Smitty, but that's beside the point. He was all nervous and jittery when I questioned him at his house earlier."

"You went to his house? He must have freaked."

"He's hiding something. I'm sure of it," Gino insisted. "Sometimes it pays to keep badgering a suspect. They get nervous and slip up. Maybe next time he'll cave. You stay away from him, and if he comes near you, I want to know about it."

I groaned. "Yes, Dad."

"Have you checked Dylan's cell phone?" Gino asked.

"No. It burned up with… I mean, it was in the car with him when he—" My heart hurt every time I let myself think about the manner in which he had died. Despite what Dylan had done, he was my husband, and I still loved him.

Gino leaned over to ruffle my hair. "If you like, I can check with the phone company and try to retrieve his texts."

"Dylan hated to text," I said. "If I sent him a message, he'd always call me back."

"Did you know his password to retrieve voicemails?" he asked.

Uneasiness washed over me like a tidal wave. I'd never been one of those wives who'd check her husband's phone on the sly when he wasn't around. It felt like a lack of trust to me. Then again, Dylan had betrayed that trust, and this might be the only way to get to the bottom of his deception. "Yeah. I know his password."

Gino drew me closer, planting a kiss on the top of my head. "You need to take a day and think about this first. What if you found out something even worse about him? Could you handle that?"

I didn't answer.

"As a cop, I'd say to check his voicemail. Speaking as your cousin, sometimes it's best to leave these things alone. Think on it before making a decision."

"I will. Thanks for the ride." Gino waited until I was inside my house before he took off. Luigi met me at the door, and I hugged him close, listening to his loud purrs, and sank down on the love seat with him in my arms. What a day. I was so exhausted I couldn't even see straight but wanted to go through the boxes, which were still in my car. For now, I was intent on closing my eyes and snuggling with Luigi, enjoying the peace and quiet.

Headlights shone through my window from the driveway and I groaned. Maybe Gino had forgotten something. When I looked out, I spotted Justin's truck. I had forgotten about asking him to stop by today when he was off work.

"Hi, stranger." I held the door open and smiled at the athletic-looking guy with the black, wavy hair jogging up my sidewalk. I hadn't realized before how much I'd missed seeing him the past few days. Justin was like a breath of fresh air—something I sorely needed right now.

"Hey yourself." He held a pizza box in one hand and a six-pack of beer in the other. "Want to join me for a slice?"

His company was always welcome, but the last thing I wanted to eat was pizza. Still, I had to let him know what I'd discovered. "Sure, come on in."

Justin put the pizza and beer on the breakfast counter while I grabbed plates and napkins from the cupboard. He removed his Carhartt jacket and tossed it on the stool next to him. Despite the cold night he was wearing a light-blue Adidas T-shirt with the sleeves cut out, his muscles bulging from the strenuous workouts he performed religiously to keep himself in shape for his job. He stooped down to pet Luigi, who rubbed affectionately against his legs. "How's it going, big guy?"

Although Justin and Dylan had both been easygoing and alike in temperament, they were total opposites when it came to looks. While Dylan had been fair-haired with crystal-blue eyes, Justin's hair was an ebony shade and always a bit disheveled, as if he'd been caught in a sudden windstorm. It went well with his Mediterranean coloring. His nose was slightly bent on one side, the result of an on-the-job injury a few years back. He'd broken it when debris had fallen on him during a house fire, and he had barely made it out of the building. Though he'd still managed to rescue two children trapped inside.

Other than his misshapen nose, it was difficult to find fault in Justin's looks. Besides his solid but lean build, he possessed an oblong face with fine, classic features and had never had trouble attracting female admirers. I'd noticed this firsthand last year when he'd gone out to dinner with Dylan and me. Several women had been eyeing him from across the room, and Dylan had teased his friend mercilessly about it.

Justin grabbed a slice of the white pie and placed it on a plate. The box was still hot to the touch and the tantalizing smell of cheese drifted upward, mixing with the faint aroma of garlic and cooked broccoli. "I checked the bathroom faucet before I went to work this morning. All fixed." He pushed my house key across the counter. "For the record, I don't like you leaving a key under the front mat. It makes me nervous."

Given everything that was going on in my life lately, he had a valid point. "Thanks. I appreciate it." I took a bite of the pizza. The crust was tender and flaky, thinner than Slice's pizzas. The cheese mixed well with the oregano and ignited my taste buds. Even though I was a big believer in tomato sauce on pizza, I could fully appreciate a creamy béchamel as well.

Justin opened a can of beer and offered it to me, but I shook my head. "So you said you were working again. I think that's terrific. Are you back at Sunnyside Up?"

I grabbed a napkin to wipe my mouth. "No. I'm working at Slice."

Justin laid his half-eaten piece back down on the plate. "The pizza place where Dylan used to go for lunch all the time? It's kind of a dump. Why would you go there?"

"There's something I need to tell you, but please don't mention it to anyone." I paused for a deep breath. "It looks like Dylan's death wasn't an accident."

He stared at me, his grayish-blue eyes darkening to the color of steel. "Please tell me you're not serious. Who the hell told you such a thing?"

I swallowed hard. "Gino did, a couple of days back. Someone tampered with Dylan's car."

Justin muttered an expletive under his breath. "I can't believe it. Hell, I don't *want* to believe it. Why would someone do this to him? And why is Gino only telling you now? Surely, he knew before."

"He said he was worried how I'd react. I don't know that Dylan's death connects with Slice in any way," I said honestly. "But he spent a lot of time there, and his car was parked in their alley right before he…crashed." I blew out a breath. "They needed a cook, so it's an angle I'm checking out."

He raised an eyebrow. "Is this why you asked me to stop by?"

I leaned forward across the counter. "Part of the reason. I'm trying to get an idea of where Dylan went and who he saw the last couple of days of his life. When's the last time you saw him? Did he seem different to you the last few months?"

A shadow passed over Justin's face. "Different how?"

"I'm not sure," I confessed. "Maybe he was worried that someone was after him or concerned about money. Was there anyone at the gym who tried to pick a fight with Dylan or didn't like him?"

Justin stared down at the counter. "We didn't really socialize with anyone else at the gym, and he stopped going with me months ago." He paused for a few seconds. "Dylan said he was too busy at work. Have you asked around there? Maybe he wasn't getting along with a coworker."

I hesitated, deciding not to tell him about the embezzlement yet. It was too much for one day, and Justin looked more exhausted than I felt. "I have a couple of boxes of his stuff in the car that I picked up earlier. Personal items from the office. I need to go through them tonight."

"I'll bring the boxes in for you before I leave." Justin came around the counter to where I was still standing and put his hands on my shoulders, pinning me with a sober expression.

"Something wrong?" I asked.

"You know that I'm always here if you need anything, right?"

"Yes, of course." Next to Gabby, he was the dearest friend I had. We'd always had such a close relationship, ever since I'd first met him when Dylan and I started dating nine years ago. Since his death, we'd grown so much closer. Justin was a rare gem of a man.

"I miss him too, Tess." His voice was gruff as he squeezed my shoulders softly, his fingers warm against my back. "Every single day. It has to be so much worse for you though. I want you to remember that Dylan always wanted what was best for you."

I started a bit at the sentence, my head still reeling with the vision of Eric's body lying on the ground. "Are you trying to tell me something?"

He cleared his throat nervously. "Sometimes husbands and wives keep secrets from one another. I'm living proof of that."

I sat down heavily on the stool he'd vacated and looked

up at him. "What are you talking about?" Maybe some wine would help. I needed something to calm my nerves.

"Dylan loved you more than anything," Justin went on. "Tess, he—"

My cell buzzed in the pocket of my jeans. I hadn't checked it for hours and figured Gabby must have been wondering what had happened to me. I held up one finger at Justin. "Hang on a second." I pressed the button. "Hey, Gabs? Can I call you—"

Gabby didn't waste time with pleasantries. "What the heck happened?" she demanded. "You never answered my texts, and when I finally got ahold of Gino, he said you were at the police station with him and there'd been a shooting."

I shuddered inwardly as I recalled Eric's body lying on the ground once again. "Eric was shot to death while making a delivery and I was waiting in the car for him."

"What?" Gabby and Justin both exclaimed in unison.

"I'm okay," I told Gabby. "Justin's with me at my house. I'll call you back later."

Justin's jaw went slack as he stared at me in confusion. "What the hell is going on? Someone you work with got shot? Why didn't you tell me about this when I first got here?"

Because I knew he'd be crazy with worry. "I'm fine. It was probably a random shooting." Deep down though, I suspected this was not the truth. Someone had it in for Eric, but why and who? And did it have anything to do with Dylan's death?

TWELVE

JUSTIN LEFT FIFTEEN MINUTES LATER, AFTER carrying Dylan's boxes in from my car. He'd offered to stay, but I'd assured him I was fine. His behavior made me a bit uneasy though. It was as if he knew something about Dylan but was hesitant to tell me what. Had Dylan already told him about the embezzlement?

I fixed myself a cup of dark-roast coffee, hoping it would help me stay awake long enough to go through Dylan's things. There probably wasn't anything incriminating to be found, especially since an employee had already checked them out. Then there was also the matter of checking his cell phone messages, but like Gino warned, what if I found something even worse? I didn't think I could handle it right now.

Dylan had been a proud man. It would have

humiliated him to tell me he'd been fired. There was no shame in losing a job under honest circumstances, but my husband had stolen from his employer, and he knew I would have been devastated to learn that. Even now, I couldn't understand what possible reason he had for doing such a thing. My mind ran through all the different scenarios. Was he in some other type of trouble? Maybe he had been planning to run away with the money and not tell me. If so, why?

Dread settled at the bottom of my stomach as I lifted the lid off the first box, rummaging through its contents. As I suspected, the few files inside contained information on his personal tax business and not the work he did for We Care. Dylan was as meticulous and thorough with his paperwork as I was about a tidy kitchen. I thumbed through every single page but found nothing significant.

Restless, I pushed the box aside and dug into the second. Luigi yawned and stretched, trotting over to see what I was up to. This box contained mostly personal items, Dylan's photos, a pencil sharpener, a large calculator, and assorted knickknacks. His cherished signed baseball from Red Sox player David Ortiz was among them, along with a picture of us on our wedding day. I placed the crystal frame on the coffee table, then continued searching through the rest of the box.

What did I expect to find? A secret bank account or maybe a handy diary where Dylan detailed each of his deceits? The last item in the bottom of the box was Dylan's day calendar and organizer. It included notes about meetings, dentist appointments, and the mention of a tennis game with Justin last spring. I flipped idly through October, although I knew Dylan had been fired roughly two or three weeks before his death, which would have put the last work-related message in September. To my surprise, I found an entry on Thursday, October 5, the day before he died.

Meeting with Ned.

That was all—only three words but powerful ones at that. I searched the rest of the year again, in case there was something I'd missed but found nothing. *Dylan met with Ned after he'd been fired? Why?* He couldn't stand the guy.

It was after one o'clock in the morning by the time I placed my mug in the sink, picked up the Ortiz baseball, and carried it into Dylan's study, which also functioned as our guest room. Luigi followed me in and rubbed against my legs as I placed the baseball on Dylan's desk. Beside it sat a twin-size bed and dresser, and a padded chair was tucked in the corner, used for Dylan's personal clients. Dylan had always done taxes for friends and family here. I never asked what he charged them, but now I realized I should have paid more attention. If Dylan had embezzled from work, there was a chance he was mixed up in some other illegal doings as well.

I opened the main drawer of the desk and started to rummage through his neat pile of papers. There was nothing of interest, normal business documents and spreadsheets, and I noticed a gold watch of Dylan's that he had said needed a new battery tucked away in the far corner. As I reached into the back of the drawer, my fingers brushed against a smooth, leather surface flush against the wood panel of the desk. Puzzled, I drew out an unfamiliar black address book. I flipped through the pages. There were names, dates, phone numbers, and one-word comments next to the names in Dylan's efficient slanted script. *Paid, Not Paid. Owes Money.* It seemed an odd way to keep track of how his customers owed him for taxes. On a hunch, I checked the Rolodex rotary business card file he kept on top of the desk for some of the names listed but didn't find any. Strange. He was always so conscientious about keeping his contacts in order. If this journal wasn't related to work, what was it for?

I was about to place the journal back in the drawer but stopped myself. Were these clients of Dylan's? If so, would they know something? I couldn't very well call them up and ask about their taxes, but maybe Gino could do some checking around. What if one of them had been involved with Dylan on a tax evasion charge?

I sorted through the other drawers of Dylan's desk and found an envelope labeled *Christmas Party* with a few pictures inside from We Care's get-together last year. Obviously, someone had made copies and given them to him because Dylan wouldn't have been interested in hunting them down himself. There was one of Dylan and me, both wearing Santa hats and with our arms around each other. A tear dropped onto the picture, and I hastily wiped at my eyes. How happy and in love we'd been then.

I let out a despondent sigh and picked up another photo of Dylan with several of his coworkers, Olivia included. Standing on the end of the row and looking particularly unhappy was Ned Reinhart. A third photo showed Ned with his head averted, as if trying to avoid the camera. His gray hair was slick from too much gel. In fact, his hair always had an unwashed look to it, almost greasy, even earlier today when I stood in front of him at We Care. The picture stirred my memory, and suddenly Archie's words from the other day returned with force. Was Ned the man with greasy-looking hair he reported seeing with my husband at the coffee shop? The date would fit with the one I'd found in his planner. My gut instinct assured me that it had to be Ned. If I showed Archie the photo, maybe he would recognize him and confirm my theory.

Luigi and I went back downstairs, and I placed the small journal and pictures in the zippered lining of my purse, intending to show Archie the photos of Ned and tell Gino about the journal tomorrow. He might be able to help me figure out if the names meant anything.

Bone tired and finally ready for bed, I glanced out the window, scanning for any cars parked out front. The street was clear, always a good sign. I double-checked the lock and chain, then turned out the light and went back to my lonely bedroom.

I snuggled under the covers and opened my steno pad

while Luigi made himself comfortable on Dylan's pillow. My eyes came to rest on Eric's name, and I shuddered. Sure, I hadn't liked the kid but didn't want to see him come to any harm. What if he'd been lying and did have something to do with Dylan's death? It was entirely possible. But it was also possible Eric knew who had killed my husband. A pang of regret shot through me. I'd been so close to discovering the truth. The opportunity, like Eric's life, had been snatched away in the blink of an eye.

After a moment's pause, I added Ned's name to the list, convinced that he was hiding something. Fortunately, I wasn't scheduled at work for the next two days. Tomorrow seemed like a good time to have another little chat with Dylan's former boss.

I tried to drift off but tossed and turned for hours. When I finally did fall asleep, Dylan was prevalent in my dreams. Dreams that I could not remember when I woke.

The buzzing of my phone startled me out of my semiconscious state. Sweat had pooled on my forehead, and for a moment, I didn't remember what day it was. I turned in the bed, almost expecting to find Dylan there, lying next to me. Instead, Luigi was curled up on his pillow, eyeing me like a bag of Meow Mix.

My phone buzzed again, and I fumbled for it on the nightstand. "Hello?"

"Did I wake you, sweetheart?" my mother wanted to know.

"Yes, but that's all right." I squinted at the time on my phone. It was almost ten o'clock. I never slept this late, but in my defense, I hadn't drifted off until sometime after five. "Actually, I'm glad you did. I have a lot to do today." My mind immediately began forming a to-do list. I thought I might de-stress with some baking, talk to Archie, and then go see Ned, if he was around. But first, how to get my mother off the phone? The less she continued to know, the better, especially about the shooting.

It was almost as if she could read my mind. "What's this I heard about a car accident? How come I always have to learn about my daughter's life from Mona? Are you all right? What else are you not telling me?"

Great. She was relentless sometimes. Heaving a sigh, I swung my legs out of bed and padded down the stairs in my bare feet, listening while she badgered me to buy a new vehicle, this time one with a five-star rating, and otherwise babbled on about meaningless gossip. I grabbed the newspaper off the front porch and scanned the front page while she continued yammering on. There was a picture of Eric and a paragraph about the shooting, causing my heart to stop beating for a moment. I read the article silently and quickly, and to my relief, my name wasn't mentioned.

"Did you hear what I said?" Mom asked suddenly.

"Sorry, what?" I was in desperate need of caffeine and turned on my Keurig. Luigi rubbed against me, yowling. His breakfast was late, and he was clearly outraged about the wait.

My mother continued as I fed the cat. "Were you aware that you hit Jenny Ravole's car? I guess you don't know her. She's an assistant at the library, but there's rumors she and her husband are moving out of state. Thank goodness no one got hurt. You know your insurance will go up, right? Oh, and don't forget about the cookies for the Altar Rosary meeting. It's only a few days away, on Saturday, remember."

"Yes, Mom. I have to go. Talk to you later."

"All right, sweetheart. Love you."

I stood in front of the bay window while I drank my coffee, exhausted and drained from lack of sleep and feeling beyond depressed after everything I'd learned yesterday. It was apparent my mother hadn't heard about the shooting because she would have gone bananas. Hopefully she wouldn't learn of it for a while. Gino had promised to try to keep my name out of the media.

My mother would have been sympathetic if I'd shared the news about Dylan, but I didn't want her pity. Or she might have gone into denial mode. *Dylan was trustworthy. Such a wonderful son-in-law. He wouldn't steal.*

As I stared at our wedding picture on the coffee table, tears welled in my eyes. Frustrated, I wiped them away in agitation. This would not do. I had to face the facts. My marriage had been a lie—as simple as that. It was time to pull up my big-girl panties and get on with my life.

I spent the next couple of hours making cookies for my mother's upcoming meeting. After yesterday's events I needed some alone time, to bask in the solace of baking as I mixed sugar and flour and lost myself in the warm, delicious smell of chocolate chips and vanilla. However, I wasn't thrilled with how the biscotti had turned out. My chocolate ones had a softer texture than most, and I wondered if I'd accidentally skimped on the baking powder, resulting in a harder consistency. I still had a couple of days to perfect another batch, but it annoyed me that distractions in life were starting to affect my cooking. By midafternoon, I decided some of Archie's specialty coffee might hit the spot, plus I needed to show him the pictures of Ned.

A soft rain had started to fall and didn't help my current mood. As I drove to Java Time, my thoughts shifted to Eric. In the newspaper article, I'd read that a relative of Eric's had given a statement but only said the family was grieving privately and planned to hold his wake tomorrow afternoon between 1:00 and 5:00 p.m.

When I arrived at Java Time, the shop was bustling with activity, and it was a few minutes before Archie could take my order. When he caught sight of me, he smiled broadly and gave me a small wink. "We made a batch of your favorite hot chocolate, honey. How about a cup?"

Rich chocolate with sugar and laden with whipped cream was definitely the way to go. "Sounds good. Make that two, with lots of whipped cream, please." Since I was already here, I decided to stop and see Gabby as well. I reached into my purse for the pictures I'd brought. "Hey, Arch. Remember that guy you told me you saw Dylan with the day before his accident? Can you look at this photo and see if it's him?"

He glanced at the picture of nonsmiling Ned, then put his glasses on to look more closely at the one of Ned's head. "I can't swear to it," he admitted, "but yeah, the hair's the same exact shade and greasy looking. I think he's the one I saw with Dylan." He lifted an eyebrow at me. "Your husband didn't like the guy."

"But you said they didn't argue," I reminded him.

Archie pursed his lips. "No, but Dylan's body language gave him away. Even though he was sitting next to the guy, he was rigid and not relaxed. I knew something was off."

Oh, something was definitely off, all right. After I saw Gabby, Ned Reinhart was going to tell me what their little meeting had been about.

\ / /

Gabby spooned some whipped cream into her mouth. "God, Tess. It wasn't bad enough that someone murdered your husband. Now you find out he was stealing from his company, one of your coworkers got shot in front of you, and you were in a car accident. How are you dealing with all of this? There can't be much room left in your freezer for more tomato sauce."

She'd meant to sound sympathetic, but despite everything, I chuckled. "Shows how much you know. I made cookies instead."

"Figures." We leaned over the front counter in her shop, sipping our hot chocolates as Liza, her lone employee, came out of the back storage room. Liza was about forty, with long auburn hair that hung down her back in a single braid. She smiled at me and adjusted the glasses she wore on her pert nose. "Nice seeing you, Tessa. Bye, Gabs. Catch you tomorrow."

"Have a good one, girl."

"So Liza's working tomorrow?" I asked. "Are you free in the afternoon?" If we went to Eric's wake, maybe we could pick up some useful information about his death and link it to Dylan's somehow.

Gabby shrugged. "She could handle the store by herself for a couple of hours. Thursday isn't usually a busy day for me. Why?"

"Oh, I don't know. Maybe we could go to a wake?"

"What am I, the grim reaper? You know I hate those things." She paused. "Wait a second. It's for Eric, the delivery guy, isn't it?"

"Correct. I want to poke around and see what we can find out."

Gabby's entire face lit up. "Oh, hell yes. The entire town is buzzing about that kid. I'll bet they even have a news crew there." She paused. "Guess that means my dear brother will stop by as well."

"Which reminds me," I said thickly. "Gino told me about his whole 'let's get Tessa back to work so she thinks she's helping with the investigation' scheme. It doesn't surprise me that Gino would do something like that, but I was really hurt to find out you'd decided to play along as well."

To Gabby's credit, she hung her head in shame. "I'm sorry, Tess. When he came to me with the idea, I was willing to try almost anything to snap you out of your depression. I've been so worried about you, hon. We all have. But I really do want to help you find out who did this to Dylan. Whatever you need, I'm here for you."

There was no denying the sincerity and affection in her voice, and it almost brought me to tears. "Let's forget about it." I glanced out the window, noting the darkening sky. "What time is it?"

Gabby stared at her watch. "Five minutes to four. Man, this day has flown."

We Care didn't close until five, so Ned should still be at his desk, but I had to be sure. I reached for Gabby's phone on the counter and dialed a number. She stared at me in confusion as I handed the receiver back to her. "Who are you calling?" she asked, taking the phone.

"Not me. You're calling We Care and asking for Ned Reinhart. I want to know if he's in the office, and Olivia might recognize my voice."

Gabby's eyes gleamed. "Awesome. Can I have a Southern accent?"

"You can speak with a Russian one for all I care."

She waved me off, indicating that the phone had been picked up. "Hey there," she drawled into the phone. "Can I speak to Neddy Reinhart?" She paused. "Yes, voicemail. Thanks y'all." Gabby disconnected and placed the phone back on the counter. "How'd I do, Nancy?"

I made a face. "Awful. And what's with the Neddy bit, anyhow? You could have made her suspicious."

"Oh chill. Like it even mattered." Gabby sipped her drink. "The girl didn't catch on. She sounded like her Happy Meal was short a few fries."

"So Ned wasn't there?"

Gabby threw her empty cup in the trash. "He was there but on the phone. She asked if I wanted his voice-mail. I said yes and then waited to hang up after she trans-ferred me."

I dug my car keys out of my purse. "I'm going over to talk to him before the office closes."

Gabby stuck her lower lip out. "Bummer. I want to go too! But I can't close the store early. Mrs. Jenson's coming in to pick up the entire Harry Potter collection for her grand-daughter in hard cover. That'll be my biggest sale of the year."

"No worries. I'll be fine." The bells over the door jingled, and we both looked up expectantly, then froze. Matt Smitty stood there, hands thrust deep in the pockets of his jeans, blond hair plastered to his head from the rain shower. He and Gabby both exchanged a frown.

Gabby placed her hands on her hips and eyed him with annoyance. "Sorry, we don't carry *Popular Mechanics* here."

He shot her a dirty look and turned to me. "Tess, I saw your car out front and was wondering if I could talk to you."

A blanket of fear wrapped around me. Why was Matt so interested in me all of a sudden? Was it because Dylan was out of the picture now? It felt a bit stalkerish. Maybe he had been the one to drive by my house the other evening. *Call me anytime, even if it's in the middle of the night.*

If Matt thought I doubted his innocence it might ruin everything, so I had to act casual and not let my concern show. "Sure. What's up?"

"Alone." He narrowed his eyes at Gabby.

"You don't think I'm going to leave my cousin here with the likes of you, do you? And, um, *hello*, this is *my* store. Forget about it. I'm staying." Gabby's voice rose.

"Gabs." Maybe Matt had remembered a detail about Dylan. "Isn't there something you could do in the storage room for a minute?" I gave my cousin a pleading look, not wanting to blow this opportunity.

"Oh, whatever," she grumbled. "He's got five minutes." She strode swiftly to the door marked *Employees Only* and slammed it behind her.

"Your cousin came to see me. *Again*." Matt jerked his head toward the door Gabby had disappeared behind. "Not that one, who obviously hates me. But come to think of it, I don't believe Gino's ever been a fan of mine either. This is the second time he's questioned me."

I had known that Matt would be ticked off, so I tried to play dumb. "What did he want?"

He laughed bitterly. "Come on. You *know* what he wanted. I tried to fool myself into thinking maybe he was suspicious of Earl, but nope. It was me he had his eye on all along."

"Matt—" I began.

He cut me off. "Gino thinks I'm the one who loosened that fitting in Dylan's engine the day before he died."

I glanced uneasily at the door where Gabby had disappeared, wondering if she had her ear pressed up against the door. "Sorry about that. Gino was doing his job. Someone wanted Dylan dead, and we have to face facts here. You guys never liked each other, and his vehicle *was* at your shop the day before he died in a car accident."

He looked at me in surprise. "You know I'd never do anything to hurt Dylan."

I didn't answer because, honestly, I didn't know. Matt hadn't liked Dylan, and everyone seemed to believe he was still carrying a torch for me. "To tell you the truth, I'm not sure what to believe anymore."

"Damn it," he whispered. "Tell Gino to back off. He came to my house, Tess. My *house*! Lila heard the whole thing, and now she thinks I'm involved too. We were already having problems before this came along. I'm afraid she's going to leave and take the boys with her. Let me tell you, I won't let that happen. I won't lose my family over this."

Matt's eyes darkened as he said the words, and I cringed, remembering that final time he'd been waiting for me at work all those years ago, begging and pleading with me to give him another chance. He'd been drinking, and it had scared me when he started crying and grabbed my arm, refusing to let go. Matt had apologized for his behavior soon afterward, and since that night, he seemed to have come full circle. Still, how well did I really know him, or for that matter, how well had I *ever* known him?

He didn't wait for me to respond. "Lila thinks I've been fooling around on her. She knows I dated you years ago. Someone must have told her about the argument Dylan and I had—you know, at On the Rocks, when I found out you guys were getting married? After we got back from Dylan's wake, she lit into me and said it was clear that I still had feelings for you."

"I don't want to get involved in your marriage."

He continued to examine my face so closely that my cheeks started to burn and were probably turning red. "Wait a second," he said slowly. "Do you actually believe I killed your husband?"

My hesitation was a second too long, and I saw a brief reminder of the sweet, hurt boy from high school before his face hardened, as if it had been carved from stone. "Try to look at this from my point of view. I'm not sure who to trust anymore. Don't you understand?"

"Yeah, I understand," he said quietly. "I understand that I apparently never meant anything to you. Now tell Gino to back off, okay? He's playing with my life, and I won't let him take everything that I love away from me."

With one last indignant glance at me, he pushed the door open and sent the bells on the door jingling merrily.

Gabby emerged from the back room and ran up the aisle. "I heard the whole thing. He's guilty as sin, Tess. I'd stake my life on it. We should call Gino and have him picked up."

"We don't have any proof." I watched Matt crossing the street, his shoulders hunched forward against the rain, and thought back again to the argument at On the Rocks that had cemented his and Dylan's dislike of each other. Shortly afterward, I'd learned Matt had left town for a while. My mother heard it was a rehab program for drug addiction but admitted she wasn't positive. He had returned to town a couple of months before my wedding and hooked up with Lila shortly afterward.

When I'd received the text from him the evening before my wedding, it had been an unwelcome surprise. Before the confrontation with Dylan, I'd convinced myself that he'd put me in his rearview mirror forever, but now I

The door was open, and Ned was staring out the window at the remainder of a brilliant orange sun that was rapidly sinking into a blackened sky. I rapped my knuckles against the doorway and he jumped in his seat, then immediately whirled around to face me.

"What are you doing here?" Ned asked, anger registering in his tone.

I folded my arms over my chest. "I thought we should have a little talk."

He drew his eyebrows together, and his expression clearly said he was not in the mood to chat. "About what? Didn't you get all of Dylan's stuff out yesterday?"

"Yes, I did." I stood tall and erect, refusing to let this man intimidate me as he'd done yesterday.

"Then why are you here?" he demanded. His dark eyes were cold and aloof, but I thought I interpreted something else in them as well. Fear?

"I need to ask you a couple more questions."

Ned frowned. "I've got a meeting."

"At five o'clock?" I asked, disbelief registering in my tone.

If looks could kill, I'd be six feet under by now. "My schedule is none of your business," he said curtly.

My temper flared. "I know why Dylan was fired, Ned. He was supposedly embezzling money from the company."

Ned inhaled sharply. "Who told you this? These are private company matters that don't concern you."

"This is my husband we're talking about," I said calmly. "Of course it concerns me. Dylan is dead. He won't tarnish your precious company's reputation anymore. What difference does it make why he was fired now?"

Understanding slowly dawned on Ned's face. "Olivia told you, didn't she? That girl is a complete moron, and I'll fire her for blabbing this all over the place."

"It wasn't Olivia." I paused before adding another lie to the mix. "And I know that Dylan didn't act alone." Time to see if my fishing expedition snagged anything.

"I will not discuss this any further with you, Mrs. Esposito. But I can assure you that whatever your husband did, he was responsible for his own actions."

"I'm not so sure." I leaned back against the wall, trying to look more confident than I felt. "I know that you met him for coffee the day before he died. He'd already been fired from his job, and let's face it, you guys were not exactly buddies, so why did you meet him?"

He scowled and shuffled some papers on his desk. "Your

husband begged for his job back. Like I'd ever consider rehiring a thief. For the record, he got what he deserved."

"What…getting fired or killed?" Ned didn't answer, so I continued. "I found a journal among his personal effects. He made notes about what was going on in the office. It proves you were also taking money from the company, and he's got dates and amounts…everything a prosecutor would need to prove you guilty." Sure, I was bluffing up a storm here, but he didn't need to know that. "I'm guessing that Dylan told you at Java Time if you didn't admit to your part, he was going to the police. I think *you* killed him."

Ned's eyes glittered as he slammed his fist down on the desk and rose to his feet, his body trembling with apparent rage. "How dare you make such assumptions."

"These are not assumptions," I said quietly. "If you come clean now and admit your part, maybe the police will go easier on you."

He let out a howl of laughter. "You're making this all up. Show me the so-called journal." Then his voice turned to a growl. "I *want* that journal."

I gave him a smug smile. "It's in a safe place. If anything happens to me, it will be sent to the cops. Specifically, my cousin Gino who's on the force." *Liar, liar, pants on fire.*

"Why are you telling me this?" he asked between clenched teeth. "Why not give it to the police then? If it exists at all, which I doubt."

I hoisted my purse over my shoulder, hoping he didn't notice my fingers shaking. "Admit your part in the plan and clear Dylan's name. It won't be long before word gets out that he was fired for embezzlement. I don't want that to be his legacy."

His smile was cold and thin. "Fine. If knowing will get rid of you, then it's worth it. I figured out what Dylan was doing but needed time to prove the deception. Once I was convinced, I alerted my boss. He ordered me to fire Dylan immediately, and I was only too happy to do so."

"Then you killed him so he couldn't reveal your involvement in the embezzlement."

Ned chuckled. "I wasn't even in town the day your husband died. Why don't you ask your so-called cop cousin to check my plane records? I had to fly to our headquarters in Michigan for an all-day conference and didn't return till the day after your husband died."

I hadn't been expecting this twist, and my stomach sank. It would be easy enough for Gino to check out if Ned was telling the truth. But if Ned didn't kill Dylan, who did?

Ned gave me a satisfied smirk as he watched my face fall, and he sat back down in his chair. He must have already figured he'd won this round. "I'm sorry for you, Mrs. Esposito."

I clenched my fists at my sides. "I don't want your sympathy."

He leaned back in the chair and studied me. "You're like a loyal dog who's been kicked around too many times and keeps going back for more. But I'm going to throw you a bone."

Uneasiness crept up my spine. "What does that mean?"

Ned picked up a pen and tapped it against his stained front teeth. "I remember Dylan saying that you were a fantastic cook. Italian food is your specialty, I believe. Can you make a pizza pie?"

What was he getting at? Did he know I was working at Slice? "Yes, I can make pizza. And your point is?"

He shook his head sadly. "Let's just say that your husband had his fingers in several pies, if you get my drift."

I exhaled deeply, and the air left my lungs in one sharp, painful movement. "Are you saying that my husband was involved in something else illegal?"

He leaned forward across the desk, his beady eyes

pinned on me. "I'm saying you'd better get out of my office now, before I call security."

"Tell me," I pleaded. "What do—"

Ned lifted up the receiver of his desk phone and pressed a button, his eyes fixed on mine the entire time, waiting for my reaction. Having no choice, I backed out of the room. A slow smile of triumph spread across his face, my last image of him as I shut the door.

I hastily made my way back to the elevator. There wasn't a soul around. Like rats, everyone scurried as soon as the workday was done. I stared out the glass-paneled wall and into the night as I rode down to the lobby. Lost in thought, I pushed through the heavy exit doors, deeply inhaling the chilly air. Ned was still hiding something, I was convinced. For all I knew, maybe he'd been the one to talk Dylan into the embezzlement scheme. It would be more than enough reason to want Dylan out of the way if he'd threatened to blow the whistle.

My biggest concern was his snide remark that hinted Dylan had been involved in something else. The dread I carried in the bottom of my stomach was heavier than a bag of rocks. Had Ned lied to me? I couldn't be sure.

I stood in front of the building for a couple of minutes,

staring at my phone and mentally trying to compose a text to Gino about Ned's alibi for the day of Dylan's death, but I was still shaking from the confrontation. As I crossed the street, the roar of an engine jerked me out of my thoughts. A dark sedan with high-intensity headlights. was moving down the one-way street at a furious pace toward me. I put a hand to my eyes to shield the brightness, but it was of no use. Instead of slowing, the car started to pick up speed as it approached. I shrieked and leaped forward, my foot catching the edge of the curb and forcing me to fall forward onto the pavement. My hands flew out in time to protect my face from any damage.

As I lay on my side on the cold, wet cement, I stared after the car, but it was too late. The license plate had been covered, and I couldn't even identify what type of model it was. Shakily, I got to my feet. Nothing seemed to be broken. I'd scraped my knees during the process, but it could have been much worse.

A woman who had been parked a few spaces away moved her car next to me and rolled her window down. "Are you okay, hon?" she asked.

I nodded, wincing from a deep cut on my palm. "I think so."

She frowned. "I saw the whole thing. Do you want me to call 911?"

"I'm all right. Thank you for stopping."

She lingered for a second, watching me with concern, then drove away while I tried to make sense of what had happened. With legs resembling Jell-O, I hobbled to my car, fully aware of a painful throbbing in my ankle. I must have twisted it when I fell. I started the engine, wanting to put distance between me and this incident. As soon as I got home, I dialed Gino's number. After I relayed what had happened, he sounded anything but pleased.

"Why were you down there?" he asked after checking to make sure that I was all right.

There was no sense in lying to him, especially if Ned went to the police about my so-called harassment. Somehow, I didn't believe he would though. "I went to see Dylan's boss, Ned Reinhart. Remember how I asked you to check him out?"

There was dead silence on the other end, and I could almost picture my cousin looking down at his shoes and cussing under his breath. "I did check him out and was going to call you shortly with my findings. The man is clean."

"I don't care. Archie thinks he's the guy Dylan met

with the day before he died. He claims that he was in Michigan the day of Dylan's death. Can you check it out? I mean, why would Dylan meet with Ned after he lost his job? It had to have something to do with the embezzlement. Even if Ned didn't kill Dylan, he had to have at least been in on the We Care scheme with him."

Gino was quiet for a few seconds. "I'll look into it. But that's still a pretty strong assumption based only on his having coffee with your husband. It doesn't make him a killer or even an embezzler."

I was growing more annoyed by the second. "What about Vince? Did you check him out too?"

"I haven't found anything yet. My sources probably won't get back to me until tomorrow."

"And Izzy?"

He sighed. "She has a rock-solid alibi for the day of Dylan's accident. She was out of town at an overnight spa."

"Which means nothing. She could've had someone do the dirty work for her."

"Try to relax, Tess. I promise we'll find out who did this."

Unconvinced, I disconnected the call. I was too stressed and upset to think straight. There was a killer walking around scot-free tonight, and the knowledge upset and frustrated me. I changed into a light-blue silk nightgown that Dylan had given me for my last birthday. I should have tried to eat something but wasn't hungry. Instead, I climbed into bed and sat there for a long time, lost in my own thoughts.

At about nine o'clock, the doorbell rang. Luigi jumped out of bed and waited for me by the front door. I glanced through the peephole. Justin. I undid the chain and opened the door. "Hi. Come on in."

"Sorry to stop by so late." Justin smiled as he followed me into the living room, but he looked even worse than he had the night before. His hair was a mess, there were dark circles under his eyes, and he smelled of smoke. It had to have been tough on Natalie while they were married, wondering if one evening he might never come home to her.

I knew that Lucy went through the same issue with Gino's job, and we'd discussed it a few times. Firefighters and police officers put their lives on the line daily, while my husband had worked behind a secure desk all day. The ironic part was that I'd always been secretly grateful I didn't have to deal with the same fears they did. But in the end, it was my husband's life that had been taken. If there was a lesson to be learned here it was to never take anything for granted.

"No problem. Come sit." I patted the seat next to me on the couch. "Didn't you have today off?"

"Yes, but we were shorthanded, and there was a huge blaze in an abandoned building on the outskirts of town. Thankfully, no one was hurt."

"You look worn out. Can I make you some coffee?"

He shook his head and sat down next to me. "No thanks. I think I need to sleep. I can barely see straight." His eyes moved down my figure, and I remembered that I was still in my nightgown. How embarrassing.

"Excuse me for a second. I'll be right back." I hurried upstairs into my bedroom and grabbed my pink satin robe off the bottom of the bed. When I went back down to the living room, Justin had his head in his hands as if it ached. "Are you sure you're okay?"

"You look pretty tired yourself," Justin remarked. "Well, what I meant is you look both pretty *and* tired. In a good way." He grinned, his cheeks becoming tinted with color.

I laughed. "Mr. Kelly, the fire department really needs to give you some time off. Those fumes must be going to your head."

Justin was silent for a moment. "I was still worried about you and what happened last night, so I wanted to stop by and make sure you were okay."

"That was thoughtful," I said. "But I'm fine." He must have sensed a shift in my tone because he continued to watch me intently. "Maybe we can talk tomorrow, if you have time."

Justin cocked an eyebrow in surprise. "I always have time for you. Come on, what's wrong? Maybe I can help. Talk to me, Tess."

"You know me too well," I sighed. "There's something I need to ask you about Dylan, and I want you to tell me the truth, no matter how difficult it might be."

A frown spread across his face, but he nodded. "Okay. Shoot."

I blew out a breath. "Did Dylan ever tell you that he was involved in something illegal?"

Justin looked at me in amazement. "Sorry, are we talking about the same guy here? Your husband. My best friend. Right?"

Flustered, I twisted a tissue between my hands. "I know this sounds crazy, but Dylan was stealing money."

His jaw dropped. "What? From who?"

"His employer." I still couldn't believe it myself. "They found out about the theft, and he was fired."

Justin swore softly. "Are you sure about this?"

"Yes." My voice shook, and he reached for my hand, encompassing it between his two strong ones. "I don't understand how he could do this or why." Ned's words echoed in my head: *Your husband had his fingers in several pies, if you get my drift.* What else had Dylan been involved in?

"When did all of this happen?" Justin asked.

"A few weeks before he died." I glanced down at his hands. He was gliding his thumb across my palm gently, and the warmth of his fingers was comforting. Suddenly, my mother's words from the other night entered my head, and for the first time ever, I found myself wondering if Justin did care for me as more than a friend. My head started to spin. Justin was a wonderful person, but I had nothing to give him or any other man right now and wouldn't for a long time. The last thing I wanted to do was lead him on, so I stiffened my hands slightly, giving his fingers an affectionate squeeze, then pulled away.

Justin shook his head emphatically. "I had no idea about the stealing or that he'd been fired. Honest." He then sat in silence for a minute, and something about the action bothered me. Finally, he spoke again. "This is so unreal, Tess. It's none of my business, but were you guys having money problems? You don't have to answer if you don't want to, but it would explain a lot."

"No. We were doing okay, so why did he have to steal? What did he plan to do with the money?"

Justin shrugged. "I don't know, but he never would have wanted to hurt you like this. I know how much Dylan loved you."

"But it does hurt me," I whispered. The spasms in my chest were suddenly so intense that I couldn't draw a deep breath without pain. Then the tears came, sliding down my cheeks like raindrops. "He's not the man I thought he was, and our marriage was a farce. I don't know what's real anymore."

Justin put his arms around me and stroked my hair as I sobbed into his shoulder. "We'll figure it out together, Tess," he said gruffly. "I'm here for you. You don't have to go through this alone. I promise."

FOURTEEN

THE NEXT MORNING, I SHOWERED, DRESSED, and planned to spend the day watching mindless television until Gabby came to pick me up at three o'clock for Eric's wake. I'd just finished my first cup of coffee when the phone rang. Anthony.

"Hi, honey, how's it going? Did you get any rest yesterday?"

"Some," I said. "How's everything at Slice?"

He hesitated on the other end. "Well, the media stopped by yesterday, about the Eric situation. Only one reporter. Of course, there's nothing to tell. It's a shame what happened to the kid, but that type of random shooting is nothing new. There's a lot of crazy people in this world."

It sounded like Anthony was trying to brush over Eric's death, and I found myself wondering why. "Well, don't worry. I'll be at work tomorrow."

Anthony cleared his throat. "I know it's your day off, but I was wondering if you might be able to make some more sauce. I'm expecting a big crowd tonight."

Again with the sauce. I suspected he didn't have a big crowd for dinner. There was no way he could have gone through the batch I'd made the other day. Vince had stored several containers in the cooler. What was Anthony really doing with my sauce? "Ah, what time?"

"I'm closing at two so that Vince and I can go to Eric's wake. No one will be back until about four. How about you come over at four thirty? Unless you want to come by now? That would be great."

I gripped the phone tightly between my hands. No one would be at Slice for two whole hours. A golden opportunity for some snooping. Quickly, I thought up a lie. "Gee, my day is pretty full, Anthony. You see, I'm having people over for dinner too. My entire family. I could stop over about three o'clock, but that's the only time that works for me."

"Damn." Anthony was silent for several seconds. "Maybe I can get Butchy or Sam to meet you there and let you in."

Shoot. That would ruin everything. "Oh, it's not

necessary. I'll be fine by myself. I'll make the sauce, clean up, and then lock the door."

He paused for a moment. "Uh, well, okay. I'll tell you what. I can leave a key in an envelope taped to the dumpster. Place it on the stove when you're done, okay?"

"I'm planning to stop by the wake for a few minutes. Shall I give it to you then? What time will you be there? Oh, and what should I do about the alarm?"

"No, leave the key in the kitchen." He paused. "The code for the alarm is Izzy's birthday, 1229. So you'll be here at three o'clock?"

It was my turn to hesitate. "Yes, at three." I'd have Gabby pick me up earlier than we planned, in case Butchy or Sam turned up to check on me. "Where would you like me to put the sauce?"

"You know what?" Anthony asked. "Why don't you call me as soon as you get to Slice, and I'll tell you where to leave it. I'll have to make some room for it first. And I'll add a little extra *dough* to your paycheck as a thank you." He laughed.

"Sure thing," I said and clicked off. Anthony didn't seem to want me at Slice alone. What was he afraid I might find? I thought about phoning Gino but knew he would not be on board with this plan of mine. Instead, I called Gabby and asked her to pick me up at 1:45 instead of 3:00, the time we'd originally planned for the wake.

Gabby groaned into the phone. "There's no way I can get to your house until two, and I need to go home and change first. We got a new shipment of books in a day ahead of schedule, so I'm here helping Liza with them. This has really messed up my entire day."

Damn. "Well, as soon as you can. We have to stop at Slice before the wake so I can let my fingers do the walking through Anthony's desk."

"Why didn't you say that in the first place? I'll be as quick as I can."

I had no intention of cooking sauce at Slice today. As I pulled ten bags from my freezer, I was grateful that I had stocked up during the dark weeks following Dylan's death. Remembering those few soothing moments at my stove, I was again happy I had never given anyone my recipe. It was a special bond between my grandmother and myself and, as far as I was concerned, would always stay that way. I hated the thought of someone confiscating our beloved creation for their own personal gain. Still, I needed to ride this out for now. I didn't want to give Anthony a reason to get rid of me until I knew exactly what was going on between Slice's four walls.

Gabby didn't arrive at my house until 2:05. As soon as she pulled in the driveway, I locked the front door behind me, hurried over to her car, and hopped in.

"Sorry," she said as she backed the vehicle out onto the street. "I did the best I could."

"I'm afraid Anthony might send someone over to see how I'm getting on. He asked me to call him when I arrived at Slice. He doesn't trust me."

A smile broke across Gabby's face as she pressed her foot down on the gas pedal. "With good reason."

"Slow down!" I said. "This is no time to get a ticket."

She laughed but eased up on the gas. "It would be just our luck if Gino was the one to pull us over. I'd get a three-hour lecture for sure."

Traffic was light, and we arrived at Slice in a few minutes. I had no idea how much time I might have until someone showed up, but one thing was for certain—I wasn't calling Anthony. At least not yet. When I spotted the dumpster, another idea crossed my mind. "Hang on one second," I told Gabby.

"What?" she asked, but I jumped out of the car without

answering. An envelope with my name on it was taped to the side of the dumpster facing the building. I removed the key and stuck it into the kitchen door. The alarm immediately started beeping when the door opened. I entered 1229 into the panel's keypad, and the noise abruptly stopped. I ran back over to Gabby's car and handed her the key. "Here. Run over to World of Hardware and have a duplicate made."

Gabby's mouth fell open in shock. "Are you sure? I'm not comfortable leaving you here alone. I can play lookout in the parking lot and—oh, I don't know, press the horn if someone comes along?"

I winked at her slyly. "Yeah, that's tactful. They know I'm making sauce, remember? It shouldn't take you more than ten minutes, and no one's due to show up until three. The hardware store's usually not crowded this time of the day either."

Gabby gave me a nervous look. "Tess, please be careful." She put the car in Drive and roared out of the parking lot.

After shutting the back door of the kitchen behind me, I quickly transferred my bags of sauce into Tupperware containers that Anthony kept in the cabinet, then placed them on the shelf inside the fridge. Mission accomplished,

I went into Anthony's office and glanced around, wondering where to start my search. There wasn't much here. Some empty pizza boxes were stacked on a small table against one of the walls. A four-shelf walnut bookcase stood against another wall, filled with binders, loose papers, and piles of mail. I reached for the main drawer of Anthony's desk. Locked. Damn. One of his jackets was lying on the swivel chair behind the desk. I moved it, planning to check the pockets, and saw a mason jar filled with tomato sauce underneath it. I unscrewed the top and sniffed, then to be certain, I grabbed a plastic spoon from the kitchen and took a small taste. Definitely mine. What was he planning to do with my sauce?

I searched Anthony's jacket pockets and came upon with a sheet of commercial labels with "Anthony's Tantalizing Tomato Sauce" printed on them. Well, at least I'd solved one mystery. I now knew why Anthony had agreed to hire me. He wanted to get his hands on my sauce and was planning to sell it as his own. Rage boiled in the bottom of my stomach. What else did this mean? Would my days be numbered at Slice once he had figured out my recipe?

I stored the anger away for later since I had more work to do. The first three drawers of the file cabinet were also locked, but the bottom one was not. I opened it and thumbed through the manila folders, recognizing Dylan's fine slanted handwriting on some of the file tabs. I looked inside the folders. Tax documents, notes, receipts from vendors. I thumbed my way through to the back of the cabinet, but nothing stood out. When I moved aside one of the files, I noticed a Post-it Note stuck to the bottom of the drawer. I reached down and removed it. This was also in Dylan's handwriting although his name wasn't on it. When I read the words he'd written, my chest constricted in pain.

Last chance if you want the pictures.
$50,000 is the lowest I'll go.

My hands shook as I stuck the note in my coat pocket. Dylan was blackmailing Anthony? What pictures did he have? Was this what Ned had meant when he'd slyly indicated Dylan was getting his hands dirty in other ways? Could Anthony have been the one to eliminate my husband?

The back door to the kitchen opened, sending a jolt of fear through my body. I shut the file cabinet noiselessly and rose to my feet. I had reached the doorway when I came face-to-face with Butchy.

He stared at me in confusion. "Hi, Mrs. Esposito. What are you doing in here?"

"Ah…Anthony asked me to drop off…err, make some sauce." I tried to keep my voice steady.

He cocked his head to one side and studied me. "Are you okay? You look like you've seen a ghost."

I managed a smile for him. "Oh, no. I'm fine, thanks."

Butchy raised his left eyebrow. "Why were you in Anthony's office?"

Shoot. He *was* suspicious. "The phone rang as I was walking past it," I lied. Then I decided to turn the tables on him. "What are *you* doing here?"

"Anthony asked me to come take orders for pizza until he got back," Butchy said smoothly. "He didn't want to miss out on any. Who was on the phone?"

"Wrong number." Who was this kid kidding? Anthony told Butchy to get his butt over here and keep an eye on me while I made the sauce. They thought I wasn't coming until three o'clock, so I was glad I'd ask Gabby to meet me earlier.

Butchy scratched his head thoughtfully. "Where's your car?"

I glanced at the wall clock. Two forty-five. Gabby

should have been back by now. "My cousin brought me. She went across the street to the drugstore for a sympathy card. We're going to Eric's wake."

Butchy smiled again, showing slightly crooked teeth this time. "Right. I'm going too, as soon as Anthony gets back to relieve me."

Before we could exchange any more lies, the back door of the kitchen stormed open, and Gabby blew in. She glanced from me to Butchy, wild eyed. "Hi. I'm back."

Nothing like a subtle entrance. "Butchy, this is my cousin, Gabby."

"Nice to meet you," Butchy said politely.

She nodded at him. "Sorry, Tess. It took longer than I thought—"

I cut her off. "That's okay. It's hard to find the right card sometimes."

Her brow wrinkled. "What?"

I shoved my cousin in the direction of the door. "Nothing. Tell Anthony the sauce is in the fridge, Butchy."

Butchy went to the fridge and looked inside. "Wow, that's a lot of sauce." He sounded impressed. "Anthony said you weren't coming until three. You must have been here a *long* time cooking."

"Oh, I managed to get here a little earlier than I thought. And it doesn't take me that long to make it," I assured him with a smile. *Crap.* He was onto my lies, I was certain of it. "Well, we'd better get going."

"Mrs. Esposito," Butchy said quietly.

I had my hand on the door and winced inwardly as I turned around. "Yes?"

Butchy held out a hand. "The key. Anthony needs it back. He said he left one for you."

Gabby gave a little nervous laugh and handed the key to Butchy. "Sorry," she said. "I figured I'd let myself in so I wouldn't disturb Tessa while she was cooking."

Butchy nodded but said nothing.

"Have a great day." I quickly shut the door behind Gabby, and we hurried to her car, both of us exhaling loudly in relief as we shut ourselves inside the vehicle. "That was close," I said.

Gabby started the engine. "I saw his car in the lot and was afraid that he'd caught you snooping. Did you find anything interesting?"

I stared in my side mirror. Butchy had opened the back door and was now standing in the doorway, hands thrust deep in the pockets of his jeans, staring after us. An icicle formed between my shoulder blades as I watched him. "No, nothing." I decided not to share my biggest concern with her right now—that my husband had been doing more at Slice than their taxes.

FIFTEEN

LIGHTING YOUR WAY FUNERAL HOME WAS on the other side of town, about ten minutes from Slice. I listened as Gabby talked excitedly about a well-known local author who would be doing a signing at her store next month. "This is groundbreaking for me," she breathed. "It should mean a lot of business for the store."

"That's awesome." I stared out the window, lost in my own thoughts.

She squeezed my hand. "So what about this Ned character you went to see before? Do you think he killed Dylan?"

"He has a motive," I admitted. "I'm almost certain he's involved in the embezzling scheme at We Care somehow. Maybe Dylan was a threat and he had to get rid of him... but he also has an alleged alibi for the day of Dylan's murder. Your brother's checking into it."

"Hmm, doesn't sound promising," Gabby said with a frown, then her face brightened. "Don't forget Matt. He's still at the top of my list."

"Jeez, you're like your brother," I complained. "Neither one of you likes Matt, so he's the first one you'd think of."

She grinned. "Can't argue with that logic. What about the employees at Slice? Who there might have tampered with Dylan's car and why?"

"Well, it seems that Anthony's daughter had taken quite a shine to Dylan, to the point of inviting him to fool around with her."

Gabby sucked in her cheeks and accelerated on the gas pedal. "Shut up. Isabella?"

"Do you know her?"

She shrugged. "Not personally, but I know who she is, and Miss Bridezilla stopped in my store last week to ask if I had the newest issue of *Put a Ring on It Magazine*. She almost threw a hissy fit when I told her no." Her eyes widened. "Let me get this straight. She's getting married but was making a play for *your* husband?"

"Sounds like she was at first, then something changed her mind and she had it in for him. At least that's what Butchy told me." I watched in horror as she ran a red light.

"Jeez, slow down! We could have gotten in an accident back there. You need to be more careful."

"Oh, stop," she groused. "Now *you* sound like my brother. And what's the deal with sexy bad boy Vince? Did you find out anything else about his restaurant?"

"Not yet. Gino is checking into a few things for me. When Vince found out who I was, he shut down completely. If Dylan was doing his taxes and ended up reporting the restaurant for larceny or embezzlement, that could explain why Vince had a huge motive to want Dylan dead. But wouldn't it be public knowledge that Dylan had turned them in?"

Gabby shook her head. "There are ways you can report your findings to the IRS anonymously, so I'm sure Dylan had that covered. It does sound like Vince is hiding something. Is anyone else there a player? What about Anthony?"

"A player? Really, Gabs. Sam and Butchy have to be considered too. There's something strange going on at Slice, but I can't put my finger on it yet. Your brother wants me out of there. I guess he thinks it's getting too personal for me."

Gabby turned into the funeral home's parking lot and glanced sideways at me. "But it *is* personal. Someone you're working with might have killed your husband or know who did."

We silently walked across the lot and toward the gray, single-story brick building. There was a large sign mounted on the side of the building with *Lighting Your Way Funeral Home* in bold block lettering, surrounded by a border of lighted candles. I shivered, thinking about how the last wake I'd been to was my husband's. We stepped onto the wide wraparound wooden porch, where two men were leaning against the rail, smoking. As we approached the front door, an older gentleman dressed in a black suit opened it and nodded politely at us. "Welcome."

We stopped to sign the registry and then took our place in the line. I glanced around at the crowd but didn't see anyone I knew.

"Didn't you say this Eric kid was a jerk?" Gabby whispered.

"Shh." I put a finger to my lips. "Don't be so disrespectful."

She surveyed the surrounding mourners. "I'm surprised he got such a good turnout. There must be twenty people ahead of us, and look in the viewing room! It's completely full."

"The obit made reference to a large, extended family."

Sure, the kid had been a creep, but someone must have loved him.

"No one looks especially broken up either," Gabby added.

The perfumed scent from the many flower arrangements was overwhelming, and I put a hand over my nose, afraid I might sneeze. We both stared with interest at the collage of pictures by the viewing room's door. There were photos of Eric from his high school graduation, a prom picture, and one of him standing in front of his vehicle, arms folded across his chest. It was the same car I'd ridden in the other night. *His last ride.* Eric wasn't smiling in any of the pictures.

"Boy, he was a happy one," Gabby remarked.

Gino had mentioned that Eric had a record and was a drug user. Was that why he'd been targeted, or could it have been related to Dylan's death?

Gabby nudged me in the ribs. "Hey, it's almost time."

The people ahead of us in line had moved from the kneeler in front of the coffin to speak to family members. Gabby and I walked toward the casket together, positioned ourselves on the kneeler, and made the sign of the cross on our chests. I'd always hated this part of a wake—not that any moments were especially enjoyable. As I feared, memories of Dylan's service came flooding back.

The pain was real and blinding and forced me to draw a deep breath. There had been such an influx of people the day of Dylan's service that for a while, it seemed like it would never end. My husband had known many people and had been liked and respected by everyone, or so I'd thought. I remembered sitting between Justin and my mother at the service, holding Justin's hand for support.

I exhaled and forced the memories away, then stared down at Eric. He looked like a different person in his impeccably pressed dark-brown suit and matching silk tie. The sullen face I remembered was peaceful, and he seemed barely older than a child. His last words continued to haunt me. *We'll talk when I get back.* What had he really known about Dylan's death?

We rose from the kneeler and paid our respects to the family, shaking hands and repeating the polite expression, "I'm sorry for your loss," to to each one—the same phrase I myself had loathed hearing. As we made our way to the back of the crowded viewing room, I turned around and scanned the mourners one last time. I nudged Gabby in the side.

"What's up?" she asked.

"Anthony and Vince are here," I whispered. "And Izzy. They're in line over there."

Izzy was wearing heavy eye makeup and a skintight black mini dress with a plunging neckline. Both men wore black slacks and blazers. They turned as we walked past, catching my gaze. Anthony waved, Izzy sneered, and Vince glared, then turned away. *Jeez, nice to see you too.*

"Wow, if looks could kill," Gabby muttered. "What's his problem?"

I didn't answer, more ideas running through my head. Anthony must have wondered how I'd arrived so soon. I'd never even called him from Slice, as he'd requested. By his calculation, I should still be making sauce. Maybe it would have been smarter if Gabby and I had stopped somewhere between Slice and the wake. Oh well. Too late now.

Someone grabbed us each by an arm from behind, and I emitted a small squeak as a familiar voice spoke low and angry into my ear.

"What the hell are you two doing here?"

"Hey, big brother." Gabby smiled winsomely at Gino, who was dressed in a conservative suit. "Nice to see you too."

Gino's face twisted into an irritated frown. "Answer the question, please."

Gabby made a *tsk-tsk* sound. "Go away now. You don't want to blow your cover, do you?"

He gave his sister a murderous glance. "There are a lot of people here who know that I'm a detective. What they don't know is that I'm related to you two, and it's probably best to keep it that way—especially since you're both trying to do *my* job."

"Tessa worked with the kid," Gabby said in my defense. "She came out of respect and has a right to be here."

His eyes shifted over to me. "Why is it that I'm having a difficult time swallowing this garbage?"

"Man, he gets so cranky some days," Gabby muttered. "Was Carlita's bakery out of doughnuts this morning?"

I glanced over my shoulder and watched Anthony and Vince approach the kneeler. Izzy had disappeared. "Did your sources get back to you about Vince yet?"

Gino pursed his lips. "Yeah. I was going to call you when I left here. Vince was co-owner of a restaurant called the Skylight in New York City, a fine-dining establishment. It started out well a couple of years ago, then slowly started going under, thanks to the senior owner, a guy named Bobby Pietro. He was dipping his hand in the register and failing to pay his employees proper wages. He's currently in prison for larceny and a bunch of other related charges."

He cleared his throat and continued. "Vince Falducci

was found not guilty and claimed he knew nothing about the goings-on. Although he had a share in the restaurant, he was also one of the chefs, so there's a possibility he was telling the truth. I can't find information on who might have blown the whistle on the place. Did you see anything in Dylan's stuff to link him to Vince's restaurant?"

I was getting nervous as Vince glanced over in our direction, and I had the weird sensation he knew we were discussing him. "No, but I found a note in the bottom of Anthony's file cabinet with Dylan's handwriting today." There was no way I was pulling it out with Anthony only a few feet away. "I think Dylan was blackmailing Anthony over some photos."

"Photos of what? And why were you snooping in Anthony's filing cabinet?" Gino asked.

"That doesn't matter," I said.

Gabby looked startled. "You didn't tell me you found anything!"

Gino's nostrils flared. "Don't play that game with me, Tess."

"Oh, leave her alone," Gabby chided her brother. "She's already found out more than the police department has." She tossed her head arrogantly. "And I helped too."

Gino's face became a bright shade of red. "Some days I want to knock both of your heads together. It's like Lucy and Ethel all over again." He turned to me. "I'm not finished with you yet. I have to work late, but expect a call from me tonight."

Gabby wrinkled her nose. "Wow. What a grouch."

He shot his sister one last irritated look and then crossed the room to speak to a white-haired gentleman in a gray suit. The older man threw his arms around Gino and kissed him on both cheeks.

Gabby shook her head. "My brother. Remember what a jerk he was as a kid to us? Now he's Mr. Law, the shining beacon of our town."

I merely nodded in reply. The smell of the flowers, the crowd, and hushed laughter were all too familiar. They brought back memories—painful memories that I longed to forget.

Gabby glanced sharply at me. "You okay, hon? You're awfully pale."

"I need some air." My head was pounding, and some aspirin might help. "Do you know where the bathroom is?"

She pointed straight ahead. "Go out and take a right down the hallway. I'll stay here and check things out." By checking out, she obviously meant the two attractive men leaning against the wall opposite us. They seemed to be interested in meeting her as well. I struggled not to roll my eyes. Leave it to Gabby to find romance at a wake.

In the bathroom, there were some plastic cups on the counter, and I filled one with water. I set my purse on the edge of the sink and rummaged through it until I found a bottle of Tylenol. After I'd swallowed the pills, I turned to throw the cup away, my right arm connecting with my purse, knocking it onto the floor. I bent down to retrieve it, and a small sound made me pause. Through a vent under the sink, I heard a muffled voice coming from what I assumed had to be the men's room and leaned in closer to listen. A chill ran down my spine when I recognized Anthony's voice.

"All you have to do is tell me the truth, son," he said. "There's nothing to be afraid of."

"I didn't tell her nothing. Honest, Anthony." The voice was young and panicked, and it sounded like Sam.

I froze and prayed no one would walk into the bathroom.

"What exactly did she ask you?"

"Nothing, I swear. I only talked to her for a couple of minutes. But Butchy said she asked him a bunch of questions about her husband. Like, if he was at Slice with another woman and how often he came by. Stuff like that."

"Anything else?" Anthony asked.

"I… No, I don't think so," Sam stuttered.

I clamped a hand over my mouth. *Holy crap. They're talking about me.*

Anthony's voice went down a notch in volume, and I pressed my ear closer to the grate. "Okay, you can leave now. But if she starts flapping her gums again, let me know right away. Understand?"

"Yes, sir," he whispered feebly.

What did Anthony not want me to find out? My stomach twisted. Had he killed Dylan and maybe Eric too? The bathroom door opened suddenly, and I jumped up, my head bashing into the sink. "Ouch!" I fell backward against the tiles and stared up into my cousin's bewildered face.

Gabby gave a bark of laughter and placed her hands on her hips. "How many times have I told you not to play on the floor in public bathrooms, Tess?"

I put a finger to my lips. "Shut the door!"

She gave me a puzzled look but did as I asked. When it had closed, I rose to my feet and straightened my slacks.

"Anthony was in the bathroom next to us. I think he was threatening the delivery kid."

Gabby's eyebrows shot up. "Are you freaking serious? But why?"

I opened the door a tiny crack and saw Anthony walking alone, back in the direction of the viewing room. As we emerged from the bathroom, I glanced down the hallway in the other direction. Through the glass-paneled door, I spotted Sam letting himself out onto the back porch. He had a cigarette and lighter in his hands.

"Go back to the viewing room," I said in a low voice. "I want to try to get Sam alone." He might not talk to me, but it was worth a shot. "Anthony and Vince can't see me. Keep your eyes on them and make sure they don't come out until I text you that I'm finished."

She wrinkled her brow. "What am I supposed to do to keep them in there? Take my clothes off?"

"It would certainly lighten the mood," I quipped, then hurried down the carpeted hallway. I pushed the door open and saw Sam striding along the side of the building, disappearing around the corner of the wraparound porch. Shoot. I hoped he wasn't leaving. Two women were sitting on a wooden bench talking, despite the forty-degree temperature. When I passed them and turned the corner, Sam was leaning over the railing, staring out at the parking lot. I was about to approach him when Izzy exited the front door. Fearing they'd spot me, I quickly retreated and peeked around the corner to watch.

My mouth dropped open as I watched Izzy cozy up alongside Sam. She snaked her arm around him and nuzzled her lips against his ear. I couldn't make out what she was saying, but Sam's face turned red and he nodded. She planted a kiss on his cheek, stroked his arm, and walked toward her car in the parking lot, with Sam staring after her.

Izzy and Sam? Sam and Izzy? What the heck could Izzy want from a pizza delivery guy who was barely old enough to shave? Whatever she wanted, it couldn't be good. Sam seemed like a decent kid, and I needed to warn him about the Italian princess. But first, I had some questions for him to answer.

He must have heard my footsteps approach, because he whirled around. When he caught sight of me, his blue eyes widened, and the freckles stood out on his face. Sam tossed the lit cigarette over the railing into one of the shrubs as he raced down the steps.

"Wait, Sam!" I pleaded and ran after him. "Please."

Sam turned around, but he wasn't looking at me. He stared at the front door of the funeral home uneasily, and I wondered what he was nervous about.

"Please go away." His voice cracked.

"What is Anthony hiding? Does he know who killed my husband?" I placed a hand on his arm. He was going to tell Anthony I'd tried to get information out of him, but at this point, I no longer cared. I was desperate for answers.

The sheer look of panic in his eyes was replaced by cold, bitter anger. He shook my arm off and gave me a shove backward. I was so surprised by the action that I nearly fell.

"Go away, Mrs. Esposito." Sam's voice was menacing. "Leave before you wind up like your husband."

In shock, I watched as Sam ran toward his car. Within seconds, he peeled out of the parking lot, tires smoking.

SIXTEEN

AFTER THE WAKE, GABBY ASKED IF I wanted to stop for food, but neither of us was hungry. As we drove home, I told her all about the note I'd found in the file cabinet. "I'm becoming more and more convinced that someone at Slice is responsible for Dylan's death."

"For what it's worth, I believe you. I have to admit, I never thought you'd find anything at Slice. Boy, were Gino and I wrong. Can we go sleuthing again tomorrow?" she asked hopefully as she turned into my driveway.

"Not trying to humor me anymore?"

Her expression sobered. "That was never my intention and you know it."

"Yeah, I do." I reached over to squeeze her hand. "Hey, why not? I don't care what Gino says, I think you're a much better sleuthing partner than Ethel Mertz."

"Damn straight," she said and pulled me into a hug. "Try not to let this get you down, Tess. Maybe Dylan's note wasn't what it seemed."

I had no answer for that. Nothing about Dylan was as it seemed anymore. "I'll call you in the morning," I said and let myself out of her car.

Luigi met me at the front door, and I picked him up, hugging him tightly against my chest. "Did you miss me?" He let out a little squeak and meowed, which I interpreted as *Feed me, human.*

I set Luigi on the floor, filled his food dish, and gave him fresh water. While he ate, I went into the bedroom, took a deep breath, and opened the left side of the closet. I stared at the hangers that still held all Dylan's clothes. Since his death, I had not touched one single item. It had been too painful, but I couldn't pretend anymore. He was gone, and it would do no good to keep his things here, like some type of shrine. Besides, all the items did was serve as a sad reminder now—of the man I never really knew. I buried my head into one of his sport jackets and caught the faintest whiff of the cologne he'd worn—a fresh, aquatic smell. Tears threatened, but I blinked them away.

Before I could change my mind, I grabbed several

hangers of clothing off the rod and placed them on our bed. I folded slacks, shirts, and blazers carefully. A memory of Dylan standing next to the ironing board in the kitchen with only a dress shirt and underwear on made me laugh. He'd always been much better at pressing clothes than me.

There were a few plastic storage boxes under the bed that I pulled out and started to line with his clothes. Next came the shoes—Dylan's three pairs of running sneakers, the New York Giants slippers I'd bought him last Christmas, six pairs of dress shoes and loafers in assorted colors that he'd worn for work, and a pair of leather sandals. I'd run everything over to Goodwill later this week. There were a few mementos from his youth on the floor of the closet—a catcher's mitt, pictures of his parents, his high school yearbook, and some other items that pained me to see. Those I stored in a separate box in the closet.

After this job was completed, I went into our spare bedroom and opened Dylan's desk, searching for the watch I'd spotted last night to add to my inventory. Scooping it from the drawer, I glanced around to see if there were any knickknacks I'd forgotten, scanning the bedroom and floor. That was when I noticed the plastic case containing his Ortiz baseball lying haphazardly on the floor.

"How strange," I murmured. I reached down to grab the baseball and placed it back on top of the desk. Maybe Luigi had jumped up on the surface and managed to knock the case off. Suddenly, the papers in the drawer seemed more cluttered than I'd remembered, but maybe I had done that. I picked them up and straightened them, hesitant to throw away any documents that had to do with his personal clients. There may be a certain period of time I needed to keep them, so I'd have to check with a CPA or the IRS first.

I sat down in the chair and thumbed idly through Dylan's Rolodex. Procrastination was my friend tonight. I didn't want to listen to Dylan's voicemail messages and was trying to put the task off for as long as I could. My heart almost stopped when I came across the name Bobby Pietro under the *P*s. I sat back in the seat, looking at the number with its 212 area code in awe. So Dylan *had* known Vince's partner, and most likely Vince, too, before he came to Harvest Park. Was Dylan the one who had turned them in?

Feeling chilled, I went to my bedroom with the Rolodex card and my cell phone. Luigi jumped up and joined me on the bed, settling on Dylan's pillow. Despite the late hour, I dialed Bobby's number. A female voice came on the line. *The number you have reached is no longer in service at this time.* That wasn't exactly a surprise if Bobby was doing time in prison like Gino had said.

I continued to sit there in the semidarkness, staring down at the phone. The time had come. Up until the other day, I never would have dreamed of checking Dylan's messages. We had no secrets from each other—or so I'd thought. But Gino was right. There could be clues as to who had rigged Dylan's car or if he'd been involved in some other type of illegal scam.

My fingers shook as I dialed the cell number and waited. We'd picked out our iPhones together last year and had decided to use each other's birthdates as passwords. Dylan could easily have checked my phone anytime he wanted to, but I knew he hadn't. There was no reason to. We'd loved and trusted each other.

When his voice came on the line asking me to leave a message, it left me breathless. Tears flooded my eyes and ran down my cheeks. I hadn't been prepared for the wave of hurt and raw emotion that hearing his voice would cause. After the beep sounded, I clicked off and then dialed the number again.

"Hi, this is Dylan Esposito. Please leave your name and number at the tone, and I'll get back to you as soon as possible. Thanks."

Dylan wasn't dead after all—it couldn't have happened. His voice was too real. I listened over and over, crying silently until I had no tears left. Finally, I stopped to wipe my eyes with a tissue and then forced myself to punch in the password while he was still talking. My heart was overwhelmed with sadness as I waited.

You have eight messages.

A shiver ran down my spine. Was I ready to face this? No, but I couldn't turn back now. My brain was flooded with too many unanswered questions. Why would Dylan steal from his employer? Why had he lied? If he loved me, how could he deliberately deceive me?

With bated breath, I waited. The messages went in order, from newest to oldest. The first one was an angry male voice that I didn't recognize. It was dated two days after the accident. There was no phone number attached.

"Esposito, it's Sobato. Where the hell is my order? Call me right away." I waited to hear more, but he didn't leave a number. Where had I heard that name before? At Slice? Was he a customer of Anthony's I'd made a pizza for? Since when did people refer to their taxes as an order?

The next message was a hang-up, and then another from a client who was afraid she was being audited and sounded panicked.

The next three messages were from yours truly, the day Dylan had died. "Where are you? The lasagna's been out of the oven for an hour, and it's ruined!" I didn't know at the time that he was already dead. Then: "Hey, are you on your way home yet?" And the first one I'd sent him that day: "Hey, babe, I didn't have time to make bread. Can you pick up a loaf?"

I shut my eyes in horror as I listened to my voice through the messages. I'd gone from tender to downright annoyed at my husband. Even though Dylan likely hadn't heard the final one, it still tortured me to know it was out there. I had been off work that day and decided to make lasagna and spent most of the afternoon experimenting with a new type of vodka crème sauce that I had eventually decided might be too zesty for the lasagna. Too late I'd realized I didn't have enough time to make bread from scratch, so I'd called Dylan and asked him to pick up a loaf from Sweet Treats. I'd already prepared the ingredients for the garlicky, buttery flavored topping. It was more than worth the trouble to watch Dylan's face light up after he'd come home and smelled it cooking, even though he'd started limiting himself to only one piece.

Shortly after I'd left the last message that day, Gino had come to my door to give me the news, and I'd crumpled in his arms. The next afternoon I'd finally remembered the lasagna, still on top of the stove, stone cold and hard as a rock. I'd tossed it and the stainless-steel pan into the trash together, wanting to forget.

The next to last message was from a woman. Her deep voice was cool and formal. "Hi, Dylan, it's Dr. Logan."

I wrinkled my brow as I listened. The woman's name was unfamiliar. She was not Dylan's general practitioner.

Dr. Logan hesitated for a brief second. "I was wondering why you never showed up for your appointment yesterday. I do have time to see you this afternoon. Please don't wait on this. Your life could depend on it." She recited her number and then clicked off.

Surprisingly, I didn't cry. I'd been expecting almost any scenario under the sun—news that he'd had an affair, another embezzlement scheme, or someone threatening his life. Everything except that Dylan might've been sick.

Spots danced before my eyes, and I inhaled sharply. For a few minutes, I sat there, frozen in time, the phone still pressed to my ear. I barely even heard the last message, which had been from Justin, three days before Dylan's death. "Hey. What's the deal with you? I've left you, like, ten messages this week. Why haven't you called me back? It's my day off, so meet me at Java Time for a coffee on your lunch hour. We need to talk."

After listening to the automated woman's voice repeat "To replay messages, press one" about fifty times, I clicked off and continued to stare into space, the doctor's words echoing in my head.

Your life could depend upon it.

I dialed his cell phone number again, this time cutting off Dylan's voice as his automated message started to play. I advanced through each message until I found Dr. Logan's. I listened for her phone number and jotted it down. If I called now, I'd probably get an answering service, so I'd try in the morning. She might not tell me anything, but I was going to do my damnedest to find out.

I turned out the light and snuggled under the comforter but already knew I wouldn't sleep. If Dylan had been sick, this would explain a lot of things, such as why he'd seemed so preoccupied, his forgetfulness, maybe even why he'd distanced himself from Justin and the gym. With me, he had been more loving, tender, and caring than ever.

What hurt the most was the knowledge that he hadn't shared the news with me. For goodness' sake, I was his wife. Hadn't we promised to love each other in sickness and in health and always be true to one another?

I stared into the dark, listening to Luigi's motorized purrs beside me. Although there was only blackness in front of me, everything had grown abundantly clear in my mind.

"I'm going to find out who did this to you," I whispered, sensing him near. "If it's the last thing that I do."

SEVENTEEN

AFTER ANOTHER RESTLESS NIGHT, I FINALLY rolled out of bed at eight o'clock. I sat in the window seat with my steaming mug of coffee and stared down at a new text on my phone that had come in from Justin at about five this morning.

> Just got in. Long night. Had an apartment build-
> ing go up in flames. Hope you're doing better
> today. Working? If not, how about I take my
> favorite cook out to dinner so she can have a
> night off for a change?

I smiled as I read the words. He was so good to me. We'd gone out for lunch a couple of times by ourselves in the past when Dylan had been out of town. We were friends, and there certainly wasn't anything wrong with accepting a dinner invitation from him, so why did this feel like more? I cared for Justin but couldn't think about him in a romantic way right now. Justin shouldn't be wasting time with me when he should be out dating some beautiful woman who could make him happy and give him the attention he deserved. But the idea of him with another gorgeous blond like Natalie caused a sharp pain in my chest. This was silly. My mother didn't know everything. Justin was only trying to comfort a friend. Eventually, he would find a girlfriend and stop coming over here as much. The thought saddened me, but I had no right to feel that way. Justin deserved a life of his own and another chance at love. God knows he'd been gypped the first time.

My fingers flew over the keyboard. Yes, working today. Will text you when I get home.

I took a shower, ate a bowl of cereal, and tidied up the living room while I planned out my strategy for the day. I hoped to talk to Sam after the way we'd left things yesterday at the funeral home. Maybe Vince would open up to me as well. It wouldn't be easy, but perhaps he'd be willing if I sounded sympathetic to his situation.

When I finally pulled up to Slice a little before noon, the parking lot was empty except for Izzy's convertible and an unfamiliar red Porsche parked next to the dumpster. Upon entering the kitchen, I heard voices coming from Anthony's office. The door was open a crack, and after hanging up my coat, I walked by it slowly, hoping to see who he was talking to. To my surprise, I spotted Izzy in the chair behind the desk, sitting on an unknown man's lap. She was busy running her fingers through his hair while his hands roamed freely over her body. My stomach churned at the sight. *Gross.* This must be the filthy rich fiancé I'd heard about. At least, I hoped so.

"But Andy and I are just friends, Rico," she insisted in a sugary voice. "He comes in here for pizza, like, every day."

"That ain't what I heard," the man grunted. "I got my watchdogs, babe, and don't like what they've been telling me. I find out you're cheating and the wedding's off. Capisce?"

"Of course, sugar," she assured him. "You know that you're the only guy for me." She leaned forward, chucked him under the chin, and giggled. "The only slice of pizza I want on my plate."

How eloquent. Maybe she could sell that line to Hallmark.

He gripped her face possessively between his hands. "I'd better be, sweet stuff. You don't want to piss me off."

"Sure." Izzy's laugh sounded a bit apprehensive.

They started kissing again. The sight was disturbing to watch, and before I could turn away, Izzy glanced toward the door and saw me.

"Can we help *you*, Tessa?"

Busted. Resigned, I pushed the door open all the way and gave a small wave. "Sorry to interrupt. I was looking for your father."

"He had to go out." Izzy got off Rico's lap and readjusted her blouse. I hated to think what else they might have been doing before I arrived.

Izzy gestured at her fiancé, who also rose to his feet and was now staring down at the iPhone in his hand. "Rico, baby, this is our newest employee, Tessa. Tessa *Esposito*."

I loved how everyone around here had to put special emphasis on my last name.

As expected, Rico's head jerked up at the word. He gave Izzy a quizzical look as I stuck my hand out. "Nice to meet you, Rico."

The dark eyes that met mine were filled with such intense hostility that I took an abrupt step back. Not missing a beat, Rico reached forward and grabbed my fingers in a tight hold. For someone whose family supposedly had a great deal of money, Rico looked like he might have been lying in a gutter somewhere. His blue jeans were full of holes, his black Metallica T-shirt threadbare. He wore his hair in a scraggly ponytail that hung down his back and sported a diamond piercing in his nose and a gold hoop above his bushy left eyebrow. For some reason, when I'd conjured up a mental image of Rico, I'd envisioned a man similar to Dylan—professional looking, in a three-piece suit. Boy, had I missed the mark on that one.

"Esposito." He frowned as he said the word and released my hand. "You any relation to—"

Izzy grinned. "Yep. See, I told you he was married."

He looked me up and down, then snorted. "If he had you at home, why was he always hounding my Izzy for a date?"

Izzy's face turned pink, and her bottom lip poked out. "It's like I said, baby, he was greedy. Always wanting more."

I knew she was lying but decided to hold my tongue.

Rico leaned forward and kissed her on the mouth. "Well, you are super sexy." He turned to glare at me. "Can't say I'm sorry to see him gone. He bothered my girl, which means he bothered me." He smirked. "No offense."

This guy was making my skin crawl. Why was Izzy lying to him about Dylan being interested in her? Because it was really the other way around? All I wanted was to disappear and let them return to their groping session. In an attempt to avoid the venom in Rico's eyes, I focused my attention on Izzy. "Will your father be back soon?"

Izzy leaned against the desk and studied her manicure. "He ran over to the post office, so it should be any time now."

"Come on." Rico grabbed her elbow. "Walk me out. I told my buddy Frankie we'd play some video games this afternoon. You wanna come along?"

Izzy ran her hands up and down the front of his shirt. "I'll meet you later. I gotta wait till Pop gets back." She gave him a wet kiss, then stood at the door with a wide grin splitting her face, waving as he roared off in his sports car. She turned around, and the fake smile disappeared as her eyes narrowed at me.

"Okay, now that Rico's gone, we can talk freely."

So now she wanted to make conversation. "Talk about what?"

"Why are you really working here?" she spat out. "I've heard you've been going around poking your nose into our business. You've got something up your sleeve. And why on earth would my father hire you when he knows how I felt about that despicable husband of yours?"

Apparently, she didn't realize that Anthony planned to make a few bucks off my tomato sauce. Something else was clearly going on. I arranged my expression into a knowing smile, hoping to bluff my way to the truth. "I think you know why."

She scanned me up and down critically. "Dylan kept secrets, you know. He probably didn't want to upset you."

I bit into my lower lip. Yes, he did keep secrets. No one knew that better than me. Was I about to learn something else earth-shattering about my husband? I steeled myself against her squeaky voice. "Dylan and I talked about everything."

She flinched slightly, and then I knew I'd struck a nerve. "Everything." I repeated the word with emphasis and waited to see if she'd take the bait.

She pursed her lips and scowled. "What did he tell you about me? Huh?"

I racked my brain trying to figure out what secret Dylan could've known about her and then remembered what Butchy had said. It was so obvious that I chuckled. "You're quite friendly with other men, aren't you?"

Izzy's eyes widened in amazement. "You have them, don't you? The pics he took?" She crossed the few paces between us like a cat and grabbed my wrist. "Where are they? Do you know how much money we gave that greedy jerk to stay quiet? I *want* those pictures!"

Jackpot. *Last chance if you want the pictures. $50,000 is the lowest I'll go.* So Dylan wasn't blackmailing Anthony at all—Izzy had been his target. I tried to shake her hand loose. "Let go of me!"

"He told you, right? He told you that he saw me with—" She clamped a hand over her mouth. "My dad knows all about it. He took care of the situation, so don't try to hit him up for any more money."

What did she mean, he took care of the situation? Had Anthony killed Dylan over the blackmailing?

Izzy's phone buzzed. She stared down at the screen, typed out a quick reply, and then narrowed her eyes at me. "I'll deal with you later. If you see my father, tell him I'll be back in a few minutes." She exhaled loudly, kicked the door open with a high heel, and stomped outside.

I blew out a shaky breath. The restaurant was eerily quiet, and I was completely alone. That was fine with me, since I needed some time to collect my thoughts.

The back door to the kitchen opened, and Anthony walked in, whistling a tune. The noise stopped abruptly when he saw me.

"Hello, Tessa." His eyes were cold and untrusting, different from before, and I wondered if Butchy had told him about my snooping yesterday.

"Hi, Anthony." My voice sounded too cheery and fake to my own ears. "I'll get started on another pot of tomato sauce right away."

Anthony grunted. "We need a twenty-four-cut pepperoni pizza for one o'clock. There's fresh dough in the prep area." He turned and walked into the office without another word to me, and his sudden change in attitude spoke volumes. I had a strange feeling that my days at Slice were numbered.

The back door of the kitchen opened, and Izzy sauntered back in. She shot me a surly look and went into her father's office. I cocked my head in that direction but couldn't hear anything. I was about to walk over and put my ear against the wall when the back door opened again and Sam rushed in, along with a gust of cold wind. He nodded at me, his face coloring in embarrassment. "Hi."

"You're early," I said. "We haven't had any calls yet."

He stared down at the floor. "Yeah, but Anthony wants me to do some cleaning in the cooler first."

I tried to put his mind at ease. "Look, let's forget about

yesterday, okay? I was upset about my husband's accident."
Every time I said the word *accident,* I cringed.

Sam looked at me expectantly, as if waiting for the
punch line. "Sure," he said. "No problem."

"Hey, I didn't know you and Izzy were such good
friends."

He shrugged. "Yeah. So? She hangs out with all us
delivery guys."

"But you two seemed particularly friendly at the wake."
I shot him a knowing look, but his expression was blank.
"She's older than you. Worldlier than you…" *More dishonest
and sneakier than you.* I smiled pleasantly. "I'm only trying
to look out for you. Be careful, okay?"

He frowned. "Careful? Izzy only acts tough. She's got
a soft side."

That was difficult to imagine. "How would you know?
She's engaged to be married."

A muscle worked on his jawbone. "Yeah, but like I
said, we're friends. Didn't you have guy friends while you
were married?"

Justin immediately came to mind, and I almost
smiled. "Of course." My tone softened. "It's good to have
friends, right?"

"Absolutely. I'd do anything for my friends." He fiddled nervously with the gold chain he wore around his neck. "I suppose you want to know what we were talking about at the wake, huh?" When I nodded, an amused expression brightened his face. "Anyone ever tell you that you're nosy?"

When he started to laugh, I joined in. "A few people. Sorry, guess I'm a naturally inquisitive person."

Sam shrugged. "No big deal. I have a friend who trains doves, and Izzy wants some for her big day."

I cocked an eyebrow in his direction. "Doves?"

He grinned. "Yeah, doves. You know, the white birds people use at their wedding sometimes?"

I shot him a quizzical look. "Izzy was discussing her wedding plans with you?"

"Not exactly," Sam said. "Izzy was hoping I could get her a discount on the birds. She wants to have them released when she and Rico exchange their I dos. Funny, I didn't think money would be an issue since Rico's rolling in the dough. Guess everyone likes a deal."

I choose my words carefully. "So, if you did this for Izzy, what was in it for you?"

His eyes lit up like a little kid's. "She said Rico would let me take his sports car for a night. You know, I could impress my girl with it. Hey, what guy doesn't like fast cars, right?" He gave me a reassuring smile, opened the door to the cooler, and disappeared inside.

I was tempted to follow him with more questions, but the steady murmur of voices in Anthony's office grew louder. I crossed the kitchen and pressed my ear up against the door.

Izzy's voice rang out loud and clear. "They need the balance by the end of this week. Call and give them your credit card number. I won't have you stressing me out like this. I have enough on my mind."

Anthony sounded frustrated. "You said twenty grand before, and now it's doubled? What have you changed, Izzy?"

"We decided to go with an open bar for the entire night and not just the bottom shelf—that looks too cheap. Prime rib and lobster are the main entrées, and we're having the dessert buffet too. Remember?"

"Sweetheart," Anthony protested. "I don't have that much cash on me right now. I'll need a few more days. Rico's family has a lot more money than I do. This is chump change to them, so why aren't they paying for anything?"

Izzy snorted. "You know that the father of the bride *always* pays, so you'd better find a way to come up with the dough. This is my day, and I won't have it ruined. Work your magic, if you get my drift."

Anthony's tone became angry. "Keep your voice down. I don't want others to hear us."

He must have meant me.

"The caterer needs the money now," Izzy insisted. "Don't disappoint me. You only get married once."

Anthony cackled out loud. "This is your old man you're talking to. I know you don't love Rico. You only care about his money. That's why you wanted Esposito out of the way."

"He was blackmailing me!" she said angrily. "Of course I wanted him taken care of. Dylan threatened to tell Rico I was cheating on him."

Did Izzy have Dylan killed, or had her father done the deed for her?

"Lower your voice," Anthony said sharply.

"You're so weak," she continued. "Instead of firing him, you kept him around. And now his wife is working here? What's the matter with you?"

"I know what I'm doing, Izzy. Dylan was taken care of," he said in a reasonable tone. "Besides, I need Tessa. That sauce of hers is a gold mine. She's also got—"

"I don't care. She has to go," Izzy insisted. Her voice

became louder, and I was afraid she might open the door at any second. I backed away, my knees threatening to buckle under me, and grabbed the work station to steady myself.

I studied the ingredients in the prep table, a desperate attempt to look busy in case Anthony or Izzy appeared. My mind was racing in a dozen different directions. Did Izzy rig Dylan's car because he'd blackmailed her? Somehow, I couldn't picture Izzy with her tight jeans and French-manicured nails opening a car hood, but perhaps someone else had done it for her, like Rico or her father. Maybe another lover? It was clear why Anthony had hired me—for my sauce. By now he must have realized it was too dangerous to keep me around, especially if Butchy told him I'd been snooping.

What the heck were you thinking, Dylan? A wave of nausea washed over me.

The door to the office opened, and Izzy flounced out. "I gotta pick up my engagement pictures from the photographer, Pop," she yelled over her shoulder, "but I'll be back later." She gave me a triumphant smile. "Have a nice life."

It looked like unemployment was in my immediate future. Still, I couldn't help myself and grinned at her in return. "Yeah, good luck to you too…with the photos."

She gave me a funny look, turned on her heel, and slammed the back door for her final dramatic act.

Anthony came out of the office hunched over, as if he'd done battle. The phone rang, and he held up a finger, indicating he'd grab it. I started to knead the dough and quickly worked myself into a rhythm, trying to shut out the atmosphere around me.

Anthony hung up the phone and crooked his finger at me. "Tessa, when you have a minute, come on into my office. I need to speak to you."

My stomach muscles tightened at his words. I wiped my hands on a dish towel and followed him inside.

Anthony sat behind his desk. "Close the door first."

I did as he asked and tried to remain calm. He gestured for me to sit on one of the chairs in front of his desk.

Anthony folded his hands on the desk's surface. "Our profits have been down lately, so unfortunately, I'm going to have to let you go. When things improve, you're more than welcome to come back."

"I don't understand." My suspicions had been correct, but Anthony couldn't have come up with a better excuse? I was convinced he'd killed Dylan or knew who had. My stubborn streak decided to kick in at that moment. "I've worked for you for only two days. What's changed so much in that short time frame? This doesn't make sense."

Anthony didn't reply. Instead, he rose from his chair and opened the door for me. "I'll put a check in the mail to you tomorrow. If you need a reference, I'm more than happy to provide one."

"What was Dylan really doing for you?" I blurted out, suddenly not caring that I was "flapping my gums" as Anthony had told Sam.

Anthony's eyes glazed over with malice, but he kept his voice on an even keel. "I don't know what you mean, honey. He did my taxes. Now if you'll excuse me, I have other matters to attend to. You can let yourself out. I'll make sure you get paid for the entire day." He closed the door in my face, successfully dismissing me from his life and his restaurant—or so he thought.

Vince had arrived while I'd been in the office. He was at the front counter, writing something down on a pad of paper, but he looked up when I came into the kitchen. Our eyes met. He continued to watch me silently for a moment and then lowered his head to the paper again.

I removed my apron and hung it on the wall, grabbed my purse and coat, and exited through the back door. The air was crisp and clean and smelled of snow. We were supposed to have frost tonight.

My lower lip started to tremble as I rummaged through my bag for my car keys. I wasn't even sure why I was crying. I'd enjoyed cooking again, but my fellow coworkers left a lot to be desired. My ego was slightly bruised, because I'd never been fired from a job before in my life. What really bothered me was that I still didn't have any concrete answers about what had happened to my husband.

However, I did have a key to the restaurant, knew the alarm code, and was prepared to take full advantage.

A soft voice spoke behind me. "Mrs. Esposito."

Butchy was standing next to my car. He must have been in his vehicle the entire time because I hadn't noticed him. "You okay?" he asked quietly.

I ran a finger under my eyes. "I'm fine, thanks."

"Where are you going?" he wanted to know.

I beeped my car open. "Today was my last day working here. I'm on my way home."

His face sobered. "Oh, wow. I'm sorry. Did Anthony fire you?"

"How did you guess?"

He shrugged. "Slice isn't doing well financially. I mean,

they do okay, but with Izzy constantly demanding money from her dad, he can barely stay afloat. Plus, he's always giving money away to the church… I was surprised he hired you in the first place. We all were. There just isn't any money."

"Right." Maybe not everyone knew about Anthony's plan to sell my sauce. "Butchy, you know Anthony well. Vince too. They like and respect you. But desperate situations can cause people to do bad things. Do you think Anthony or Vince had something to do with my husband and Eric's deaths?"

Butchy's smile faltered. "What are you talking about? Dylan died in an accident."

"Level with me," I said. "Does Anthony have something illegal going on inside Slice?"

He shook his head in confusion. "Illegal? I don't understand what you mean."

This kid needed to wake up and smell the tomato sauce. "What's really going on, Butchy? I think my husband was blackmailing Izzy and also angered Anthony in the process. Anthony has a lot to answer for. He's been hiring people who were using drugs too. Did you realize that? I saw some white powder in the cooler and know it wasn't sugar."

Butchy's eyes widened in horror. "No, ma'am. You've got it all wrong. Anthony runs a clean business."

"Tell me the truth," I implored. "My cousin is a cop. If you're involved, I'll ask him to go easy on you, provided you help us catch whoever is responsible. Dylan was involved too. Wasn't he?"

Frustrated, he backed away from me. "You're wrong, Mrs. Esposito. Dylan wouldn't have done something like that, and neither would Anthony. Please don't worry about the job. You're an awesome cook, and I know you'll find another one soon."

His denial was starting to agitate me. "Talk to me."

Butchy climbed back into his car. He rolled the window down and spoke as his vehicle came to life. "Anthony's like a father to me. The only one I have. He'd never do that."

"Listen to me!" I yelled to be heard over the rumbling of his engine. "You need to get out while you can. He killed Eric or had him killed. What if you're next?"

"No." The sunlight from above glistened off a fresh tear that landed on Butchy's cheek. "You shouldn't tell lies like that, Mrs. Esposito."

With that, his car roared out of the parking lot.

EIGHTEEN

I PULLED INTO MY DRIVEWAY AND shut off the engine, not even bothering to place the car in the garage. For several minutes I continued to sit there, despite the chilly temperature, and contemplated what to do next. I was still trying to come to terms with the fact that my husband had lied to me and embezzled. How many more bombshells did I have to endure?

Time seemed to stand still while I continued to sit there, lost in thought. I might have blown my last opportunity to find out who had killed my husband. So far, I'd managed to successfully alienate several people—Butchy, Vince, and probably Matt as well. Anthony, who'd been a friend before, couldn't wait to shove me out of his restaurant. Where did I go from here?

The car was getting cold, and I eased myself out of the seat, my mind still in a blur. I fumbled with my keys. *Don't do this. You've come so far in the last few days.* A couple of weeks ago, I couldn't even get out of bed. *Don't lose it now.* I inhaled several gulps of fresh air, then inserted my key into the front door.

Luigi greeted me with a perfunctory meow. I patted him on the head absently but made no attempt to pick him up. I needed something to calm my nerves. There was still some wine left from Sunday night's dinner, and I poured myself a jumbo-size glass of merlot. Although not much of a drinker, I desperately needed something to dull the pain. I gulped down half a glass in one swallow and went into Dylan's study. I stood in the doorway for several minutes, staring at the surroundings. I'd known this man intimately for nine years, but overnight, he'd become a stranger to me.

My phone buzzed, and Gino's name popped up on the screen. "Sorry I didn't get a chance to call you last night. Are you at work?" he wanted to know.

"No. I just got home."

He must have sensed something was wrong. "Are you all right?"

"Great. Never better. What did you want?"

"I wanted to tell you that Ned Reinhart's being brought in for questioning some time later today."

I sucked in a deep breath. "For Dylan's murder?"

"Don't think so," Gino replied. "His alibi checks out. He was definitely in Michigan at the time of Dylan's death. But a buddy of mine on the Albany force left me a message a little while ago. Sounds like it has more to do with the embezzlement at We Care. He promised to let me know when it all goes down."

"That snake. He swore he had nothing to do with it, but I knew he was lying. I want to be there when he's questioned."

He snorted into the phone. "Sorry, Tess. It's not my precinct, so I don't call the shots. But I'll call you as soon as I know anything."

"Gee, thanks for that," I said, not even attempting to hide my sarcasm.

He paused. "You sure you're okay?"

"I've got something on the stove. Talk to you later." I hung up before he could say another word. I should have told Gino about being fired. It would have made his day, but I was annoyed with him. It was ridiculous of me to be angry at him about the questioning, but I couldn't help myself. Right now, I was angry at the world.

I scrolled through the contact information on my

phone and redialed Dr. Logan's number. I'd tried her before I left for work that morning but had only gotten the answering service. It was early enough in the afternoon that someone should be there now.

Thankfully, a live receptionist answered. "Dr. Kelly Logan's office."

"Hello." I tried to keep my voice steady. "Uh, I…would like to speak to Dr. Logan, please."

"She's with a patient right now, ma'am. Is this regarding an appointment?"

"No." My mouth was dry as a stale cracker, and as a result, the words came out with difficulty. "I… My husband… He was a patient of hers."

There was silence on the other end. "Ma'am, HIPAA regulations prohibit Dr. Logan from discussing another patient's condition."

"But my husband is dead," I protested. "What does that even matter?"

"I'm afraid that makes no difference," the woman replied. "Unless there is something in your husband's file to indicate Dr. Logan can consult with you regarding his medical state?"

That was highly doubtful. Dylan hadn't bothered to

tell me he might be sick, so why would there be anything in his records to allow me to converse with his doctor? We'd never gotten around to healthcare proxies. "I just want some answers," I whispered into the phone. "I *need* some answers."

The receptionist sighed heavily on her end. "I'm sorry, ma'am. I do wish I could help you. Now if there's nothing else—"

"Wait. One more thing. What type of doctor is Dr. Logan?"

There was another pause. "She's a cardiologist, ma'am. Have a nice day." The receptionist clicked off.

Blood roared in my ears. The secrets kept on coming. What more was there that Dylan hadn't told me? He'd stolen money and been fired from his job as result. I was positive he'd been blackmailing Izzy over intimate photos of her and other men. Now he might have had a heart condition as well. How serious had it been?

Dylan had always been fit and in excellent health. Then again, if he'd been sick, that might explain his attempt to control his weight in the past few months. Perhaps he'd stopped working out at the gym because he wasn't supposed to exert himself?

"Oh God," I whimpered. How could I have slept

next to this man for almost six years and never really have known him at all?

If Dylan wouldn't tell me—his own wife—that he was sick, was there anyone else he might have confided in?

The answer was obvious. Justin.

I sat there in silence, holding my phone. It pinged with a text message, but I tossed it onto the bed. I didn't want to look at it, much less see or talk to anyone. I went into the kitchen, grabbed the bottle of merlot I'd been drinking, and brought it into the living room with me. I sat down and flicked on the television, and Luigi jumped on my lap. I patted his soft fur absently as we both watched the screen. I refilled my glass.

Emotions and the wine flowed freely through my veins, and I soon became sleepy. My face was still damp with tears as I stretched out and pulled the afghan off the back of the couch around me. Luigi snuggled next to me, purring away contentedly. I slept and dreamed about our wedding day, as Dylan promised to love me forever. He leaned down to kiss me, happiness shining in his sky-blue eyes. I sighed and wanted nothing but for the dream to go on forever.

Someone was shaking me, and my eyelids refused to move. "Stop," I mumbled, but the shaking continued. I opened my eyes slowly and saw Justin's concerned face next to mine.

"Tessa, are you all right?"

I glanced at him through a foggy haze. "What time is it?"

"After midnight. You look like you've had a rough night." He was in jeans and a dark-blue Under Armour T-shirt. He always changed at the firehouse before coming home, and his handsome face was tired and drawn.

"So do you." I forced myself into a sitting position.

His expression was grave. "I'm fine. I texted you hours ago to see if you wanted some company. When you didn't answer, I got worried."

I let out a mammoth-sized yawn and stretched. Such a lady. "There's no need. Sorry if I scared you. Everything's dandy."

Doubt registered in his eyes. "Yeah, sure it is. I'm glad I stopped over before going home, because you left your key in the front door. Any psycho could have gotten in." He eyed the bottle and empty wineglass on the coffee table. "What's this?"

"What does it look like? I was having a drink. I am an adult, you know, and can have a drink if I want to."

Justin sat down on the couch next to me and reached for my hand. "But you hardly ever drink, Tess. Did something happen?"

As I stared into his smoky-gray eyes full of concern, I was afraid I might lose it again. "You should go home. I said I'm fine."

He ignored my request and instead put an arm around my shoulders, making it even more difficult to keep the tears at bay.

"Come on," he said. "I happen to care about you. Let someone help you for once, Tess. There's no shame in that."

He smelled of smoke and sweat, with the faint aroma of his woodsy cologne mixed in. An odd combination but nevertheless strangely addicting. I clung to him, and he moved closer to me on the couch, wrapping his strong arms around me tighter. It felt good to have someone hold me, but at the same time, it made me miss Dylan even more, and I started to sob.

Justin said nothing as I cried. He patted my back and stroked my hair at different intervals, then his soft lips connected with my cheek. They stayed there for several seconds.

I gently released his hold and sank back into the

couch cushion, exhausted from my pity party. He kept a protective arm around my shoulders. I reached for the wine bottle. There was still a little left.

Justin placed his hand over mine. "Maybe that's not such a good idea. How will you go to work tomorrow?"

I hiccupped back a laugh. "That won't be a problem. I got fired today."

He pressed his lips together. "Sorry to say this, but that's the best news I've heard all day. I didn't like the idea of you working there—especially after you had to watch your coworker get shot."

"They were getting suspicious of me. I'd been asking too many questions…and snooping. Must have put them on alert." It was tough to keep my eyes open. "Something's going on at Slice. Dylan was involved too."

Justin narrowed his eyes. "What are you talking about?"

My eyelids grew heavy, and I tried not to slur my words. "It looks like Dylan was blackmailing Anthony's daughter."

Justin's face was grim. "Tess, you're not making any sense."

"It's too much to take in right now." Talking was becoming more difficult as the wine took over. I needed to ask him about the voicemail message he'd left for Dylan but couldn't get the words out. Regardless, I reached for the bottle again. "He had a bad heart. M—my entire marriage was a lie."

He reached for my hand. "No more. The wine won't solve anything, believe me. I've been there myself."

Angrily, I pulled my hand away. "Dylan was a hypocrite. Mr. Honesty, Mr. Stand-up Guy. All I ever did was brag to everyone about his squeaky-clean image. What a dope I was." I didn't even bother with the glass and instead drank right from the bottle.

"I know how you feel, but don't torture yourself like this."

"Dylan didn't know who he was dealing with, and because of that, he managed to throw his life away." I stared down at my hands, which had begun to tremble. "We had a good marriage. We should have had children and grown old together. And please don't say you know how I feel because you don't."

His face fell, and I winced. Crap. He didn't deserve this treatment. "Sorry. I shouldn't have said that."

Justin rubbed a hand over the scruff on his chin. "No worries. Maybe we should talk about this in the morning, okay? We can have breakfast together. You need to sleep that wine off." He rose.

"Sure." I attempted to get to my feet, but someone had moved the floor. I wobbled back and forth for a minute, trying to steady myself, and then giggled. "It must be something I ate."

"You never could hold your liquor." Justin shook his head ruefully as he reached down and picked me up in his arms as if I weighed nothing. He carried me up the stairs to my bedroom, and I didn't even attempt to stop him.

After he deposited me on the bed and pulled the covers up around me, I yawned in his face. "Thanks for the lift."

He touched my cheek lightly with his fingers and smiled. "Anytime. Go to sleep. We'll talk in the morning."

Like an early morning mist, fear settled over me, and I found myself afraid to be alone. How ridiculous. I'd been alone for weeks, so what did one more night matter? For some reason though, it did matter. Despite what I'd said and the reassurances to everyone that I was fine, I needed someone—a friend to help me through this. Someone like Justin.

"Will you stay with me?" I asked and reached my hand out to him, silently willing for him to take it.

This time he brought it to his mouth. "For as long as you need me to."

NINETEEN

THE SMELL OF COFFEE AND FRYING bacon woke me from a deep, dreamless sleep. Luigi was curled up on Dylan's pillow, purring away. I opened one eye, and the numbing pain in my head would not be ignored. Tiny little men with hammers pounded away endlessly at the surface. This was why I did not—correction, *should not*—drink. Ever. I tried to remember the events from last night, but only bits and pieces came back to me.

Someone was whistling downstairs. For one brief moment, I thought it was Dylan, then remembered that wasn't possible. Justin had stayed here last night, but where? I turned to Luigi for confirmation. He opened one eye, stared at me, and then, presumably bored, closed it again.

My cheeks burned when I thought back to my pathetic drunken state last night. I recalled Justin picking me up in his arms and feeling safe and warm, but the rest of the details were sketchy. There had been wine, crying, and more wine. I'd woken once during the night, and he'd been sitting next to my bed. Something must have startled me out of sleep because he'd been quick to put his arm around me and reassure me.

"I'm here, don't worry. No one's going to hurt you again. I promise." My pulse quickened when I remembered how he'd gently stroked my hair until I'd gone back to sleep.

Justin appeared in the doorway with two mugs of coffee. His T-shirt was wrinkled, and I was pretty certain it was the same one he'd been wearing last night, which helped further convince me that it hadn't all been a dream.

"Good morning." He handed me a steaming mug. "Cream and two sugars, right?"

I gratefully accepted the drink. "Good memory." The coffee was hot and strong, exactly the way I liked it.

"How's the head?" Justin sat down next to me on the bed.

"Still attached." I watched him sip his coffee and prayed I hadn't made a total fool out of myself last night. There was only one way to find out. "You didn't go home." It was a simple statement.

He shook his head. "I didn't want to leave you."

"I was a mess," I admitted. "It was nice of you to stay with me."

"No problem." His face broke out in a wide grin. "Hungry? I made you some breakfast."

I raised an eyebrow. "But you don't cook."

Justin laughed and took another sip from his mug. "I can manage bacon and eggs, but that's pretty much the extent of it. Oh, and I can boil water—sometimes." He tucked a stray curl behind my ear. "Everyone needs a day off once in a while, and you've certainly cooked enough meals for me."

"But I love cooking," I protested. "It's not really work when you enjoy something so much."

"Well, it shows. You're an amazing cook, even better than my own mother, and that's really saying something."

"Thank you." The room was too warm, intense, and suddenly, I felt awkward. In a desperate attempt to distract myself, I sipped from my mug again. Even though he'd seen me during my worst moments after Dylan's death, I knew I was far from glamorous right now, with messy hair, no makeup, and red-rimmed eyes from crying last night. "I should take a shower and clean up. I must be a disaster."

His gaze didn't waver from my face. "Far from it."

There was another awkward pause as I noted the truth in his voice and my face heated as a result. The only man who consumed my thoughts was my husband, yet here was Justin sitting next to me, and I suddenly realized that I needed him too, but in a different way. Justin was attractive, thoughtful, and kind, a wonderful man I'd loved and trusted as a friend for years, but I couldn't think about him in any other manner. It was too soon and seemed disloyal to Dylan.

Justin studied me, noting my embarrassment. "Don't worry, I was the perfect gentleman," he said breezily, trying to relieve some of the tension from the room. I let out the breath I was holding in, happy to get back on secure ground, but his gray eyes quickly turned smoky as he added, "But you didn't make it easy for me."

Oh boy. I gulped and took another sip from my mug, at a loss for what else to say.

Mercifully, he changed the subject. "Come on. Let's get some food into you. Maybe it will help that headache go away, and then you can take a shower afterward." He stood and offered a hand to me, and like that, the tension disappeared. We were back to being friends again.

After I was on my feet, Luigi meowed loudly, and

Justin picked him up in his arms. "I already fed the boss. He was looking for breakfast at six."

"I owe you," I said gratefully.

Justin shook his head. "You don't owe me anything. We're friends, remember? This is what friends do for each other. I'll never forget how good you and Dylan were to me after Natalie moved out, especially you—always inviting me for dinner or sending Dylan over with a plate. That meant a lot to me."

"It wasn't a big deal. You hardly ever came by anymore, and I...well, *we* worried and wanted to make sure you took care of yourself."

He averted his eyes. "I think it's obvious why I avoided coming here after Natalie left, isn't it?"

Silence filled the room before I managed an answer. "Yes." It hadn't occurred to me before that Justin might have been nursing a crush on me. Dylan and I had been in love, so why would I have even considered it? Still, when I looked back, there were signs that I must have chosen to ignore, like the time Dylan had been in the hospital for an appendectomy last year and Justin kept me company in the waiting room. He'd held my hand as I worried and asked what had first attracted me to Dylan. He'd wanted to know everything—what I loved most about him, why I'd decided to go out with him. At the time, I'd attributed it to his recent breakup with Natalie. Now, I wasn't so sure.

He paused in the doorway, Luigi lying contentedly in his arms. "We'll talk more during breakfast."

"Let me brush my teeth first. I'll meet you downstairs." I walked into the bathroom and glanced at my reflection in the mirror, blowing out a sigh. As I'd suspected, my eyes were bloodshot from crying, my hair was mussed, and my face had a haggard appearance compounded from lack of sleep. The sad part was that I didn't even care anymore. I splashed water on my face and pinned the unruly curls back in a clip. I brushed my teeth, tasting last night's wine during the process. Ugh. I tried to remember our conversation and recalled that Justin seemed to be holding something back. Did he know more about Dylan's lies than he was letting on?

When I went into the kitchen, he was standing next to the breakfast counter, coffee mug in hand, reading the paper. He looked up when I entered the room and gave me a warm smile. "Feel better?"

"Somewhat." I waited as he pulled out a stool for me and then glanced down at my plate. There were scrambled eggs, bacon, and an English muffin. "It looks wonderful. Thank you."

His eyes softened as he refilled my coffee mug. "I was happy to do it."

I took a bite of the muffin. "Last night, I must have said some things that sounded pretty strange, but they happen to be true. Dylan was embezzling from We Care. I also think he was blackmailing Anthony's daughter at Slice. Dylan never told me he'd been fired. He kept a lot of secrets from me."

Justin said nothing, and the silence was deafening.

I blew out a steady breath. "I want to ask you something and need you to please be honest with me, okay?"

He drew his brows together. "You know I will."

"I checked Dylan's voicemail messages," I said. "There was one from you, about getting together for coffee. It was a few days before he died. You sounded worried about him. Did you ever meet up with him?"

To his credit, he didn't look away from me. "Yes, we talked."

"Tell me what was going on with him," I implored.

"Tess, I—"

"Tell me," I pleaded. "He was sick, wasn't he?"

Sadness crept into his eyes as he nodded. "I thought maybe he'd told you, but you never mentioned it, so I wasn't sure. He had a condition called hypertrophic cardiomyopathy. A form of heart disease."

"He was only thirty," I protested. "How could he have had heart disease?"

Justin held fast to my hand. "Apparently, it's not uncommon for someone our age. He started having shortness of breath a few months back and stopped working out with me at the gym. I'm guessing he never told you about the breathing problems."

"No," I whispered. "He kept me completely in the dark." We were quiet for a few seconds, then I managed to choke out three words. "Was he dying?"

His face was full of misery. "I don't know. He said the doctor wanted him to have open-heart surgery. She thought he had a good chance, but I think Dylan was putting her off. He mentioned getting a second opinion." He paused. "Honest, he didn't tell me much, Tess. I practically had to force it out of him."

"But at least *you* knew." I wasn't sure who to be angry with now—Justin or Dylan. "I was his wife, and he never told me anything. Did I mean that little to him?"

"I think it was the opposite," he said solemnly. "I'm sure he would have told you eventually."

My body jolted upright, as if he'd given me an electric shock. "*Eventually?* Eventually doesn't cut it. He could have gotten sick some night when we were in bed together. I could have woken up to find him—oh God." Like a waterfall, the tears stared again. "I don't believe this."

I had thought things couldn't get any worse. Being fired from a job, embezzling, and murder apparently weren't enough to deal with. How much more did I have to take?

Justin squeezed my hand. "I'm so sorry you're going through this. If it helps, I told him he should talk to you right away. I didn't see him again after we got together for coffee at Java Time. Three days later, Dylan—" He didn't finish the sentence.

I wiped away my tears and stared at him. "How could you not tell me?"

His tanned face turned crimson. "I wanted to, but Dylan made me promise not to."

"He's been dead over a month," I protested. "You've had plenty of time. I told you last night that he had a bad heart. Why didn't you tell me then?"

Justin rose to his full six-foot height and paused for a

second too long. "I—I wasn't sure what you were talking about last night. It... You weren't making much sense. And I did try to tell you the other night—after the shooting. But then Gabby called, and I figured maybe it would be too much for you to deal with in one day."

Anger formed a ball in the pit of my stomach. "This is great. I guess there really is no one that I can trust."

Justin's mouth dropped open in amazement. "How can you say that? I'd never deliberately do anything to hurt you." He reached out to take my hand again. "Don't you realize how much you mean to me?"

The truth was I did have an idea, but that didn't make any difference. Maybe deep down I realized I was being unreasonable, but it still felt like a betrayal. I pushed his hand away. "Go home."

He shook his head vehemently. "Forget it. I'm not leaving. Someone has to look after you."

"I can take care of myself. Now please respect my wishes and leave." It hurt me to say the words out loud, and from the look on his face, it bothered him as well.

After a long moment of silence, he straightened up again, his jaw set in a determined lock. "Sure. You know where to find me if you need anything."

I remained in my seat, staring straight ahead into the kitchen, when I heard the front door close behind me a few seconds later.

I marched upstairs into the bathroom to take a shower, angry at the world. Why did everyone insist on treating me like a delicate flower? *Poor Tessa can't handle it. We have to protect her.* Gino, Justin, and Dylan had all lied to me. Even Matt fell into that category, if I was allowed to go back in time. What was it with men? Weren't any of them capable of telling the truth?

With a sigh, I stepped into the shower and turned the spray on as hot as I could stand it, hoping it would make the cold, sickening feeling in my stomach dissipate. Ten minutes later, I dried off, grabbed my pink robe from the hook, and opened the door.

Luigi was slumbering away on Dylan's pillow, without a care in the world. I went back downstairs, suddenly unsure of what to do with myself. The house seemed too empty and quiet with Justin gone. My cold breakfast was still sitting on the breakfast counter, waiting for me.

Guilt set in and my eyes began to grow moist. Fighting back the tears, I opened the wastebasket and slowly lowered the food inside.

An hour later, the sauce had started to simmer on the stove. As I inhaled the smell of fresh tomatoes, onions, and basil, I almost felt like my old self again. My wooden spoon went around the inside of the steel pot as I adjusted the flame underneath for fear of burning my delectable creation. I scooped up a spoonful, blew on it, and savored the taste. It was satisfying yet a tiny bit greasy and not as thick as usual. Had I forgotten an ingredient? Impossible. I could make this sauce blindfolded. Still, it needed something. I went to the fridge and added a half cup of chianti wine to the mixture, then breathed in the heavenly aroma. Somehow, I'd get through this day.

My cell buzzed from the counter, and I was tempted to ignore it. From a few feet away, I saw Gino's name pop up on the screen. *Another liar.* "Leave me alone," I whispered to the phone.

After I had finished cutting up a tiny piece of braciole for Luigi, there was a banging on my front door. Cripes. No one would let me be for one lousy, stinking day. Like the sauce, my anger bubbled dangerously close to the surface. I knew who it was even before I heard his voice.

"Tess?" Gino shouted. "Let me in."

Having no choice, I unlocked the door and opened it. Gino stepped in the entranceway and put a hand on my shoulder. "You okay?" he asked.

"No, I'm not okay. What do you want?"

He seemed taken aback by my attitude. "I'd like you to come down to the station with me."

"For what? I've told you everything I know so far." My voice cracked. "Oh, except for the newest bulletin. It seems that my husband was very ill. So if someone hadn't rigged his car, he might have died anyway."

Gino's expression was puzzled. "What the hell are you talking about?"

"He had a heart condition and needed surgery." Despite everything, I let out a hollow, bitter laugh. "Wow. You think you know a person, especially after you've been together for almost ten years. Boy, was I wrong."

His mouth dropped open. "God, Tess. I had no idea. How did you find out?"

"There was a message on Dylan's phone from his doctor about a missed appointment. The office wouldn't give me any information, so I asked Justin. Dylan told his best friend but couldn't be bothered to tell me."

"I wish to hell this wasn't happening to you," he said grimly. "But there's a chance we might have solved the mystery of Dylan's death. That's why I want you to come with me."

"What are you talking about?"

"I went back to talk to Earl Horowitz," Gino explained. "The guy cracked like an egg this time. He said that Matt was at the shop the day Dylan brought his car in."

My heart sank. "I don't understand. Why would Matt lie about it?"

"You can find out for yourself," Gino replied. "He's down at the station and has asked to see you."

TWENTY

SERGEANT RAY WARNER, GINO'S BOSS, WAS waiting for us. He was accompanied by Matt, sitting in a rigid position in front of Gino's desk. Matt's hands gripped the sides of the chair so tightly that his knuckles had turned white. His face was drawn and his skin an ashen tone. He looked up expectantly as Gino and I entered the room.

Gino gestured toward his boss. "Tess, do you know Sergeant Warner?"

I nodded. "Yes, we've met." He'd been nice enough to come to Dylan's wake and had brought his wife with him.

Ray Warner was in his late fifties with thick, salt-and-pepper hair and emerald-colored eyes that didn't seem to miss much. He extended a cool, strong hand to shake mine. "Nice to see you again, Mrs. Esposito." He cut his eyes to Matt. "It appears our visitor has requested your presence."

Matt wasted no time in getting to his feet and walking over to us. Gino positioned his body in front of mine.

"Mancusi, I just want to talk to her."

"It's all right," I assured Gino. "Can we have a minute alone?"

"Absolutely not," Gino said. "I'm not leaving you in this room with him."

Matt shot him a death glare. "Come on. How long have you known me? I'd never do anything to hurt Tessa."

"Maybe not," Gino conceded. "But what about her husband? Did you want to hurt him—or perhaps even kill him?"

Matt stared down at his oil-stained hands and finger-nails outlined in black. Signs of a true mechanic. "No," he said in a low voice. "I didn't do anything to Dylan."

Gino folded his arms over his chest. "Why did you lie about being off from work the day Dylan brought his car in?"

Matt flashed him a look of contempt. "I didn't lie. I *was* scheduled off that day. I'm usually at the shop six days a week. Hell, it belongs to me, so that's the way it's supposed to be, right? Blood, sweat, and tears are what it takes to make a successful business. Earl was in charge of the place that day because Lila needed me to drive her to the hospital for some outpatient surgery. I've got a part-time guy, Jeb, who was there as well. Sure, I figured they could take care of things, but this is my bread and butter we're talking about. After we got home that afternoon and Lila fell asleep, I figured I'd run over to see how everything was going. Earl's a great mechanic, but he's not the best at managing money. Do you get what I'm saying?"

Gino straightened up. "No, I don't. Get to the point, please."

"What I mean," Matt said, "is that he likes to give everyone a discount. Now, I don't mind a 10 percent discount for your wife or kids. But not for every damn uncle, aunt, or cousin who comes down the pike. I can't afford that."

"Did you talk to Dylan that day?" Gino asked, impatience seeping into his voice.

Matt shook his head. "I slipped in to check things out and was gone ten minutes later."

"So Earl lied when he told Gino that you weren't around that day," I broke in. "He did see you there."

Matt hung his head. "That's my fault. I asked him to. When this all went down and your cousin here came to the shop to question us, I begged Earl not to say anything about me being there. I even had to give the guy a raise so he'd keep his big mouth shut." He glared up at Gino. "Some trusting employee. I should have known he'd cave and you'd suspect me instead."

Gino didn't reply.

Matt watched me, his hazel eyes round and innocent. "I didn't do anything to Dylan's car, I swear it. For God's sake, you guys have all been bringing your vehicles to me for years. Even you, Mancusi."

"You never liked Dylan, and we know why," Gino said, his eyes flicking to my face.

Deep in my heart, I didn't believe Matt had done this. Still, his actions were making me uneasy. There was a desperate look on his face, like a trapped wild animal waiting to flee at any second. Yes, I'd heard the rumors about Matt's drug problems and his going into rehab, but I was a firm believer people could change, and you should give them the benefit of the doubt. But what if I was wrong? I didn't know Lila or what their relationship was like. The text he'd sent me on the eve of my wedding still gnawed at my brain. If he was using again, could he have somehow been involved with the dealings at Anthony's along with Dylan? Had they argued over it? Or had Matt merely hoped that with my husband out of the picture, we could find our way back to one another?

"Okay, I admit I didn't like him." Matt addressed Gino, but his eyes were focused on me. "I'm never going to think that any man is good enough for Tessa. She belonged to me first."

"*Belonged* to you?" Gino's face hardened as he echoed the word. Not a smart thing for Matt to say in front of my cousin.

"We broke up twelve years ago, Matt," I said calmly. "You've been married for what—five years now? You have three kids to worry about. No offense, but why should you care whom I'm with?"

"Of course I care," Matt insisted. "I love Lila and don't want to lose her, but I'll always care what happens to you." His voice reeked of desperation as he continued. "Lila threw me out. She's planning to go back to Georgia to her folks and take the kids."

Gino put his hands on his hips. "She's leaving you? Hard to imagine why."

"Damn it!" Matt said angrily. "It wasn't me, I swear. Why don't you take a look at Dylan's so-called buddies—specifically the pizza king of Harvest Park himself?"

"What are you saying?" Gino asked.

Matt kept his gaze pinned on me. "Dylan spent a lot of time at Slice. He even came into my shop once with that delivery kid...the one who got shot."

"Eric," I murmured.

He went on. "They were dropping Dylan's car off. And another time, your husband came in with Anthony, and they looked pretty chummy together."

"Dylan did Anthony's taxes. They were friends for a long time." I tried to act calm, but his words sent a chill through me.

"I'm not a fool, Tess," he said. "I know that Eric kid was a user and also selling, so I have a pretty good idea of how Anthony might be supplementing his pizza income at Slice. Maybe Eric was...ah...assisting him. Dylan might have been in on it too."

"Where did you hear this?" Gino demanded.

"Let's just say that I have my sources," he said tightly. "I run a business, too, and know how helpless it feels when you think the place might go under. Have you ever asked yourself how Anthony's making a living? There's never anyone in that dive."

Gino rocked back on his heels and studied Matt. "Please go on."

"Everyone thinks that Anthony's pure as the driven snow," Matt chortled. "Well, that's not the case."

"Okay, Smitty," Gino said. "Time to come clean. Is Anthony Falducci running some kind of drug operation from Slice?"

Matt stared down at the floor. "I can't answer that."

"Can't or won't?" Gino insisted. "How did you know about Anthony's operation? If there's a chance he was selling drugs, you need to tell me everything. Unless, of course, you were in on it too."

Matt's face turned beet red. "No! I'm done with that part of my life. I never actually saw drugs there. Once in a while, we get takeout from Slice over at the garage. I'd make small talk with Eric. He asked me how business was, and if I still had a…uh…certain kind of bad habit." Matt hesitated before he went on. "Someone must have told him that I'd been a user in the past. The kid was clearly offering, and I have to admit, it was damn hard to say no. But I didn't want to fall back into that again, because I have too much to lose now. I've been clean for over five years now. Swear to God."

"Eric never actually said the word drugs, did he?" I asked.

Matt looked at me sadly. "He didn't have to, Tessa."

Fair enough. "When was this?"

"A couple of weeks back," Matt replied.

Gino's brown eyes locked on him. "Why didn't you mention this before?"

"Because I wasn't certain that Dylan's death might be connected to Slice." Matt sneered at him. "And I don't make a habit of offering up information to pigs like you either. I'm not a snitch."

Gino glared at him but said nothing. I knew that look well. He was fighting to control his temper. Things were about to turn ugly.

Matt returned Gino's scathing look with one of his own. "Why the hell did you have to come to my house to question me? It's your fault Lila threw me out." He gave me a pleading look. "I asked your cousin if he would bring you by so I could tell you face-to-face, with him here." Matt reached for my hand. "Please believe me."

Gino smacked his arm away. "Don't touch her."

Enraged, Matt pushed Gino backward. Before I even understood what was happening, Gino shoved Matt up against the wall and placed him in handcuffs. Matt swore angrily as Sergeant Warner opened the door and shouted to someone in the hall. He was quickly escorted out of the room by another officer.

Gino watched me closely. "Are you okay?"

I nodded mutely, shocked over what had transpired.

Sergeant Warner cleared his throat. "I'll give you two some privacy." He nodded politely at me and then left the room, shutting the door quietly behind him.

"I'm sorry you had to go through that, Tess," Gino said. "This is unusual practice, I'll admit. Matt came down here to confront me. He was pissed off that I'd gone to his house and accused me of badgering him. Matt said he could prove he was innocent and asked me to call you. Apparently, he figured you'd believe him. I thought he might show his true colors in your presence."

"I think he was telling the truth. Eric *was* using and probably dealing drugs at Slice too. I'm guessing the others were in on it as well." I heaved a long sigh. "Dylan included."

Gino stroked his chin and watched me thoughtfully, saying nothing.

"How long are you going to keep Matt here?"

He gave me a smug smile. "As long as I want to. Nah, I'm kidding. An hour maybe."

"So you used me as bait for him?"

He looked guilty. "In a sense, yes. But you did say you wanted to be here if I questioned him."

"Yes. Thank you for that." I was glad it was over.

He slung an arm around my shoulders. "Come on. I'll take you home."

When we were settled in his car, Gino glanced briefly at his phone and dashed off a quick text to someone, then started the engine. "Tell me more about Dylan's condition."

"He had something called hypertrophic cardiomyopathy. The doctor wanted him to have open-heart surgery. I looked it up online, and it's a hereditary disease. I guess there's no cure, but surgery could have prevented further complications." It may, in fact, have saved his life. I didn't know how bad things were, since Dr. Logan's office wouldn't divulge any details.

Despair settled on my chest like a heavy boulder. Dylan must have been terrified when the doctor had told him. My mood quickly soured to anger. "Why wouldn't he let me be there when he found out? When the doctor explained everything. That's what your spouse is supposed to be for, yet Dylan didn't even want me to know."

"He asked Justin to keep it a secret from you?"

I nodded. "Justin should have told me. I had a right to know."

Gino clenched his jaw and stared straight ahead. It

was a beautiful, sunny day but chilly, with the temperature hovering at about thirty degrees and supposed to dip into the teens tonight. "Of course you had a right to know," he said. "But don't put it all on Justin. When someone makes a promise to a friend or a loved one, they're supposed to honor it."

For some reason, I had expected Gino to agree with me. "Well then, he should have told me after Dylan died. There was no reason for him not to."

He turned his head slightly. "Maybe so, but that's not always an easy thing to do, especially when you have deep feelings for that person."

I sighed heavily. "Gino, I can't get into this with you."

A sly smile tugged at the corners of his mouth. "As a cop, I've learned to read other people's faces pretty well, and it's no secret the way he looks at you—has always looked at you. I never said anything because he was Dylan's pal and I know how happy you two were together. But I always suspected he had feelings for you. I'm actually kind of surprised that Dylan never noticed."

"There was no reason for him to," I said honestly. "I've never loved another man besides him."

He cocked a fine, arched eyebrow at me. "Not even Matt?"

"No. He never came close."

"Gabby hated it when you guys were dating," Gino commented. "She used to come and complain to me about him all the time. I think she was afraid you'd end up marrying the guy."

I smiled. "Gabby should learn to stop gabbing so much."

He laughed, then his expression grew serious. "Try not to be so hard on Justin, Tess."

"In all honesty, I'm angrier at Dylan."

"I don't know his reasoning for what he did," Gino commented. "It's easy to hurt the ones you love, no matter how hard you try not to. Getting back to your buddy Matt. Do you really think he's telling the truth?"

I hesitated, not wanting to set Gino off again. "Yes. He's not a killer, Gino. And I think he's right about the goings-on at Slice. I'm convinced Anthony knew something about Dylan's death, and he fired me because I was asking too many questions. It also looks like Dylan knew Vince's partner, Bobby. I found his name in Dylan's Rolodex."

"So Dylan was doing their taxes?" Gino asked. "Maybe Anthony had recommended Dylan to his brother."

"It's possible. Carlita told me they didn't seem happy when they ran into each other in the bakery one day. And what about the white powder I found? Say what you want, but I know it was drugs, and Matt confirmed back there that Eric was dealing. Dylan was definitely involved—in a blackmailing scheme and possibly with the drugs. He had to have at least known about them if Anthony was supplementing his revenue from the sales. He was the one looking at their books for goodness' sake! Slice is hurting for money, and Vince might be, too, since his restaurant had to close. How else would Slice even stay in business? They get a decent takeout crowd but not enough to support it. Anthony was even planning to bottle my sauce and sell it. That's why he hired me."

Gino looked impressed. "You've found out a lot to help us. We'll start watching the place and see what it gets us. We can't go in there and search without proof first. I'm kind of embarrassed I didn't put this together myself. When I get back to the station, I'll talk to Warner. You have to admit, with Dylan embezzling and now blackmailing...seems like he was focused on stockpiling a lot of money."

"Well, I don't know where it could be. I haven't seen any of it. But I think we can narrow the killer down to Slice now. Almost everyone there had it in for Dylan, and they all had a different reason to want him dead."

He nodded. "Makes sense to me."

It should have made me feel better that we were getting closer to an answer, but I was overcome with sadness. No matter how you sliced the pizza, the facts remained the same. My husband may have been sick or dying, but he'd still stolen money that hadn't belonged to him. Plus, I was devastated that he hadn't told me any of it in the first place.

"I'll let you know what I find out about Ned," he promised. "We're close on this, Tess. I can feel it. Now, for your part, stay home until I call you. Don't go back to Slice, understand? Make sure to lock your—"

"For God's sake," I snapped. "Stop treating me like I'm five. I'm not your responsibility. If I want to go back to Anthony's and find out what's going on, I will. And I don't need your permission either!"

He grabbed my arm, but I was quicker. I let myself out of the car and ran for the front door.

"Tessa," Gino shouted, but I ignored him. As soon as I was inside and had locked the door, I heard his car drive away. *Good.* I hadn't meant to hurt my cousin but was so overwhelmed with grief and shock, I wasn't sure what to do anymore.

Distracted, I went into the kitchen and opened the

freezer. There was still part of an apple pie in there if I wanted to indulge in another pity party. No, I refused to eat my feelings. On top of the kitchen counter was an unopened bottle of pinot grigio that my mother had brought over. My hand started to pull it forward, then I stopped myself. Instead, I settled on a cup of peppermint herbal tea.

When I walked back into the living room, my eyes fell upon our wedding picture. I picked the frame up off the coffee table and studied the photo carefully. I'd looked at it a million times, but it no longer evoked the same warm sensation. There was no more experience of euphoria or contentment as I stared at it. Anger was the prevalent emotion and threatened to consume me.

Dylan and I were smiling into each other's eyes and holding hands, deeply in love. He looked so handsome in his black tuxedo, while I wore a white lace gown with an antique veil covering my head. It was almost six years since the photo had been taken but somehow seemed longer. Things had been so perfect back then. If you have true love, what else did you need? For some reason, Dylan hadn't shared my view. He'd wanted more, and his greed had ended up costing him his life and me the man that I loved.

I removed the lid off one of the boxes I'd brought from

We Care and stared down inside. I'd intended to place the wedding picture in there because I couldn't bear to look at it any longer. Still, I continued to clutch it to my chest. Everything inside the box was as neat and orderly as I'd left it the other night. Dylan would have been pleased to see that I'd made the effort—dear, organized, meticulous Dylan. He'd kept everything so pristine, with the exception of his own life, which contained more secrets and lies than a dirty politician's.

Consumed with rage, I picked up the picture and hurled it at the wall. The glass broke and shattered into a hundred tiny pieces, its symbolism not lost on me. Then I sank to the floor and began to sob.

There were streaks of blood on my palm where a shard of flying glass must have landed. Numb to the pain, I continued to cry in anger at the circumstances—of how Dylan had let himself be put in this position. If he'd told me what was going on, we might have been able to work things out. I'd loved him more than anything in this world and never would have left him. Perhaps that's what he'd been afraid of.

If Dylan had only come to me with the truth, he might still be alive today.

TWENTY-ONE

FOR THE NEXT COUPLE OF HOURS, I sat in the window seat and stared numbly out onto the street. A few of the neighborhood children were outside, riding their bikes despite the cold, with a parent watching nearby. This might be one of the last opportunities they'd have to ride their bikes this year. Rumor had it that we'd be getting our first snowstorm this weekend. The sound of their innocent laughter hit my ears, reminding me of happier times that were now beyond my reach.

As I watched the sun disappear behind the clouds, I knew I had to redirect my anger, but at who? Justin? Gino? The police department? Dylan was dead. It solved nothing to be angry at him, but still, I couldn't help myself.

Justin had meant well, but knowing that he had been privy to Dylan's secret, or at least part of it, continued to eat away at me. He cared for me, but I couldn't let myself think about that.

Justin wanted more than friendship, and I had nothing to give. It might be a long time—if ever—until that changed.

My head was pounding, and I needed some aspirin. It was Saturday, and my mother's Altar Rosary Society meeting was being held tonight, which meant she'd be stopping by for her cookies soon, bad batch of chocolate biscotti and all. It was tempting to leave them on the porch. I didn't want to see or talk to anyone.

As I reached into my purse, my hand brushed against a smooth leather surface. It was the journal I'd tucked inside the other day. I'd forgotten to give it to Gino. I sat down on the couch and opened it. My eyes ran through the names, and one immediately stood out. Johnny Sobato. The man who'd left a message on Dylan's phone. Was he a drug client? Had Dylan been in on the sales with Anthony? Nothing would surprise me anymore. Without stopping to think first, I dialed the number.

A man picked up after the second ring. "Yeah," he grunted in greeting.

"Is this Mr. Sobato?"

He didn't answer right away. "Who wants to know?"

I went with the first name that popped into my head. "Isabella."

Another pause. "You sound different."

"I have a cold."

"Why's your father got you calling? He never does that," the man said.

"Uh," I hedged. "He's been busy, so I'm taking over. What'll it be?"

An uncomfortable silence met my ears. "What do you mean? It's always the same. Hey, what are you trying to pull? Are you working with the police or something?"

Oh crap. *Stupid, stupid, stupid.* My heart knocked so loudly against the wall of my chest, I was positive he could hear and clicked off in a sudden panic, then chided myself. I should have called from a number that couldn't be traced. He'd all but confirmed my previous suspicion. Anthony *was* running some type of illegal ring—and Dylan had been in on it too. Any doubt I'd had before was gone. So what did this mean for Dylan's death? Who at Slice had killed him?

I went into my bedroom, grabbed the steno pad still sitting on my nightstand, and scanned through the names again. *Izzy.* How was she involved? Was she so afraid of losing her meal ticket that she'd killed or asked somebody to kill Dylan to protect her cheating ways?

Then there was Anthony. He claimed to have adored

Dylan, but maybe he wanted him out of the picture. How far would he go to protect his precious daughter from a blackmailer?

Vince. Someone had blabbed about the illegal goings-on at his restaurant in New York City, and there was a good chance it might have been Dylan. Had Vince returned to Harvest Park to start over or to settle the score with my husband?

There was a knock on my door. Good grief, what now? Then I remembered. My mother had arrived for the cookies. Before I reached the door, her shrill voice echoed from the other side. "Tessa? Honey, we're running late here!"

I unlocked the door to my mother, who gave me a swift kiss on the cheek. Aunt Mona and Mrs. DeNovo crowded into my living room behind her.

Mom glanced around the room anxiously. "I'm sorry, darling. The meeting starts at eight, and we're terribly late."

"How nice to see you, dear." Mrs. DeNovo gave me a little wave. "It's been a long time. Have you turned atheist?"

A subtle hint that I hadn't been to church lately. "Ah, no. I do need to start going to Mass more often. How are you, Mrs. DeNovo?"

"Call me Angela," she said and beamed.

My mother was shifting from one foot to another in impatience. "Are they in the kitchen, dear?"

Gee, the world was certain to end if she couldn't have the chocolate biscotti right away. "Yes, in two trays on the breakfast counter."

"I'll help," Aunt Mona offered. "But I need to call Gabby before we go anywhere. I forgot to ask her earlier to bring home the newest Danielle Steel novel. It came out this morning."

My mother rolled her eyes at the ceiling as they walked toward the kitchen and left me alone with Mrs. DeNovo. She was a petite thing who only came up to my shoulder, and although she wasn't much older than my own mother, she looked as if she'd aged twenty years since the last time I'd seen her. The woman's hair was a tangled grayish-white mixture, and her entire face was etched with fine deep wrinkles. She smiled at me and took my hand between her two tiny, liver-spotted ones. Her fingers were ice cold, and I almost yelped as they brushed against mine.

"I hope Butchy's been taking good care of you," she said.

Puzzled, I stared at her. "Excuse me?"

She gave me a little, playful nudge. "Well, since you are his employee."

"Oh, right." The poor woman was clearly delusional.

Mrs. DeNovo patted my hand again. "I'm going to tell him to give you a raise. I'm sure you've earned it."

"He's the best boss I've ever had." Good lord. Why was I playing along?

"I'm so glad Anthony promoted him. I always knew he was management material. Plus, we do need the extra money he's bringing in."

I nodded and then paused, absorbing Mrs. DeNovo's words. Wait—where was Butchy getting the extra money from? Then it dawned on me. This wasn't only about Anthony, Izzy, or Vince—it involved all of them. Every person at Slice had something to hide.

Mrs. DeNovo prattled on. "I'm so glad he quit that other job. Not that I have anything against mechanics, mind you. But who could turn down a job as a manager?"

I glanced at her in surprise. "Butchy was a mechanic? At the Car Doctor?"

"Oh no. He worked for Central Motors in Albany. That boy does such good work," she said proudly. "He always tells me that he never met an engine he didn't like."

TWENTY-TWO

I DIDN'T EVEN REMEMBER WHAT I said to my mother after Mrs. DeNovo's revelation, but I shuffled the women out of my house as fast as possible. My mind was racing in a dozen different directions. After they departed, I tried Gino's cell, but he didn't pick up. I left a message, asking him to call me back immediately.

The pieces were starting to fit together. I didn't have solid proof that Butchy had killed Dylan, but he had jumped to the top of my suspect list. Butchy could have easily tampered with Dylan's car, thanks to his past experience. But what was the motive? *Anthony's like a father to me*, he'd said. His own father had died years ago, so perhaps that part was true. Maybe he'd resented Dylan and Anthony's close relationship. If Dylan had taken on a bigger part in

Anthony's drug business after he was fired, he could have stepped on Butchy's toes in the process.

Then there was the matter of Eric's death. He had wanted to tell me something that night in the car, right before he was shot. Could he have seen Butchy tamper with the car?

A half hour passed with me doing little else but pacing back and forth. I tried Gino again, but there was still no answer. I sent him a text. Call me asap. Why was there never a cop around when you needed one?

It was almost nine o'clock, which meant that Slice would be deserted soon. Gino might cuss me out later or even arrest me, but I didn't care. If Anthony and company got wind that the police were on to them, the drugs, or any evidence of them, might disappear from Slice forever. If I could get inside the restaurant and find something incriminating, though, one of the employees might crack in an attempt to save their own skin.

I hunted through the junk drawer in my kitchen until I found a flashlight, then went upstairs to my room to get changed. My plan was crazy and dangerous, and a mental image of Gino yelling at me passed before my eyes. But if I was right and the information Matt relayed had been truthful, everything might finally fall into place.

I threw on my jacket and gathered up my purse and flashlight, opening the front door to find Gabby on my porch, her hand raised in the air as if to knock. I let out a small squeak of alarm.

"Holy cow." I placed a hand over my heart. "I didn't even see you drive up. You scared the daylights out of me."

"Obviously. I parked at the curb." She narrowed her eyes. "And where are you off to this time of night, sweet cuz?"

I hesitated. "Taking a walk."

"Right." She pushed past me into the living room. "At nine o'clock when it's twenty degrees outside? Puh-leeze." Her eyes took in my getup—black leather jacket, black jeans, and low-heeled boots. "Looks like you're going on a stakeout or something."

Damn it. I'd never been able to hide anything from my cousin. She could always read me like a book. I shut the door behind her. "Well, what are *you* doing here at this hour?"

She placed her hands on her hips. "I didn't hear from you all day, so I thought I'd stop by and make sure you were okay. Something's up, and I want to know what. I texted you earlier, and you never responded. What's going on?"

I reached into my purse for my phone. Sure enough,

there were texts from Gabby and one from my mother but still nothing from Gino. "Oh. Sorry about that."

Gabby continued to watch me, her dark eyes filled with doubt. "I went into the pizzeria today to pick up a pie and asked for you. Sexy Vince said you didn't work there anymore. I tried to reach my brother, but he's not answering his phone. Lucy said he had some kind of emergency call. I thought I was your partner! Tell me what's going on."

Of all days for her to go into the pizzeria, it had to be today. "I hope you didn't tell them that you were related to me. I don't want you involved in this, Gabs."

"Involved in what?" she demanded. "What else is going on that I don't know about?"

Defeated, I threw my car keys and purse back on the coffee table. "Yes, I was fired. They were getting suspicious. I also discovered that Dylan was sick, which might have been his reason for joining forces with Anthony."

Her eyes widened in horror. "Hang on. Dylan was sick? What do you mean, *joining forces*? I don't see you for one day and all hell breaks loose. Talk to me!"

"Gabs, I don't have time for this. I think Anthony was selling drugs at the restaurant, and Dylan was involved."

My voice started to falter. "I also have an idea who might have rigged Dylan's car."

Gabby brought a hand to her mouth. "Oh my God, Tess. Was it Anthony? They could be coming after you next. What did Gino say?"

"I haven't been able to reach him either."

She snorted and echoed my earlier thoughts. "Yep. That figures. He only shows up when you'd rather *not* see him. Tell me who rigged Dylan's car."

I was anxious to get going but needed to tell someone my theory. "I think it might have been Butchy."

She swore under her breath. "Shut up. The DeNovo kid? Your mother always talked about that family like they were saints."

"I'm not positive," I admitted. "But it would fit. If Dylan was involved with the drug dealings, Anthony or Butchy might have wanted him out of the picture. Eric may have been blackmailing whoever rigged Dylan's car, so someone took him out as well. I'm going to Slice to see if I can find anything—drugs, money, whatever. I'll start my search in the cooler, where I found the bag of cocaine. I have a feeling there's more in the boxes, unless someone's cleaned them out already. Don't waste your time trying to talk me out of it either."

Her eyes almost popped out of her head. "Are you nuts? You're going to break in? What if you get caught?"

"Remember, I still have the spare key from the other day. As long as Anthony didn't change the alarm code yet, I'll still be able to get in. So it's not really breaking and entering."

Gabby grinned. "I do like the way you think. But what if one of those creeps happens to come back to the restaurant and finds you there?"

"I'll tell them I forgot something at work yesterday."

She looked at me like I was a moron. "You can't be serious. You think they're going to believe that?"

I shot her a death glare. "You don't understand what this is like for me. I can't reach Gino, and I'm tired of waiting. I want answers now. Dylan might have done some terrible things, but he didn't deserve to die because of them. I know this is risky, but I'm willing to take that chance."

"Darn right it's risky," she agreed. "What if something goes wrong with the alarm or the police are already there watching the place? Do you really want my brother carting you off to jail?"

"I'll deal with it when or if it happens."

Gabby held up her hand. "Well, you see, I kind of have a problem with that."

Ugh. Not her too. Gabby was the one person who I thought would understand, and now she was giving me grief as well? "Forget it. You're not going to change my mind."

"Who said anything about changing your mind?" She shot me a sly grin. "I want to go too."

"Absolutely not." I should have realized that Gabby would have demanded to be let in on the action. Even though I was scared to go alone, involving her in this mess was not an option. "Your brother will go ballistic if he finds out that I dragged you into this."

"You didn't drag me into anything. I applied for the job as your assistant, remember? I'm the Ethel to your Lucy. So if you don't take me along"—she shrugged, then drew her cell phone out of her jacket—"I'd have no choice but to tell Gino. He might not be reachable, but I can always leave a message. So you see, there's no winning for you."

"Well, gee, thanks for making this so easy for me."

"Not a problem." Her tone became serious. "Tess, if you think for one minute I'd let you go there alone, then you really don't know me at all. Besides, I'm kind of intrigued by this. It's like going on a scavenger hunt or something."

"Okay. First off, this is not the land of pretend, like in

those Harry Potter books you love so much. This is real life, cuz." And a scary one at that.

Gabby's full red lips formed a delicate pout. "Forget it. And for the record, some of those books are pretty damn scary. I'm going with you, and that's the end of the discussion."

Having no choice, I grudgingly relented. "Fine, but you're to wait in the car for me. If Gino arrests us, no complaints from you."

Gabby winked. "Hey, being arrested might not be so bad. My brother works with some hot-looking cops." She stared at the leather jacket I was wearing. "It's freezing out. You'd better get something heavier."

"Maybe you're right. Be right back." Upstairs in my bedroom, Luigi was curled up on the quilt, sound asleep. How I envied his simple, comfortable life. I grabbed my wool coat and searched through the pockets for my gloves. Not there, but I did find some tissues, a tube of lip balm, and my license that I'd shoved in there after the car accident the other day. Scooping it all back in, I slid the heavy coat on and went back to the landing.

"Hey, Gabs? Are my gloves in the living room?" I shouted down to my cousin.

There was no answer. "Gabs?" I switched off the light and hurried down the stairs.

Gabby was standing in front of the couch, flanked by Butchy on one side of her and Anthony on the other. Butchy had a gun pointed at the side of her head. She stood there motionless, staring straight ahead. Her eyes shifted slightly when she caught sight of me, and the panic in them must have mirrored my own.

"Well, well, Mrs. Esposito," Butchy greeted me. "Where are you off to so late at night?"

TWENTY-THREE

IT TOOK ME A MOMENT TO answer. "How...how did you get in here?"

Butchy held up my house key. "I made a copy of this little gem the other night after I found it in your coat pocket at Slice. Guess I'm not the only one good at detective work, huh?"

Anthony held out his hand. "The journal, honey. We know you've got it."

There was no choice but to try playing dumb. "I have no idea what you're talking about."

Anthony rolled his eyes, a clear indication that I wasn't fooling him. "There were two reasons I hired you. One, because of your sauce, which is going to make me a nice little profit once I start selling it to distributors. The other was to get my journal back. At first, I thought maybe you didn't have it after all, but then you called one of our customers today—a Mr. Sobato. He had your number traced and then reported it back to me." He made a *tsk-tsk* sound. "Not a smart thing to do, Tessa."

Another moment when I'd acted without thinking first. "He… I thought he was a client of my husband's," I lied. "Dylan was doing his taxes, right?"

Butchy laughed. "Oh, he was a client all right. But he belonged to us, not your greedy old man."

"What Butchy means," Anthony said quietly, "is that all those clients belonged to *me*." He took a step toward me. "But you'd already figured out that your loving hubby was in on my family operation. Did you also know that he decided to make his own deals and eliminate us from the equation? Real nice, huh?"

When Anthony had first offered me the job, I'd been struck by his eyes—caring and kind, big pools of warm chocolate. Now they were as dark and cold as an abyss.

Anthony kept his voice low and on an even keel. "I don't want to hurt you or your friend, Tessa, but you aren't giving me much choice here."

"I threw it away," I lied. How I wished I'd given the

journal to Gino, but I hadn't known exactly what it was. Now it was too late.

"The jig is up, doll," Butchy said. "I admire what you did though. Really, I do. Trying to find out who did your man wrong. It gets me"—he patted his chest—"right here." A sadistic smile played across his lips while his amber eyes shone like a cat's, rendering Butchy almost unrecognizable. He was clearly enjoying this. With a twinge I thought of his poor mother and what the truth would do to her. "Now that you know our secret, we've got to take care of you."

Gabby's eyes met mine, full of terror. How were we going to get out of this one? There was no doubt in my mind that they planned to kill us. They couldn't afford not to. I knew a little about guns from a self-defense class I'd taken and this one didn't appear to have a silencer. Still, I had no idea if my neighbors would hear the weapon should Butchy try to use it.

My phone was inside my purse on the coffee table. If I could distract them for a second, maybe I could dial 911, or if Gino had texted back, I could easily alert him.

Butchy grabbed Gabby's arm and twisted it behind her back as she yelped in pain. "Hand over the journal and we'll let your friend go. If not, you both die. Simple as that."

"No need to get rough with the girl," Anthony said quietly. "*Not yet.* You're too high-strung, kid."

"Don't call me kid, old man," Butchy retorted.

Anthony shook his head at him. "You've got a lot to learn. You can't go around killing people whenever the mood strikes. It doesn't work that way." He kept his voice calm and steady, as if he'd asked me to whip up a batch of sauce.

My initial emotion of fear gave way to anger. "Let Gabby go. She has nothing to do with this. You can take me instead."

Butchy shot me a sly wink. "Looks like your friend was in the wrong place at the wrong time. If you don't cooperate, she's going to end up dead like your husband."

"Why did you rig Dylan's car?" I asked hoarsely.

Anthony held out a hand calmly. "The journal, Tessa. My patience is wearing thin."

"Okay." I blew out a sharp breath. "I'll get it." There was no way I would risk Gabby's safety. The nose of the gun followed my every movement as I lifted my purse off the coffee table. With shaking fingers, I grabbed the journal and defiantly threw it on the floor.

Muttering under his breath, Anthony snatched up the

leather book and began flipping through the pages. I kept a hand inside my purse until my fingers connected with the phone.

Butchy kept the gun pointed at Gabby as he leaned over Anthony's shoulder to read along. "All that time wasted looking around in here the other day when she had it on her all along." He glared at me with obvious contempt. "Your husband had no right to try cutting us out of these deals. He stole thousands from us! His death was karma, pure and simple. Put down the purse, sweetheart. No need to make yourself pretty where you're going."

Anthony looked up from the journal at the same moment, and our eyes met. In desperation, I stared down into the purse, intending to press the *1* on my phone. My finger never made it. Anthony lunged forward and shoved me backward. I lost my balance and fell as both the purse and phone shot out of my hands.

Terrified, I lay there for a moment, unsure of what he might do next. Anthony reached down and roughly yanked me to my feet. The room started to spin as I tried to maintain my balance. Anthony pushed me again, and I fell against Gabby, who wrapped her arms around me in support.

"Are you okay?" she whispered in my ear.

I managed to nod. Neither one of us was okay, but telling her that solved nothing. We had to get away from them.

"Enough of the small talk." Anthony walked over to my phone and stared down at it. We all watched mystified as he slammed the heel of his black leather shoe down on its surface, resulting in a definitive crunch. My heart sank as he grunted in satisfaction. "There. Now you won't be tempted to do anything else stupid. Looks like we're ready to go, ladies."

"Where are we going?" Gabby asked, her eyes large and round with terror.

The two men exchanged a knowing look, and then Butchy flashed us an evil smile. "It's a nice night for a drive."

Panic seized me. "You promised to let Gabby go."

"Forget it, Tess! I'm not going anywhere without you," she said.

Anthony shook his head sadly. "I'm very disappointed in you, Tessa."

How was this even the same man that Dylan had always spoken so highly of? Anthony had sent flowers and food after my husband died. He'd offered monetary support at his wake. Now I knew why—it was an attempt to ease his guilty conscience. If he even had a conscience, that is.

Anthony must have guessed my thoughts. "I really liked Dylan. He was the son I never had."

I clenched my fists at my sides. "Tell me, who'd kill their own son? You're nothing but an animal, Anthony."

The smile fell from his lips. "I didn't kill him. I couldn't do something like that to Dylan."

Right. That only left one alternative, if he was in fact telling the truth. I still wasn't sure how Dylan's death had come to be but could wager a guess and took a step toward Butchy. He pointed the gun in warning while Gabby attempted to hold me back, but I shook her off. Even though I wasn't thinking straight, everything else had become clear in my mind. "You killed my husband?"

Butchy laughed. "I wish I could take credit for it. You two will be my very first fatalities. To tell you the truth, it kind of excites me. No one would ever take me for as a killer. Little Butchy DeNovo. What a nice Italian boy," he mimicked. "Hey, I'm sick and tired of having nothing in this world. Your husband had a lot of nerve working his way in and taking a job that was supposed to be *mine*."

Anthony clenched his teeth together in anger. "I never promised you anything. Tell the girl the truth about her husband. You must have been the one to kill him. I know that Izzy and Rico had no part in it."

Butchy ignored him. "I've had to help support seven brothers and sisters since my father died. My mother thinks Anthony made me his manager and that's why we've suddenly got money coming in. She's sick and can't work. When I scrape a little more bread together, I'm out of this country. It's time to put myself first."

"What about Eric?" I said in disgust.

Butchy waved me off. "What about him? That kid was a major scumbag. He got what was coming to him."

"Eric saw you tamper with Dylan's car, didn't he? He was blackmailing you."

Butchy's eyes resembled stone. "I didn't tamper with the car."

Why do they keep denying it?

"He's right. Eric was nothing but trouble from the beginning," Anthony agreed. "Always asking for money or part of the stash. We'd send him to make a drop, but lots of times the punk would help himself first. You can't trust no one these days."

Rage burned inside my brain. "You're nothing but cowards. Dirty, pathetic cowards."

Anthony's nostrils flared in anger as his hand shot up and caught me on the side of my mouth, his onyx ring cutting into my lip. Gabby screamed and reached for me, but Butchy shoved her to the floor. My lip started to bleed. I brought a hand to my mouth but didn't fall down this time. They weren't going to break me.

"Why did you make me hit you?" Anthony whined, using the anguished tone of a jilted lover or an abusive parent. He didn't wait for my response as he jerked Gabby to her feet, then gripped her tightly by the forearm. "Butchy, you take the troublemaker. I don't want to even look at her anymore. If she does something else, shoot her in the back. We can put her body in the trunk."

"Works for me," Butchy said cheerfully. "This is gonna be fun." His casual attitude horrified me. Butchy was barely out of his teens and already a full-fledged monster.

Butchy opened his coat and then pulled me in front of him. The gun pressed hard into the small of my back and was now hidden from view. I stiffened and refused to budge, but he pushed me forward. "Out the front door, and no funny stuff," he grunted. "If you do, I'll shoot your friend. That's a good girl."

"You said you'd let her go!" I cried.

"Shut up and walk," Butchy snarled and lifted his other hand as if he intended to strike me. He shoved me out the door and down the steps of the porch, with Anthony and Gabby bringing up the rear. I glanced across the road at Stacia's house and the one next to it where Lyle and Anna Hansen lived with their two little girls. Everyone was most likely down for the night. I looked up and down the darkened street, but there was not a soul in sight.

Butchy handed me my car keys. "You're gonna drive."

I trembled from the cold, with fear added into the mix. The frigid air along with his menacing tone sent a jagged chill through me. God knows where they were planning to take us. Maybe Gino or Justin would stop by and see Gabby's car at the curb. But it was after ten, and the chances of visitors wasn't likely, especially when Justin thought I was still mad at him.

"Why my car?" I tried to stall for time.

"Mine's parked over on the next block. Besides, I don't want to get blood in it," Butchy said simply. "That lip of yours is spewing it everywhere. Haven't you got a tissue?"

"There's one in my pocket." I reached down into my coat pocket until my fingers connected with my driver's license. I let the card flutter to the ground in the driveway, relieved that it made no noise and appeared to go unnoticed. It wasn't much of a clue to leave, but if someone happened to stop by, maybe they would find it and put two and two together. I reached into the other pocket and produced a tissue that I held to my lip in a futile attempt to stop the bleeding. Annoyed, Butchy pushed me into the driver's seat and then made his way around to the passenger side.

All I could do was pray that someone would find us in time. But how? Where was Gino when we needed him? Butchy kept the gun pointed at me from the front seat while Gabby and Anthony settled themselves in the back.

"Take a left," Butchy ordered after the car crept out of the driveway. As we pulled on to the main road, Justin's truck passed us in the other lane, and my heart raced. Had he seen us? I glanced in the rearview mirror. Maybe he would turn around and go back to my house. I tried not to get my hopes up, but we needed to get out of this mess before—

"Step on it!" Butchy yelled, interrupting my thoughts. "Stop stalling."

Anthony spoke quietly from the back seat. "You see, Tessa, Dylan was trying to take over our little business venture and lifted a bunch of my important contacts. Your husband disrespected me and betrayed my trust."

I clutched the steering wheel tightly between my hands. "You didn't have to kill him or Eric over it."

Anthony shook his head. "That Eric was a real piece of work. He threatened to squeal on us if we didn't give him a bigger cut of the profits. He was costing me big time. Take a right here."

The car was quiet, except for Gabby's heavy breathing. She sounded like she was about to hyperventilate. "Let me stop the car so Gabby can get out. You said if I gave you the journal, you'd let her go."

"Sorry but it's not gonna happen now," Butchy said. "She'll run right to the cops for sure."

Anthony's breath was hot against the back of my neck, forcing the hair on it to rise. "When Dylan started doing my taxes, he figured out what was going on right away. Smart boy. At first, he wanted no part of it, but then, a few weeks before he died, he had a sudden change of heart. He said that he needed money—badly. A shame that he went and got himself killed."

I shook my head, not wanting to hear any more. Most likely, Dylan's illness had come into play, and his main concern had been leaving me with a bunch of bills to pay. My blood ran cold with the sudden realization. That was why he'd done these things—*for me*. Didn't Dylan realize that he was all I wanted and not the money? If he'd only confided in me, I was positive that I could have talked him out of it.

"He told me that his wife deserved to have the best." There was a sudden lilt to Anthony's voice, as if he knew the direction my mind was running and enjoyed hurting me. "Too bad that he got too damn greedy. We would have made a good team."

The words were like a dagger to my heart, but I was determined not to give Anthony the satisfaction of seeing me cry.

Butchy chuckled. "Yeah, how freaking sweet. Your husband was an arrogant putz, honey. He didn't deserve to be Anthony's middleman. That job had been promised to me."

"Quiet," Anthony growled. "You're too young. I told you to be patient, and it would happen eventually."

My skin prickled at his words. With new defiance, I pinned Anthony with my gaze in the rearview mirror. "You're a phony. You didn't care about Dylan at all. After you got what you could from him, you murdered him in cold blood." I clenched the steering wheel between my hands and kept staring at him. "You're not a man—just a monster."

Anthony sighed and shook his head. "You shouldn't disrespect me, Tessa. It's making things worse for you and your friend. Now take a right here."

We were off the highway, and it didn't take a genius to figure out where we were headed. The Hudson River stretched out to our left for miles—dark, cold, and foreboding. I slowed the car to a crawl.

The speed limit along the embankment was fifteen miles per hour, but I was only going about ten. Fear had lodged itself in my throat as we drove along. A potential getaway plan took shape in my head, but it could easily backfire. I needed to wait for the right moment, and we didn't have much time.

"Drive until I tell you to stop," Anthony ordered. "We need a more isolated spot. Keep moving."

TWENTY-FOUR

I COULDN'T BELIEVE THAT OUR LIVES were going to end like this. Even if Gino had received my earlier message by now, he didn't know where we were and wouldn't reach us in time. We'd be dead within minutes.

Butchy looked out the window at the endless body of water. "It's frozen, ain't it?"

"Only partially. Don't worry. It'll get the job done," Anthony assured him. "Stop the car, Tessa."

I continued to keep my foot on the gas pedal but slowed my pace until we were at a crawl along the marshy bank of water.

"Please," Gabby whispered. "Don't do this."

Anthony's tone remained calm but with an icier edge than before. "Listen, lady. I don't want to kill anyone, especially women. Your friend here isn't giving me much choice." He glared over the seat at me. "You brought this on yourself, Tessa. If you'd left well enough alone, things could have been different."

"Damn straight," Butchy agreed.

Anthony held up a hand in an attempt to silence him. "Stop talking," he commanded quietly. "Remember who's still in charge—who is *always* in charge. You're another taker, like my daughter. I never should have let you help make the sales. And I warned you not to touch Esposito. I said I'd deal with him in my own way. All you've done is make things worse and opened a bigger can of worms."

"Oh, for God's sake," Butchy snapped. "Stop with the clichés, old man. If it wasn't for me, Slice would have folded long ago."

"Don't speak to me that way," Anthony warned. His eyes were dark, dangerous pools of water, eerily similar to the river in front of us.

"'Remember, respect is key,'" Butchy mocked. "Maybe *you* fell for it, but I never trusted Esposito." He thrust a finger in my direction. "Then you had to hire his wife. Didn't you think she might be looking into his death and cause us more headaches? Hell, I figured that out right from the beginning. That's why I started following her around. With her résumé, why would she want to come to your dump for a job? Boy, you're stupider than I thought."

Gabby whimpered again, then grew silent. I continued to crawl along, praying for another car to appear, but there was no one in sight.

Anthony's lips curled back in distaste, but he kept his voice low. "Oh, you've gone too far, kid. But I'll deal with you later." He turned his head back in my direction. "Are you deaf? I said to stop the car!"

Having no choice, I positioned the vehicle so that it was pointed toward the river, only a few feet away. I kept my foot on the brake and pretended to place the car in Park. I stared at Anthony through the rearview mirror, hoping for some faint glimmer of humanity in his eyes, but they remained cold and expressionless. We were merely another job to him. Gabby started to cry again, and Dylan's face flashed before me.

Butchy pointed the gun at Gabby and clicked the hammer. "Any last words?"

It was now or never. My heart thumped wildly against the wall of my chest as I pressed the pedal to the floor. My little beauty of a car reacted as I'd hoped. The Toyota sputtered, wheels spinning in the mud for a moment before it jerked forward into the river near the boat launch. A deafening splash filled my ears, and my vision was temporarily blinded by the rush of water hitting the windshield.

"What the hell are you doing?" Butchy yelled and reached over to yank the wheel from me. My right hand shot up and connected with his face. The sting was unbearable but worth it when he hit the back of his seat with a groan. The gun flew out of his hands from the impact, and a shot rang out, shattering the front windshield. Gabby and I both screamed.

A flash of bright, colorful lights appeared in my rearview mirror. Butchy whipped his head around in a sudden panic. "The cops!" The window whirred down in seconds, and Butchy jumped out of it into the knee-high water. Anthony swore from the back seat and did the same, while Gabby and I sat there, shell-shocked, watching them go. I reached for her, ignoring the water sloshing inside the car. "You okay?"

She nodded shakily, and before we could attempt to get out of the car, our doors were wrenched open. I shrieked in surprise, afraid for a second that Butchy and Anthony had come back. Gino appeared at my side while Lou guided Gabby through the freezing water.

"Don't let them get away!" I screamed and shielded my

eyes against the lights, which were everywhere. I spotted several figures on the shore, but it was difficult to tell what was happening.

"Relax." Gino put his arm around my waist and reached for his sister while Lou ran off in the direction of the squad cars. "They're both already in cuffs." We reached solid ground, and Gabby and I both sagged against him. Concern and alarm were etched on Gino's face as he continued to hold us both tightly against him. "Thank God," he murmured.

"I can't breathe, bro." Gabby's voice was muffled against his jacket.

He loosened his grip and examined our faces closely. "You both look like you've been through a war. Are you sure you're okay?"

"We are now that you're here," I said gratefully.

Gino opened the back door to his vehicle as Lou handed each of us a blanket. "Thanks, Sawyer," he said and turned to us. "You two climb inside and get warm. We need to talk to the other officers for a few minutes, and then I'll take you both over to the hospital to get checked out."

"How did you find us?" I asked as Gabby slumped in the back seat.

Gino exchanged a glance with Lou and smiled. "Let's just say that the GPS tracker I installed on your car when you thought I was checking the tire's air might have helped some."

TWENTY-FIVE

GINO WAITED AT THE HOSPITAL WHILE the doctors examined Gabby and me. He called my mother and Aunt Mona, assured them that we were fine, and urged them to stay put, which they thankfully did. When I came out to the waiting room, Gabby was already sitting there with her brother. They both stood when they saw me.

"What'd the doctor say?" He was staring at my swollen lip. Without waiting for my reply, he handed me a cup of coffee from Java Time. "Lou stopped in a little while ago with these for you and Gabs."

Grateful, I inserted the straw he'd also brought into the cup and took a large sip from the hot beverage. "Since when is Archie open so late at night?"

"He was hosting a private party for a friend," Gino explained. "Lou drove by and saw the lights on. He said you guys were at the hospital, and Archie gave him the beverages on the house for his, I quote, 'two favorite ladies.'"

Gabby sighed. "Well, I guess we know who's going to be the topic of conversation at Java Time tomorrow."

That didn't bother me in the least. I was simply relieved to have made it out of the night alive. "I'll bake him some chocolate biscotti this week as a thank-you." I swallowed another mouthful of the rich, dark-roast coffee.

"Forget that." Gino waved a hand. "I asked you what the doctor said."

"It was only a couple of stitches in my lip. I'll be fine."

He drew his eyebrows together in concern. "Your mother said to drop you off at her house. She's waiting up, and I promised to deliver her daughter safely."

It would be useless to argue. "All right, thanks. I fed Luigi before I left, so he should be okay until the morning."

Gino's dark gaze rested on me solemnly. "I spoke to Justin a little while ago. He's been worried sick about you."

I spotted a flicker of interest in Gabby's wide-set eyes, but it disappeared when I shot her a death glare. "Where is he?"

"At work," Gino said. "He refused to go in until I had called and told you were safe. Honestly, if it wasn't for him, we probably wouldn't have made it to you guys on time. He stopped over at your house and found your driver's license in the driveway. When he saw that the front door was unlocked and your phone had been smashed, he called me right away."

Justin had certainly come through for me—*for us*. I realized that I'd had no right to be angry with him earlier. He'd made a promise to a friend and had kept his word. Undoubtedly, he would have done the same thing for me too. I'd talk to him later and straighten everything out.

"Well, thank goodness for him," Gabby chimed in. "But where were *you* all evening, dear big brother? Tessa tried to call you, and so did I."

Gino shot her an annoyed look. "I was actually at Slice. Before Justin called, we spotted Isabella's fiancé, Rico, leaving the shop with a stack of pizza boxes. The place had already closed, and no one else was around. When we called out to him, he freaked and took off in his car. Then we had probable cause to go after him. After we pulled his Porsche over, we found drugs inside the boxes. Heroin, cocaine, LSD, you name it. Pretty much everything but anchovies."

"Damn," Gabby breathed, and we exchanged horrified knowing glances. If we'd made it to Slice as planned, it was safe to say things might not have ended well. We could have botched up the police's plans or, depending on the timing, found ourselves alone with Rico and, as a result, might not be here to tell the tale.

"Rico told us what we wanted to know. He was more than happy to cooperate in exchange for us going easier on him. He gave up everyone—Butchy, Eric, and Anthony."

I paused and took stock. "But not Sam?"

"Nope. Apparently, he was the only one of the group who actually delivered pizzas."

"Well, at least they're not all bad," I sighed.

"Rico even told me how Dylan blackmailed Anthony into cutting him into the drug ring. He threatened to go to the IRS with everything he knew if he couldn't profit from the deals too. Quite the busy guy." His face reddened. "I'm sorry, Tess."

Despite my initial suspicions, it still hurt to hear that my husband had been involved in Anthony's shady dealings as well. "Go on with the story."

"Rico said that Butchy blabbed to Anthony about you snooping in his office. He also said that you asked Butchy if they were dealing drugs there. Anthony must have figured you'd tell the police your theory," Gino said. "The DEA is at Slice right now, going through the place."

Even though I was exhausted and my body sore, I wanted to see for myself. "Can we stop there on the way home?"

Gino looked at me in amazement. "No."

"Come on," Gabby pleaded. "We'll wait in the car."

Maybe Gino felt bad about what we'd endured tonight, because to my surprise, he let out a long, exasperated sigh. "Okay, but only for a minute, and you'd better make sure to stay in the car."

We went outside and piled into the back of Gino's sedan. He continued talking as we drove along. "Lou's back at Slice, watching it all play out. I think they're almost done."

Gabby placed a protective arm around my shoulders. "You know, I always thought it would be such a thrill to be involved in detective work and go on a high-speed chase. After tonight, I'm not so sure. I plan to appreciate the simple things in life for a while. A book, a cup of hot chocolate on a chilly evening, and good friends and family to laugh with."

"Does that mean not having a different boyfriend every month?" Gino quipped.

She ignored him. "Suddenly, my little bookstore doesn't seem so unexciting anymore. I need to start focusing more on marketing it anyway."

Slice was ablaze with light—inside and out. Two men in navy-blue Drug Enforcement Administration jackets were standing in the open doorway of the kitchen, deep in conversation. A squad car was parked in the lot next to their van. Lou was standing at the side of the cruiser, chatting with a cop behind the wheel. Both men looked up briefly when we pulled in, then resumed talking.

Gino turned around in his seat. "I could kick myself, thinking how Anthony managed to fool us. Him and his little family-run business. I should have seen through it." He shook his head ruefully.

"Don't blame yourself," I said.

"Rico said that Anthony told him he'd gotten the idea a few years ago about dealing drugs. This was when Slice was in the red and he'd thought about closing it down. Anthony knew someone who imported the stuff, and it was easy to find a supplier."

My heart was heavy with sadness. "I wish Dylan had told me the truth."

"We'll probably never know exactly what he was think-ing," Gino admitted. "When I question Anthony and Butchy further, they might be able to shed some more light on everything. Greed can work like a disease, Tess. It's probably of little comfort, but maybe Dylan figured if something happened to him, at least you'd be well provided for."

"Yes, I'd thought of that too." I had no idea what Dylan might have done with the money. Was it hidden somewhere? The cash meant nothing to me—it never had. All I'd wanted was Dylan. Now that he was gone, I had to move forward and try to find a way to live my life—without him.

"What about Vince and Isabella?" Gabby asked. "They must have been in on it too. Italian families always stick together."

"Yeah," Gino said. "Sort of like those meatballs you made last Christmas."

"Hey," she protested. "They weren't that bad."

He suppressed a smile. "Rico said that Isabella knew about the drug ring but, unlike him, wasn't actually involved. Her girlfriends threw her a bachelorette party at a casino earlier tonight, so we'll be making a little visit to her house tomorrow when she gets back. Strange as it sounds, Vince is clean. Warner—my boss—just got done with him. Vince is the one who actually owns Slice's building. Anthony's his half brother."

That explained the considerable age difference between the two men. "But I thought Anthony was the owner."

"He was originally, but he sold it to Vince a few years back when he needed the cash. That makes Vince his landlord, but it doesn't appear that he's ever had a genuine interest in running the business."

"Was Dylan doing taxes for his restaurant in New York City?"

Gino nodded. "Briefly. When their former accountant retired, Anthony recommended Dylan, but after doing their return for one year, Dylan suddenly told them he had too large of a client list and recommended some other guy he knew. Shortly afterward, someone blew the whistle on the place, and Vince thought Dylan was responsible. He might have been, but reporting to the IRS can be done anonymously, so we may never know for sure."

It did sound like something Dylan would have done—the old, honest Dylan, who I'd known and loved for so long. That was the memory of him I wanted to keep in my heart—not what he'd become since then.

Lou walked over to Gino's side of the vehicle and leaned his arms against the open window. His green eyes shimmered with warmth as he stared in at us. "You two are looking much better than the last time I saw you. How are we feeling, ladies?"

Gabby smiled at him. "Excellent—*now*."

Gino twisted in his seat and glared at his sister. "Gabs." His tone was a warning, as if he knew exactly what Gabby was thinking. I was pretty sure that I did too.

Lou turned his attention back to Gino. "They're about done, so I'll be taking off shortly." At that moment, another man in a DEA windbreaker came out of the building with two German shepherds.

Gino watched as they passed our car and got into their white paneled van. "Did they find more drugs?"

Lou nodded. "There were some buried inside coffee cans in the cooler. Guess they figured no one would look for drugs there. The dogs sniffed them out right away."

"Getting back to the building for a second," I said. "Did Vince happen to tell Sergeant Warner what he was going to do with it?"

Gino shook his head. "No idea. Warner didn't mention anything to me, but I assume Vince will close it down. Guess we'll be coming to your house for pizza from now on, Tess. How about tomorrow night for starters?"

We all laughed, but my mind was still preoccupied with thoughts of Slice. My dream of it as a cozy restaurant with families enjoying homemade chicken parmigiana, pizza, and penne started to fade into the recesses of my mind. It saddened me to think of all that potential going to waste.

"What's wrong, hon?" Gabby asked me.

I smiled at her. "Nothing. I'm fine." They had no way of knowing how much I wanted that building. It was calling to me in my mind—a voice that refused to be ignored. Someday, somehow, I vowed to make my dream happen.

Lou leaned further in the window. "So, what are you doing next weekend, Gabs?"

"No," Gino grunted.

Gabby ignored her brother and batted her eyelashes at Lou. "What'd you have in mind, handsome?"

"If you date her," Gino warned, "I'll have to shoot you."

TWENTY-SIX

WHEN I WOKE THE NEXT MORNING, it took a moment for me remember where I was—in my childhood bedroom. I glanced down at my watch to check the time, but my wrist was bare. Shoot. I must have lost it last night. And where was my phone? An image of Anthony stomping on it came to mind, and I shuddered inwardly. Oops, no phone either. Yes, I was on a roll already.

I stumbled into the connecting bathroom to take a shower. When I emerged ten minutes later wrapped in one of my mom's thick cotton pink towels, I stole a glance in the full-length mirror on the back of the door. *Yikes.* My lip, underneath the two Steri-Strips, was double its usual size, and my face looked drawn and pale. I was sorely tempted to lie back down and sleep the entire day away, but there was no chance of that happening. A nagging sensation in my brain alerted me to the fact that I'd forgotten something important about today, but for the life of me, I couldn't remember what it was.

There were a few items of my clothing in the closet from the last time I'd stayed here, when Dylan had been away on a business trip over a year ago. To my amazement, the pair of jeans in the closet was baggy on me. I knew that I'd lost weight since Dylan's death but hadn't realized how much.

My mother knocked on the door and came in with a mug of coffee and a straw. "Here, sweetheart. Drink this."

"Thanks, Mom." The coffee was hot and strong, and I sipped it carefully. I'd been told by the doctor not to get the dressing on my lip wet for forty-eight hours.

My mom reached over to cup my face between her hands. "You've been through so much, my girl. I wish that I could take all the pain away. I also wish you hadn't kept this a secret from me."

"I didn't want to worry you."

She frowned. "I'm always going to worry about you. You're my only child. I love you and know how much you're hurting." Her voice faltered. "I still hurt too." She didn't go on, but there was no need to. It was evident how much she missed my father.

"I know that and love you too."

She kissed my cheek. "Maybe you'd like to come stay with me for a while? You and Luigi, of course. We'd figure out a private room for him away from the dogs. You could put the house up for sale and move in permanently. I'd love the company."

As much as I loved my mother, I had no desire to live with her again. "Thanks, Mom. I appreciate the offer, but I'm going to be fine on my own. It's time to start rebuilding my life."

Mom smiled in that knowing way of hers. "I understand. If you'll remember, I had to do the same thing after your father died. It's difficult but necessary." She sighed. "Now, what would you like for breakfast?"

I shook my head. "I'd rather go home, if that's okay. I want to see Luigi. Maybe we could make a quick stop first and see about me getting a new phone?"

"Of course. Let me get my keys."

I finished my coffee, rinsed out the mug, and followed my mom to the curb where her SUV was parked. When we stopped at the provider's store, I was relieved to discover that my contacts and photos would transfer over with no issues.

My mom glanced at me as she started the engine.

"Justin called the house this morning. He wanted to know if you were okay. I offered to wake you, but he said no, that he would talk to you later."

Lost in thought, I stared out the window. "He saved our lives last night. If Justin hadn't come to the house and found my license and phone, no one would have even known that Gabby and I were missing until it was too late."

A small smile formed at the corners of her mouth. "That man is in love with you, Theresa. I've always suspected, but it was obvious from his voice this morning."

Incredulous, I stared at her. "How can you tell that from someone's voice? Never mind. He pretty much told me already."

She whipped her head around, startled, and barely missed hitting a car parked on the side of the road. "Mom! Watch the road, not me."

My mother laughed. "I remember telling you the very same thing when you first started driving." She paused for a moment. "I know it's far too soon for you to even think about dating someone else. You still need time to grieve and decide where to go from here. It was hard for me too, remember? All I want is for you to be happy."

"I know, and I appreciate you saying so. But I'd rather

not talk about this anymore today because—" I stopped midsentence. Of course. With everything else that had happened, I'd almost forgotten what day it was. Today was Dylan's birthday. "Dylan would have been thirty-one today," I whispered.

Mom pulled the car into my driveway and patted my hand. "It will get easier. I promise. I won't lie to you—it will take a long time, but hopefully one day, you can look back and remember the good times. Would you like me to stay with you?" She handed me the spare key to my house.

"Thanks, but I think I need to be alone for a while."

She nodded. "Of course. How about going out for dinner tonight? My treat."

I hesitated. "Maybe tomorrow instead?"

"Perfect. I'll pick you up around seven." She blew me a kiss before taking off.

I unlocked the front door and threw yesterday's envelopes from my mailbox down on the coffee table, adding to the stack that had already formed the last couple of days. Luigi must have been asleep upstairs, because he didn't appear to greet me. My new phone buzzed, and I lifted it out of my pocket and glanced down at the screen. Gino.

"Hey."

"Are you home yet?" he asked.

"Yes, my mother dropped me off. What's up?"

He cleared his throat. "Ned Reinhart spilled the beans and admitted to his part in We Care's embezzlement scheme."

"He confessed? Why now?"

Gino went on. "He didn't have much choice. We Care sprung another surprise audit after they got an anonymous tip that Reinhart was involved in the first theft with Dylan."

"I knew he was in on it."

"Well, you were right," Gino admitted. "When Dylan got wind of the whole thing, Reinhart bribed him to keep it a secret. Then We Care got suspicious, so he threw Dylan under the bus. Dylan wanted his share and threatened to go to the police. I've got a feeling Ned will be going away for a long time."

I sucked in a deep breath. "I see. Thanks." What else was there left to say? It was still painful having to face the truth about my husband's deceitfulness.

Gino cleared his throat. "Oh, I almost forgot. Your watch must have fallen off last night when you were in the back of my car. I'll bring it by later."

"Thanks. Come over for lunch. I'll make you some penne with tomato sauce."

"Tess, don't go to any trouble," he said. "You've had a rough night."

While he spoke, I was already taking a saucepan out of the cupboard. "It will help me to unwind."

He chuckled. "Well, I haven't eaten yet and happen to be starving, so you've got yourself a deal. I've got a meeting scheduled with my boss first. How does an hour sound?"

"Perfect." I disconnected and was about to remove a package of sauce from the freezer when I recalled the batch from yesterday. Gino had arrived to escort me to the police station, and I'd left it in the fridge. I emptied the container into the pot and put water on for the penne.

As I stirred the sauce, my thoughts returned to last night. An involuntary shudder went through me when I remembered Butchy with the gun. Thank goodness the police had shown up when they did.

I drained the penne and set it aside. When the sauce started to bubble, I adjusted the burner to its lowest setting. Butchy's face continued to haunt me, and my heart ached for his mother. As Butchy had been led away to the squad car, he'd kept insisting in a childlike voice that he had never killed anyone. His words from last night repeated in my head.

I'm looking forward to killing someone for the first time.

There was no doubt in my mind that Anthony and Butchy would have finished the job if given the opportunity. They were confident we wouldn't be around to see the light of day, so why lie about Dylan's murder? Why not brag about their conquests instead?

If they hadn't killed Dylan or Eric, that meant a killer was still lurking out there somewhere.

Goose bumps arose on my arms. I rubbed at them viciously and wandered back into the living room. My eyes came to rest on the boxes from Dylan's office still sitting on the floor. The lid on the top box was slightly crooked. Had Luigi been sitting on it? With my heart thumping against the wall of my chest, I slowly lifted the lid and gasped out loud.

The papers inside were a mess. When I'd opened the box yesterday afternoon, everything had been in order. Someone had been in this box while Gabby and I were fighting for our lives last night. But who? What did it all mean? Had Butchy been telling the truth when he said he'd never killed before? A nagging sensation swept over me. If Anthony or Butchy hadn't killed Dylan, then the killer was still out there—somewhere.

I was done taking chances. With my fingers shaking, I removed the cell from the pocket of my jeans to call Gino. A step sounded on the stairs behind me, and the air went out of my lungs. Fear lodged in my throat, and I couldn't breathe.

Please don't let this be happening.

Something cold, hard, and now familiar pressed into my back as a deep voice rumbled in my ear. "Drop the phone and hand over the pictures, or I'll shoot you."

Like fog lifting from the sky, everything had become abundantly clear. Of course. There was someone else who'd wanted my husband out of the way—someone who had been jealous of the attention Izzy had given him. Another man who wanted to claim the Italian princess as his own. His statement from the other day burned into my brain.

I'd do anything for my friends.

Sweat trickled down the small of my back as I obeyed his command. The man grabbed me roughly by the shoulder and whirled me around to face him. For the second time in two days, I found myself staring down the barrel of a gun.

Sam sighed with mock disgust. "Oh, Mrs. Esposito. It seems that you're just as stupid as your husband."

TWENTY-SEVEN

"HOW DID YOU GET IN?" I managed to say.

Sam's chest heaved with laughter. "You should have invested a few dollars in a more complex lock. My pick worked in less than a minute. You might as well have left the door open. Thanks for making it so easy for me."

His blue eyes were dark, endless pools of insanity. He grabbed me by the arm and jerked me forward, pressing the gun against my forehead. "Out all night, huh? I was about to pull into your driveway when some guy in a truck zoomed out of here. Guess he got his night confused with your other lovers. You surprise me, Mrs. Esposito. I didn't think you'd be sleeping around so soon after your husband's death."

So he didn't know what had happened with Butchy and Anthony yet. It was difficult to breathe or concentrate with the gun pressed against my face. "You've been waiting for me all night?" From his rumpled clothing and the thick smell of sweat permeating from him, it seemed a safe assumption.

"Yeah. I need those pictures Dylan left for you." Sam's hot, sour breath invaded my nostrils. "But I didn't go hungry. You might be stupid, but at least you're a pretty good cook. I even fed the cat. Such a nice little kitty."

Alarm rose from the pit of my stomach. "Where is he? What have you done with him?"

"Relax. Your cat's fine. I shut him in the bathroom upstairs because he hissed at me. I'd never hurt an innocent animal. What kind of a guy do you think I am?"

A psychotic freak. "You killed my husband."

He moved the gun away from my head and studied me for a moment. "I didn't have a choice. Dylan was black-mailing Izzy, upsetting her, making her sad. I had to put a smile back on her face."

Oh boy. Sympathy, disbelief, and disgust all mixed together in my stomach as I watched him. "You care for her."

He shot me a *duh* look. "I *love* her."

"What about her fiancé?" I asked.

Sam shook his head, looking at me as if he were explaining geometry to a three-year-old and I didn't understand. "That's just business. Izzy needs his money for her father's company. Anthony's a horrible manager. She's sacrificing her happiness for her family."

Did he actually believe that garbage? If so, Izzy had succeeded in doing quite a number on him. "Is that what she told you?"

"It's what I *know*. That husband of yours was going to ruin everything she's worked so hard to build. Dylan got what he deserved for trying to blackmail her."

"You're sick," I whispered.

"And you're an idiot," he chortled. "You actually believed my story about the doves."

"Why did you shoot Eric? Did he see you tamper with Dylan's car?"

Sam laughed. "That loser wasn't even around when I did it. But I bet he told you he knew who did, right? What a jerk, trying to make a few bucks off a grieving widow. No, that was an unfortunate accident. I was aiming for you. I had a feeling from the beginning you might be a problem. That night when you left the office building in Albany? It was me who tried to run you down. Izzy and I both wondered if you took the job at Slice to continue Dylan's dirty work."

"I didn't know anything about it."

"Right." He exhaled loudly. "Dylan was always talking about how much he loved you. How you two could tell each other anything." His upper lip twisted into a snarl. "I figured he would have shown you the pictures of Izzy with other guys. Turns out I was right to be worried."

This kid was deluding himself. "You think she loves you? She's using you to get the evidence of her cheating ways. You don't think Izzy's fooling around on you too?"

"That's different," Sam insisted. "Those guys in the pictures are marks. She gets stuff from them. Money. Clothes. Jewelry. Things she'll need when we run off together. You think a fine girl like that can live off my pizza delivery money?"

He was crazy; that was for certain. Or gullible. Or maybe just plain stupid. Perhaps a little of all three? "She's going to marry Rico, you know." When the police were done with him, that is. Sam must not have known that Rico had been arrested last night, and I didn't volunteer the information.

Sam shook his head stubbornly. "Izzy's going to leave him after the wedding. Rico promised she'd get her own bank account with one hundred grand as soon as they're married. When she's got the money, we're taking a cruise to Milan," he bragged.

"Sure. Okay." I took a deep breath and tried to remain calm. Once again, I had to figure out how to get away from a lunatic. Another thought occurred to me. Gino was stopping by for lunch in less an hour. Somehow, I had to keep Sam talking until he arrived.

His smile was evil. "Now, hand over the pictures. My girl can't rest until she gets them. Which means I won't rest either."

"There are no pictures," I whispered. "It turns out Dylan didn't tell me everything. If he had them, he kept it to himself. He had secrets—lots and lots of secrets." I tried to change the subject. "Dylan was blackmailing Anthony too, right? That's why Anthony didn't fire him when Izzy told her father about the pictures."

He smiled. "Yeah. I guess he figured out Anthony's little side business from doing his taxes. Dylan threatened to go to the cops and the IRS if he didn't cut him into the deal."

"But why? Did he say why he was keeping secrets and blackmailing everyone?"

Sam looked at me in disbelief. "For you, of course. Your husband needed to make sure you were well provided for. He told Izzy once that he didn't want you to have any debts when he was gone." He laughed. "Was he psychic? Did he know I was going to kill him? The guy made it sound like he was going somewhere permanently. Which didn't make sense, you know? Because if he loved you so much, why leave you behind?"

A sob escaped from my mouth before I could stop it.

"That's when I knew we had to get him out of the way. I told Izzy that joker is leaving town, and if I don't take care of him now, we may never get those pics. That auto mechanic class in high school turned out to be pretty useful after all." He raised the gun and pressed it against my chest. "Now, hand them over."

"I don't have any pictures."

"If you don't have them, that would be bad. See, it would mean I'd have to kill you for no reason."

Fear lodged in my throat. "My cousin will know. You won't get away with it."

"Oh, but I will," Sam insisted. "I've got a gas can in my car down the street. After I shoot you, I'll strike a match, and you and kitty will go up in flames. I'll make it look like you had an unfortunate cooking accident. Now for the last time, hand over the pictures."

In desperation, my eyes darted around the room, hoping for some type of escape or weapon, but there was none. For the second time in as many days, my life was being threatened. Except this time there was no Gabby as an ally.

Think, think. A light switch clicked on in my brain. "Okay. They're in the kitchen."

He pushed me roughly in front of him. "Move. And don't try anything stupid or I'll kill you."

Sam really must have thought I *was* stupid. Pictures or no, it was clear that he was going to kill me. I shuffled one foot in front of the other as he kept the gun pressed into my back. I was terrified he might stumble and the gun would go off. Blood pounded noisily in my ears, and I tried to remain calm. I thought of Dylan and how his obsession with money had cumulated into his death. It might end up doing the same thing to me as well.

No. I couldn't let this monster win again.

We reached the kitchen, and then Sam shoved me against the counter. "Where are they?" he snapped.

"In the drawer by the stove."

"I already looked there."

My hands were shaking as I started to pull it open.

How could I move quickly enough without him firing the gun first? "They're taped to the underside."

Meow. I glanced down at the floor to see Luigi rubbing up against my legs.

Sam stared at the cat in disbelief. "How did he get down here?"

It was the split second that I needed. I grabbed the steel pot by its warm handle and threw it at Sam's head. The gun dropped from his hand, and he screamed in agony as the hot, red liquid cascaded down his face. He started to dance around the room, arms flailing in the air. The gun slid across the room and under the fridge. I picked up Luigi, who was unharmed, rushed to the living room, and flung open the front door.

"Help!" I screamed over and over, hoping that someone would hear me. As I ran down the driveway I saw Gino's car pulling onto the street and rushed toward it. He screeched the vehicle to a stop at the side of the road and quickly got out, accompanied by Lou.

"Tess, what's wrong?" He drew his gun.

"Sam," I gasped. "In my house. He had a gun—it went under the fridge. He's the one who killed Dylan. I threw a pan of hot sauce at him."

Lou was already rushing toward my house, gun positioned at his side. Gino gave my arm a little shake. "Stay here." He took off running after Lou.

I buried my face into Luigi's soft fur. He immediately started to wriggle in my arms, so I opened the back door of Gino's car and placed him on the seat. I leaned against the vehicle and waited for my body to stop shaking.

A few minutes later, Gino came out of the house and strode over to me. "Lou's got him in cuffs on the floor. We found the gun too."

My shoulders sagged with relief. "How did you get here so quickly?"

"Warner went home sick and canceled my meeting. Lou stopped by and asked me to go to lunch with him. He said he wanted Italian, so I brought him along. I knew you'd have more than enough, but food will have to wait now. We need to take a formal statement from you down at the station."

"I'll make it up to both of you," I promised.

His mouth crinkled into a smile. "I'm sorry if I ever doubted you could take care of yourself. But I have to confess that I never thought of your tomato sauce as a lethal weapon, Tess."

TWENTY-EIGHT

BY THE TIME I HAD GIVEN my statement to the police and Gino had dropped me off at my house, it was after two o'clock. Sam had second-degree burns on his face and neck and was being treated at Harvest Park Hospital. He'd confessed to both murders and insisted that Izzy was not involved, that he'd acted on his own. While I still believed Anthony's selfish, money-grubbing daughter was somehow complicit in my husband's murder, it was only Sam that was on his way to his new home—a jail cell. The nightmare was finally over.

The first thing I did after slipping my shoes off was to check on Luigi, who was curled up in a ball on the couch. He purred with contentment as I stroked his soft head and rewarded me with a sleepy meow. My wonder kitty. If he hadn't distracted Sam, things could have ended very differently.

I cleaned up the mess in the kitchen and sat down next to Luigi with my phone and pile of unread mail. I scrolled through the texts that Justin had sent last night.

At 10:30: I'd like to stop by and see you, if that's okay.

At 11:05: Found your license outside but your car is gone. Everything all right? Did you and Gabby go somewhere?

After that, he must have found my phone, because I didn't receive another text until 1:30.

It's crazy to send this because I don't know if you'll see it. I found your phone—that scared the hell out of me. Gino just told me you're okay. Thank God. If you need me, call. Any time of day or night. I'll always be here for you.

The words tugged at my heart. Luigi began to knead my lap with his paws, and I absently scratched him behind his ears. "I was too hard on him."

Luigi emitted a squeak, as if to say he agreed with me. "He's a good guy, isn't he?" Despite my sentiment, the cat had already lost interest. He jumped off my lap in search of a more interesting place to snooze.

I typed out a quick text. I have to go out for a little while but can I make you dinner tonight? I owe you.

There was a knock at my door, and I glanced up with a start. After everything that had happened in the past couple of days, my nerves were shot. I glanced out the peephole in the door, smiled, and opened it. My neighbor Stacia was standing on my porch in a pink housecoat and matching foam rollers. She had a sympathetic smile on her face and a glass pie plate in hand.

"Looks like you had a rough day, honey. Saw all the police cars and flashing lights earlier. You okay?"

Nodding, I gestured for her to come in. "Everything is fine."

"Well, I thought after all that trouble, you could use something sweet to eat, so I made you another apple pie. I thought it might remind you of Dylan, in a good way." Stacia followed me into the kitchen and set the plate on the counter.

"That was so thoughtful of you. I'm not really hungry right now, but I'll have a slice later for sure."

"Of course. I always have a tough time eating when I'm upset too." She patted her rollers, as if to make sure they were still there, her face lighting up like a Christmas tree. "There was another reason I stopped by. I did that thing Dylan asked me to do."

My eyebrows lifted. "What thing?"

"He gave me a sealed envelope about a week before he died. He said it was our little secret, and I shouldn't mention it to anyone. You know, like working undercover." Stacia giggled. "It was already addressed with the correct amount of postage. That young man of yours was always so thoughtful. He told me that if anything ever happened to him, wait a few weeks and then drop it into the mail. The envelope should be arriving at its destination today."

Pain settled in my chest. Why would Dylan have a neighbor send a package, and what could have been in it? Finally, I'd thought there were no more secrets. "Do you remember who the envelope was addressed to?"

"Oh sure, to a Rico Lucchese. Dylan wrote on it *Do Not Bend, Photographs Inside.*"

For the first time since Dylan's death, I laughed with a true sensation of joy. Rico was going to receive the photos, and Izzy would not get her fairy-tale wedding after all. Karma could be a wonderful thing. "That's the best news I've heard all day. Thank you so much for the pie and the… um…update."

Stacia looked surprised. "Oh, of course, dear. I mean, who doesn't like apple pie, right?" She waved and then headed for the door. "Sorry to rush off, but I've got trays of cookies in the oven. My son and his wife are coming for a visit, and he asked me to make him some. I've got a busy afternoon of baking ahead for me."

"Sounds like fun." I watched her cross the street, thinking of Sam's earlier words—how Dylan wanted to take care of me. I still had no idea what he had done with the money he'd coerced from Izzy or the cash Anthony had given him for his part in the drug ring. Had he bought a yacht or a new sports car? If so, where did he hide it?

My gaze fell upon the stack of mail that had been accumulating on the coffee table for a few days. I shifted though it, then finally decided to open a large manila envelope from our mortgage company. I hoped that the payment wasn't going up. I slid my nail through the flap and pulled out a letter, quickly skimming its content. It congratulated me on paying off our mortgage.

There had to be a mistake. We were only two years into a thirty-year loan with $200,000 still owed on it. I flipped through the rest of the papers and stopped when I saw the original promissory note and mortgage we'd signed together. A large red *PAID* and *CANCELLED* had been stamped on the top. Dylan had made enough payments in the last six months to completely pay the loan off.

The papers slipped from my shaking fingers, and I closed my eyelids against the tears building inside. *This was why he was blackmailing Ned, Anthony, and Izzy.* This was why he'd wanted in on Anthony's drug ring. I could barely swallow around the lump in my throat. Our home was paid in full. I summoned an image of Dylan in my mind, one with the wind blowing in his hair and a smile on his face. "Thank you," I whispered out loud. "Thank you for taking care of me."

I opened another envelope from our life insurance company. There was a letter inside, and a check was attached, made out to me. The amount was $200,000. I blinked twice—okay, maybe three times. This couldn't be right. We'd both had policies for $100,000. Was this some type of mistake? Dylan might have tried to increase it after he found out he was sick, but good luck doing that with a preexisting medical condition. There was a toll-free number on the letter that I went ahead and dialed. The agent asked me for some personal information and then assured me that the amount was correct.

"According to our records, Mr. Esposito doubled the policy amount about a year ago," she said. "He even prepaid it five years in advance. Is there anything else I can do for you?"

"No," I whispered into the phone. "Thank you."

After she'd clicked off, I continued to stare at the check. How ironic. Today was Dylan's birthday, but he'd given me a present instead. Two presents. A house to call my own and an insurance payment large enough that I could pay off all our bills, including what I owed the funeral home, and buy a new vehicle.

This wouldn't do though. The money he'd used to pay off the house had been gained illegally. Somehow, I was going to pay it back, or perhaps pay it forward instead, to some local organizations. Silently, I vowed to replace every single dollar he had taken.

The insurance money was mine to do with as I pleased though. I'd donate a good share of it, but I planned to set some aside for a new project—something I'd been dreaming about for a long time.

Dylan had worried that his illness might take him from me too soon and wanted to make sure that I was well provided for financially. He'd tried to think of everything ahead of time so that I'd never want for anything. As with his paperwork, he'd been meticulous about every detail. Tears rolled down my cheeks as I realized I'd never have what I truly wanted more than anything else—him.

My cell buzzed again, and I wiped my eyes and glanced down at the screen. The number was local but not one that I recognized, and I prayed there wasn't a reporter on the other end. Word had already leaked about Anthony, Butchy, and the pizza parlor's dealings. No doubt Sam would follow. With hesitation, I pressed Accept Call. "Hello?"

"Tessa, it's Vince. Vince Falducci."

He was about the last person I had expected to hear from. "Hi."

There was a long pause. "Look, I wanted to apologize. When I found out you were Dylan's wife, I was pissed off. I guess I blamed him for the restaurant going under, when in truth, I should have blamed my so-called partner instead—and myself. I was a schmuck who let myself be taken advantage of. I didn't have my eyes wide open, and that wasn't fair to you."

"There's no need for you to apologize."

"Yes, there is. You have my word that I wasn't involved with Anthony's side business either and knew nothing about what happened to Dylan. I—" He stopped to catch his breath. "I feel like a complete idiot. This is the second time I've been screwed over. I didn't even know about Anthony's goings-on at the restaurant until a couple of days ago when I first became suspicious."

Doubt hung heavy in the air, and I was silent, not knowing what else to say.

Vince must have guessed my thoughts. "I have only been back at Slice for a few weeks, since right before Dylan died. Anthony first recommended Dylan to us as an accountant a couple of years ago. Before I even knew what happened, the place had closed down, and I decided to come back here. You must think I'm a real lowlife."

I exhaled sharply. "Let's just say that I'm not exactly in a position to criticize anyone. Dylan knew about Anthony's side business and was blackmailing him. He did have his reasons, but that still doesn't make what he did right. You really didn't know?"

"No, I didn't. Honest. I don't condone drug dealings. The entire family is torn up over this."

I had no doubt. It wasn't my place to judge Vince, and if Gino said he was clean, it must be true. "Thank you for letting me know."

There was another awkward silence. "I'm truly sorry about what happened to your husband. It was a complete shock when the cops came to my door in the middle of the night to tell me what Anthony had done. Frankly, I hope he rots in jail for a long time. Are you and your cousin okay?"

"We're fine, thanks." I was about to hang up when another thought occurred to me. "What are you going to do with the place?"

His voice sounded puzzled. "Excuse me?"

"I heard you own Slice. What are you planning to do with the building now?"

"I haven't really thought about it yet," he confessed. "Are you interested in buying the place?"

Excitement soared through me. Oh heck yes, I was interested. Suddenly, my dream was once again within reach, the perfect restaurant that Dylan and I had been working toward. I tried to steady my voice. "It depends on the price. I don't have much money to sink into it. The building alone needs a lot of cosmetic work."

"Perhaps we can work something out," he said. "I might be willing to lease it to the right person. Say, oh… someone who's a fantastic cook and I know would do the place proud."

My body tingled with excitement as I did a silent little happy dance. It was a good thing Vince couldn't see me, and I struggled to keep my voice on an even note. "That would be wonderful."

"Would you like to meet me for coffee later?" he asked. "How about we get together at Java Time, say, at three o'clock, to discuss this further?"

"I can't today. How about tomorrow?"

"That works for me." Vince paused for a moment. "I'll look forward to it."

I sat very still, enjoying the happiness blooming in my chest. How I wished Dylan was here to share in this moment. Sadly, he wasn't, so I tried to relish the thought alone.

Yes, it's finally happening. I'm going to have my very own restaurant.

TWENTY-NINE

I PICKED UP MY PHONE AND called a cab. There was somewhere I needed to be and no transportation available after my Toyota had been half submerged in a river. I'd have to go car shopping tomorrow.

After changing into comfortable jeans and a wool sweater, I had barely enough time to get downstairs before the cab's horn tooted from my driveway. Except for a slight headache, I felt fine. I promised Luigi that I'd be back soon, but he didn't seem concerned.

I opened my front door and was surprised to see Matt on my doorstep, a yellow taxi idling behind him in the driveway. Then I noticed the flowers in his hands. Oh, no. My heart started to beat a little faster, and I gripped the doorknob tightly in my hand. I didn't want a scene with him. What was he planning now?

I took a deep breath and smiled. "Are those for me?"

He nodded shyly and held out the bouquet of white and pink chrysanthemums. "I never sent flowers after Dylan... died. Ellie at the Flower Girl said they meant sympathy... and friendship. I miss being friends with you, Tessa."

I tried to ignore the mournful look in his eyes. "Ellie certainly knows her flowers." The arrangement was beautiful, full of large, fluffy blooms and wrapped with a blue silk ribbon. The sentiment was sweet, but I didn't take the flowers and gave him a shrewd look instead. "Before I got married, you sent me a text that said I'd be sorry if I went through with my wedding. What did you mean by that?"

Matt's cheeks burned bright red as he bowed his head. "In hindsight, I know how that must have looked, but I only meant you'd be sorry you broke up with me, that you'd miss me one day." He stared up at me then, a slight smile on his lips. "It turns out I'm the one who's sorry. Sorry that I messed things up so badly. I'm sorry, Tess... about everything."

I gazed into his wide hazel eyes and saw genuine sincerity there. With a sigh, I took the flowers from his outstretched hand. "I accept your apology, Matt."

"You do?" He sounded stunned.

The taxi tooted its horn again, and I looked past Matt's shoulder to wave at the driver in a *just-one-minute* gesture. "Yes. It was a long time ago. Water under the bridge now."

He looked slightly relieved but shifted his weight from his right to left foot—something I remembered him doing when he was nervous.

"Listen, would it help if I talked to Lila for you? I'd be glad to tell her there was nothing going on between us, that you had nothing to do with Dylan's—"

"She's gone," he said abruptly. "She left and took the kids with her."

His face was full of pain, and it saddened me. "Oh…I'm so sorry."

"It's not your fault. We've been having problems for a while. This investigation was the straw that broke the camel's back." He cleared his throat. "But it's fine. Maybe I can convince her to try counseling. In the meantime, I still get to see the kids."

I patted his arm awkwardly. "I'm glad to hear that. If you'll excuse me, I really have to get going."

Matt glanced back at the taxi, then at me. "Right. Of course. Sorry to keep you." He stepped off the porch, then looked at me again. "Please take care of yourself." His eyes twinkled. "Not that I should be worrying though. The word around town is that you're pretty good with a pot of tomato sauce."

Boy, news traveled fast in Harvest Park.

He waved at me again before trotting toward his car parked across the street. With a smile, I watched him drive away. I truly hoped for his sake that he and Lila could work things out. Matt wasn't a bad person. He'd made mistakes in life—like Dylan, like me. No one was perfect. Hopefully, he would learn from them, and his life would be better for it.

I closed and locked the door behind me. Flowers still in hand, I gave the cab driver my destination and then settled back in the seat, thinking about all the things I needed to do today—cash the check, grocery shopping, and laundry. Maybe tomorrow night I would take my mother out to dinner instead of her treating me. There was something else that I needed to do right now though—an event that I'd been putting off for over a month, and it couldn't wait any longer.

No one else knew about the secret I'd kept since Dylan's death. My mother might have become suspicious in the last few weeks. She would casually ask how I liked the roses or peonies she'd placed by Dylan's headstone. In return, I would mutter some lame reply about what a beautiful color they were.

The truth of the matter was that I had not been out to Dylan's gravesite since his funeral. It had been too difficult, too painful and permanent for me. But I had realized that this was only putting off the inevitable. After the last few days, I'd become aware that I could no longer avoid the past. Facing it would help me find my way to the future.

Besides, there were a few other things that I needed to say to my husband.

THIRTY

THE CAB DROVE THROUGH THE OPEN metal gate slowly as the driver gave me a questioning look in the rearview mirror.

"This is fine here," I assured him. He told me the amount, and I added five dollars for a tip.

"Thank you, miss." To my surprise, the driver seemed concerned as he watched me. "Do you want me to wait for you?"

I shook my head. "Not necessary, but thanks."

He gave a perfunctory nod, and as soon as I stepped out of the vehicle, the cab drove away. I planned to stay here for a while and could always call another cab or ask Gabby to come and get me. The bookstore was closed on Sundays, and she'd said last night that she planned on sleeping in and binge-watching television, but I knew she'd be available if I needed her.

The sun cascaded down on my face, and a gentle breeze whipped my hair around my shoulders. For a November day in Upstate New York, the temperature was mild, hovering in the low fifties, quite a change from last night's icy cold water and the below-freezing temperatures. That was one of the beauties about New York weather. It might be ninety degrees one day and forty the next. Unpredictable, the same as life.

I was ashamed that it took me a minute to recall where Dylan's grave was. *Two rows up. That's right, isn't it?* Leaves crunched beneath my sneakers. As I went down the second row, my memory kicked in, and then I spotted the beechnut tree. Although bare now, it had still been in full bloom on that awful but mild October day. There wasn't much else I remembered about the funeral, except the sickeningly sweet smell of flowers that had permeated the air around me. They say that grief helps a person to block out certain memories. I'd tried that mechanism for a while, but no more.

Dylan's resting place was at the end of the row. The entire cemetery was peaceful and sedate, with no one in sight. Snow would be in the air soon, and it saddened me to realize that most people didn't come out as often to visit their loved ones during the winter months. Or, if they were like me, they avoided coming at all. My Catholic upbringing had originally reassured me that it didn't matter if I came to visit because only Dylan's body was buried here. His spirit lived on elsewhere.

I knelt on the damp ground, running my hands over the smooth, granite surface of his headstone. I laid the flowers alongside it. They were lovely and perfect for this moment. This was the first time I'd seen the stone, since it hadn't been ready in time for the funeral. As the undertaker had promised, it looked beautiful. My fingers traced his name, engraved in raised black letters. *Dylan Lawrence Esposito. Born November 15, 1987. Died October 6, 2018. Devoted husband, son, and friend.*

That was all it said, but it was more than enough.

Devoted husband. Yes, he had been that. There was no doubt in my mind that he had loved me as a person desires and needs to be loved. Still, the lies and the secrets would weigh on my heart forever. I didn't know if I could ever fully come to terms with it, but maybe I wasn't supposed to.

"I don't understand why you thought you had to do those things. You could have told me the truth. If you got sick, I would have taken care of you. Every minute of every day. That's how much I loved you."

Defeated, I allowed myself tears one final time. As they rolled down my cheeks and onto his headstone, the wind began to pick up speed, and a glorious array of yellow, red, and orange leaves whirled around me. Dylan knew how much I enjoyed the leaves in autumn and how I could stare at them falling from their branches for hours on end. We'd done that one autumn when we'd visited the Poconos in October. Dylan and I had spent an entire day sitting on the porch of our rented cabin, holding hands and sipping hot apple cider while watching the leaves. A lump formed in my throat at the memory.

That day, I had told Dylan that watching the wind make the leaves dance was one of my favorite things to see. At this moment, the leaves were dancing. For *me*, at Dylan's grave. Maybe this was Dylan's way of letting me know that he was okay, and I would be too.

"Luigi and I are fine," I assured him. "I may even be able to open our restaurant soon. Things are starting to fall into place. I'm much stronger now, so there's no need for you to worry about me."

I waited, but nothing happened. He was so vivid in my mind—his blond hair blowing in the wind, and those clear-blue eyes the color of the sky on a cloudless day. With a smile, I remembered those obsessive-compulsive habits of his that could drive me to distraction but were all part of his charm and another reason why I had loved him. Life without Dylan would prove to be very different from what I'd known before.

"Happy birthday." I touched my hand to my lips and then to his headstone. The wind died down, and the leaves finally settled on the ground. As I rose to my feet, I saw a man leaning against a tree, watching me. My heart gave a jolt.

Justin was unshaven, his dark hair adorably messy. He was wearing a gray jacket the exact color of his eyes. His expression was somber, and I remembered that I was not the only one who had lost someone they loved. Losing Dylan for him must have been the equivalent of my losing Gabby, something I couldn't bear to think about. No matter what happened, we would always be drawn together because of our mutual love for him. Maybe it was meant to be that way.

He smiled but waited for me to come to him. "I knew you'd be here. Are you okay?"

"You remembered." My voice came out in a breathless whisper.

Justin nodded soberly. "Of course. I'm glad you finally came. I know it wasn't easy for you."

I stared at him. "You knew it was my first time here?"

Justin placed his hands on my shoulders. "It's nothing to be ashamed of. Right after Dylan's funeral, I came out here a few times. Today is the first day I've been here in over two weeks. It doesn't mean that you don't care, Tess. Everyone handles grief differently."

"Thanks. I needed to hear that."

Justin pushed a loose piece of hair back from my face. "Last night I went out looking for you myself and drove to Slice. When I saw all the commotion, I was afraid you were mixed up in the middle of it, but then Gino called to say they'd found you and Gabby." His jaw hardened. "I was so worried about you."

"You saved our lives. If you hadn't found my driver's license, no one would have known—until it was too late."

A shadow lifted from his face. "Does this mean you're not mad at me anymore?"

I shook my head. "I understand why you didn't tell me. You were honoring a promise to a friend."

Justin's tone was gentle. "I guess we'll never know what was running through Dylan's mind, but you should always remember how much he cared about you. Do you think you can forgive him?"

It took a few seconds for me to respond. "Yes, but forgetting will take a long time, maybe forever. I can't dwell on it any longer though. I need to move forward with my life."

He covered my hand with his. "I'm happy to hear that."

There was a question in his eyes that he dared not ask, but nevertheless, I felt I should address it. "I care for you very much. Next to Gabby, you're the dearest friend I have, but I can't promise you anything else right now. It's too soon for me."

Justin's smoky eyes observed me thoughtfully for a moment, then he leaned down to place a light kiss on my forehead. "I'm a very patient man, Tess. Especially when it's something that's well worth waiting for."

I lowered my eyes to the ground and had no response for that.

"I know how much you loved Dylan and that you aren't done grieving for him," Justin continued. "But I'd like to be there if you need a shoulder to cry on, or anything else, for that matter. It's the thought of you *not* in my life that's unbearable."

I reached for Justin's hand, and he squeezed mine

in return. "Okay, enough serious talk for now." I smiled, pulling him forward. We walked toward his truck together in comfortable silence. "I'm free today." Laundry and grocery shopping could always wait. "What would you like to do?" We both needed something to lighten the mood and rid ourselves of the heartache that threatened to descend upon us again.

"Hmm." He grinned at me sheepishly. "I did get this text a little while ago from an incredibly beautiful, talented woman who offered to make me dinner. So I might not be free after all."

I struggled not to roll my eyes. "You're a regular comedian these days."

Justin opened the passenger door of his truck for me. "No jokes here. I happen to be starving and would love a good, home-cooked meal. Does this invitation mean that I get my choice of what I'd like to eat?"

I climbed inside the vehicle. "Of course. What will it be—stromboli, lasagna, eggplant parmigiana? Or something else?"

He shook his head. "None of the above. Come on, keep guessing. The choice should be obvious."

Then it finally dawned on me. "No way. You want pizza?"

He flashed me a lopsided smile that reminded me of an excited little boy. "Hey, I can't help myself. All this talk about it lately has given me a craving for one mean pie."

I started to laugh. "As long as you don't mind giving me a lift to the store so I can pick up some ingredients."

"Wow. Some cook," he teased. "Here I thought you always had everything on hand."

"Hey, never underestimate an Italian chef. We can always come up with a solution." I chuckled.

He shut my door and went around the truck to get in, giving my hand a little squeeze after he pulled his seat belt around him. As we drove away from the cemetery, I continued to watch the sky. Even with winter imminent, this was a day that refused to be ignored as sunshine radiated the earth. We passed a large elm tree with a few remaining leaves attached. They refused to let go—a sign of hope that did not escape my notice.

I would continue to carry Dylan in my heart forever, but it was time to look ahead—for my own well-being. A new day had dawned, and I was determined to make every minute of it count.

NEVER-FAIL PIZZA CRUST AND PEPPERONI PIZZA

Crust

Ingredients

- 1 .25-ounce package active dry yeast
- 1 teaspoon sugar
- 1 cup warm water
- 2½ cups bread flour
- ½ teaspoon salt
- 2 tablespoons olive oil

Directions

Preheat the oven to 450 degrees. In a medium-sized bowl, dissolve the yeast and sugar in warm water. Wait about 10 minutes or until the mixture looks creamy. Stir in the flour, salt, and olive oil, beating by hand until smooth. Let the mixture sit for about 5 minutes.

Lightly flour a surface on your counter, then roll out

the dough, patting or rolling it into a round. Transfer the crust to a lightly greased pizza pan, and spread the desired toppings on top of the crust. Bake for 15 to 20 minutes or until the crust is golden brown. Let the pie cool about five minutes before serving. Makes about 8 servings.

Pepperoni Pizza

Ingredients

- 6-ounce can tomato paste (preferably Contadina)
- 1 teaspoon dried oregano, crushed
- 1 teaspoon dried basil, crushed
- ½ teaspoon garlic powder
- ½ teaspoon onion powder
- ½ teaspoon salt
- ¼ teaspoon black pepper

Toppings

- ¾ pound pepperoni (stick) or 6-ounce package sliced pepperoni (if slicing your own, make them on the thin side)
- 1 cup shredded mozzarella cheese, or more to taste

Directions

After the crust is prepared, combine all sauce ingredients with ½ cup water in a medium bowl. Top the crust with sauce, pepperoni, and cheese. Bake for 18 to 20 minutes until crust is browned and cheese is bubbly. For best results, rotate the pizza pan between the top and bottom oven racks halfway through the baking cycle. Extra sauce can be frozen.

TESSA'S TANTALIZING TOMATO SAUCE

Ingredients

- 1 medium to large onion, sliced
- ¼ cup olive oil
- Pork butt (small piece, about 3 pounds) or 6 boneless spare ribs (both optional)
- 2 28-ounce cans crushed tomatoes
- 1 28-ounce can tomato puree
- Garlic powder
- Black pepper
- Dry parsley
- Dry basil
- Dry oregano
- 6 6-ounce cans tomato paste (preferably Contadina brand)

- 1 28-ounce can Hunt's tomato sauce
- 1 tablespoon sugar

Directions

Sauté the onion slices in the olive oil in the pot that will be used to make the sauce. Once the onion is translucent, remove from the oil, making sure you do not burn it. Discard onion. In the same oil, brown the boneless spare ribs or pork butt if using. Afterward, set the meat aside, but do not discard the oil.

Add 2 cans crushed tomatoes and 1 can tomato puree to the oil you have been using. Season with pinches of garlic powder, black pepper, and dry parsley, as well as a pinch of dry basil and a little dry oregano to preferred taste. Let the mixture come to a low boil, add all the meat back in, and stir it regularly, about 15 to 20 minutes. Continue to simmer for at least 1 hour, stirring often. Sauce will bubble—do not let it burn. After the sauce has cooked for an hour, remove the meat and set aside.

Add tomato paste, using 2 6-ounce cans for every 28-ounce can of tomatoes. Stir constantly to blend the paste into the sauce. Add in can of Hunt's tomato sauce. Season with more garlic powder, black pepper, dry parsley, and dry basil, and let the mixture come to a low boil, which should take about 20 to 30 minutes. If sauce is still very thick, add more water and one additional can of Hunt's tomato sauce.

Add the meat back into the sauce and cook for another hour, then add 1 tablespoon of sugar (optional.)

GOOD TO THE LAST BITE STROMBOLI

Ingredients

- ½ pound lean ground beef
- 1 cup chopped cooked ham
- 1 green bell pepper, chopped
- 1 red onion, finely chopped
- 1 14-ounce jar pizza sauce
- 1 4.5-ounce can mushrooms, drained
- 10-ounce package pizza crust dough (or use earlier recipe)
- 1 8-ounce package sliced pepperoni or sausage
- 1 cup shredded mozzarella cheese
- ¼ cup butter, melted

Directions

Preheat the oven to 400 degrees. In a skillet over medium heat, brown the ground beef until no pink shows, then drain. Mix in the ham, bell pepper, onions, pizza sauce, and mushrooms. Lay the pizza dough flat on a cookie sheet. Distribute the pepperoni slices over all the dough. Place a heaping pile of the sauce mixture on one side of the dough (some may be left over). Sprinkle with mozzarella cheese. Fold the dough over, and pinch the ends and sides together. Poke holes in the top of the dough, and brush melted butter over the surface. Cook for 30 minutes or until golden brown. Slice into individual sections to serve. Makes about 6 to 8 servings.

ACKNOWLEDGMENTS

A story needs many willing hands to make it into an actual book. I'm fortunate that I get to do something I genuinely love and have the following people to thank for their assistance:

My publisher, Sourcebooks, for making this an incredible experience, and especially my editor, Anna Michels, for taking a chance on me and helping to shape this book into one I'm proud of. A very special thank-you to Margaret Johnston, as well, for her invaluable help and marvelous ideas.

To my literary agent, Nikki Terpilowski, for her patience, guidance, and honesty. I'm so fortunate to have you in my corner.

Kudos to retired Troy police captain Terrance Buchanan, who willingly answered rounds and rounds of endless questions. Your help is appreciated more than you know.

Thank you to my awesome beta readers, Constance

Atwater and Kathy Kennedy, who always give it to me straight and never let me down.

My friends Sue Bellai and Amy Reger, who were thoughtful enough to share their amazing recipes with me and the rest of the world. You guys can cook for me anytime!

Last but not least, thank you to Phillip for sharing his "pizza" knowledge with me. You'll always be my favorite delivery guy.